Timmy & The Quibbleberry

By

Justin B. Black

Timmy and the Quibbleberry

COPYRIGHT © 2024 by J. Barrett-Brown & Justin B. Black. All rights reserved.

No part of this publication may be reproduced, distributed, or transmitted in any form or by any means, including photocopying, recording, or other electronic or mechanical methods, without the express prior written permission of the Author and/or the publisher, except in the case of brief quotations embodied in critical reviews and certain other non-commercial uses permitted by copyright law. For permission requests, write to the publisher.

ISBN: 9798322514053

The following is a work of fiction. The story, all names, characters, and incidents portrayed in this production are fictitious. No identification with actual persons (living or deceased), places, buildings, and products are intended or should be inferred. All names, characters and places are products of the author's imagination, and should be regarded as such.

Illustrations and book design assisted by DALL-E 3

First Edition Printing 2024

For more information from the author, email TheQuibbleberry@Gmail.com

Timmy and the Quibbleberry

*'Don't just be careful what you wish for…
…But be cautious of how you wish for it!'*
- Jason Barrett-Brown

Justin B. Black

To Katherine,

Keep being random!

I hope you enjoy reading about ↩

TIMMY & THE QUIBBLEBERRY

Best Wishes,

Justin Black

28/05/24

TABLE OF CONTENTS

Prologue 7

Chapter 1: Hi There 14

Chapter 2: I Feel all Fizzy 28

Chapter 3: Slice, Swoosh, Slice, Swoosh, Slice 44

Chapter 4: That Wasn't Me, Was It? 54

Chapter 5: Bluey, Purpley, Greeny, Brown Mulch 68

Chapter 6: The Snarl Had Turned to A Smile 78

Chapter 7: Looked Like the Number '8' 91

Chapter 8: Survival of The Fittest 101

Chapter 9: I Don't Think It Is, I'm Afraid 108

Chapter 10: A Hint of Blue…BLUE! 116

Chapter 11: You Said a Mouthful 122

Chapter 12: Here He Comes 132

Chapter 13: A Very Strange Looking Train 142

Chapter 14: Strength & Honor 153

Chapter 15: It's your Gra… 163

Chapter 16: We May Have a Problem, Mrs Bongo ... 173

Chapter 17: C'mon You's Two! 181

Chapter 18: My Grog 190

Chapter 19: Oooomph 200

Chapter 20: Shut Her Eyes with A Smile 210

Chapter 21: Her Villainy Undone 219

Chapter 22: The M.O.U 228

Chapter 23: A More Dangerous Alarm 238

Chapter 24: Descendants of A Wizard 249

Chapter 25: Pob's Rest 262

Epilogue 272

Acknowledgments 276

About the Author 278

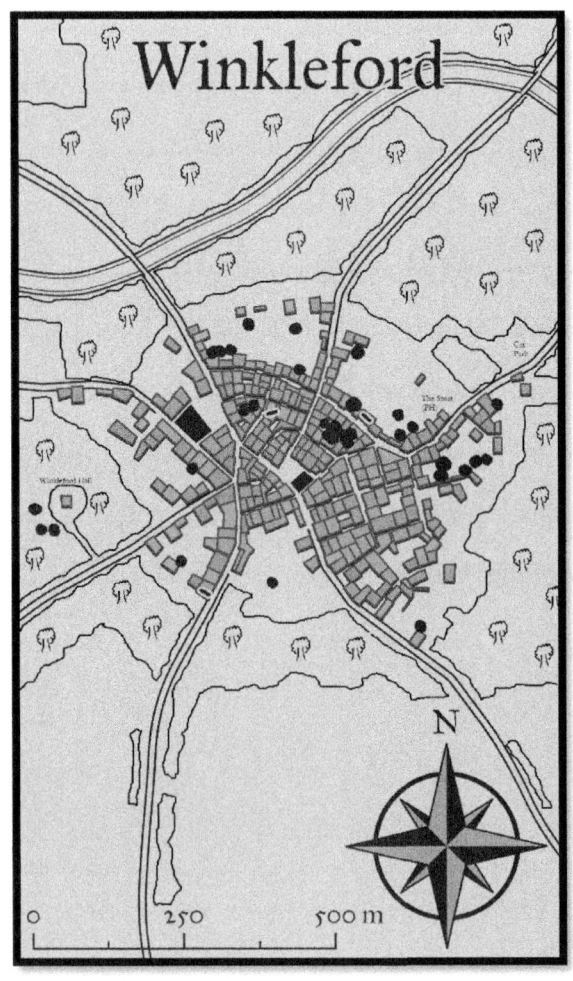

Justin B. Black

Timmy and the Quibbleberry

Prologue

Pitch black. A very faint glow from the moonlight obstructed by storm clouds on the branches and reflected from the puddles of rain. The deafening noise of leaves blowing from side to side, branches smashing into each other, and the wind blowing through the trees like a giant untuned wind instrument, interspersed with the rhythmical surges of rain smashing into the ground. Not a very pleasant environment, void of any human interference, and any life nearby is safely burrowed away from the storm.

A mighty black stallion pulling a tattered wooden carriage with a bearded, cloaked driver controlling the vehicle, rages passed. Screams of 'H-YAA!' breaks natures orchestra as the driver of the chariot pushes to go faster. The wooden cart has seen better days, clearly called into service as a last resort. A collection of hastily packed boxes, bags, bottles, and rags thrown into the back with no thought or consideration of protecting the items, or the best use of the space available within the tattered confines of the carriage. The large wooden wheels clattered and bounce, installing no confidence that each impact won't shatter the wheel into hundreds of pieces, a problem the cloaked figure at the helm clearly has no concern for.

The powerful horse pulling the cart, narrowly avoiding trees and burrows, wilfully obeying the commands of the whip to pull as fast as possible, onward, that's all that mattered, onward as fast as possible. A faint suggestion of a track is followed and forged as they push their way through the forest. The urgency of the driver to escape and run from something is clear, pushing the horse and carriage to breaking point, taking corners to the brink of catastrophe, and skilfully rescuing and saving the cart at the last second. Anything to push it to its breaking point and get away from… something, as fast as possible. 'Onward Merlin' screamed the driver.

Their experience has not failed either the horse or the driver until an unseen fallen tree which spans the path comes

into view immediately in front of them. The Stallion's reflex actions react quickly, and its front legs are launched off the ground by its back legs, and it jumps the obstruction with impressive ease. If any spectators had been fortunate enough to witness this performance, it would have been met with an 'Ahhhh' of appreciation as the front legs landed safely followed by the back legs.

However, this manoeuvre was not enough to save the tender vehicle being pulled, which was unable to avoid the obstacle. The front wheels smashed into the side of the log with a crash, catapulting the front of the carriage a few feet into the air, shortly followed by the back wheels. For a split second, the horse was pulling a weightless, floating cart, until the front wheels landed, briefly winding the driver who hadn't had enough time to prepare for the impact. As the rest of the cart landed, however not all the contents were so lucky to survive intact, or where they were a few moments earlier.

An old wooden box containing half a dozen small bottles of potions of various colours and shapes smashed into the ground, blending, and mixing their content into a shallow puddle, along with several unmarked homemade sachets, and packets of powders, and a collection of dried berries. By the time, the ingredients had been dispersed, there was more mixture than water. The horse and cart raced off into the distance, blissfully unaware of the missing contents, but with a wave of relief to have survived the jump, and continue at pace to escape something, that was all that mattered. The mixture stewed for a moment, as the storm raged through, thunder and lightning became more prominent with rain splashing into the ground.

A clash of light and noise as the area is illuminated by a bright white electric flash. A branch above is struck and ignited. As the flaming limb of the tree hurtled to the ground, embers scattering and warming the concoction below before the rain gently extinguishes and dilutes the mix. As the storm subsides, and the rain all but stops, and the various woodland creatures emerge from their individual sanctuaries to survey the damage and look for food. The sun breaks through the canopy with an intense beam of light, focused on the area of unintentionally discarded ingredients.

The puddle level almost entirely dried out, dried berries semi submerged into the mud, in the perfect storm of unintentional cooking and photo-synthesis, spawns a new and unique life, the process had started, now all it needed was time, all the time in the world, This was never going to be a quick process and this is no exception, but there was no rush at all, as much time as it needed to become what it was destined to, was now available. The Quibbleberry bush was born.

Chapter 1:
Hi There

Quibbleton Forest was a vast woodland of every different type of tree you could imagine, north of the quaint forgotten village of Winkleford, in the east of England. The village fell into forgotten history, so much so it rarely even appeared on some maps anymore. There were all the usual services you would expect to see in a village of its comparable size, there was a small corner shop called 'The Corner Shop,' the closest thing to a post office was a small post-box on the corner of 'Drabble Ln' and 'The Street.' A small children's park adjacent the main road, and the stapple of any British community, an old pub call 'The Stoat' run by old Mr Shuttleworse, and his wife. There wasn't a town square so-to-speak, but the car park to the village hall was as close as it got.

The river Winkle ran through the village following the line parallel with the road. The roaring Mississippi it <u>WAS NOT</u>, about thirty-five inches deep at its sump; not even deep enough for fish to take residence. The river itself was the only thing that regularly visited the village, and just as quickly left. There were a collection of half a dozen houses, some holiday lets which only saw action 2-3 weeks of the year, which gathered around the pub, in the village that any kind of town planning forgot.

Timmy Tumblewhisk lived on Wobble Lane, a quaint street lined with houses that seemed to sway and dance in the gentle breeze, unimaginative buildings of buff coloured brick and ironstone panels. Timmy had never known anything different, nor had he cared to, there was no need for anything else. He had his mum and dad, and his oversized Rabbit Bongo. He never knew his grandparents, and his parents seldom spoke of them. He was only aware of their existence by the arrival of a card at Christmas, and Timmy's dad telling him 'Your grandparents have sent you £20' on his birthday and or Christmas, which usually got spent on something for his online gaming.

It was any other Wednesday, nothing exceptional about today. It was the summer holidays, so while Timmy's parents were at work, and if the weather would allow it, he would play in the garden with Bongo. To be fair, most of the playing was done by Timmy, Bongo, with his rusty brown fur, was rarely interested in anything that wasn't a lettuce leaf. 'Bongo? Bongo, would you like to play fetch? Would you like to do… anything? I wish I knew what you wanted' Timmy had often wished he could talk to Bongo, instead of chasing him a few steps back and forth, but Timmy's imagination was all he needed, and it had never failed him before.

Timmy Tumblewhisk was only 11 and 5/8th but as he grew older, he was starting to be a little more daring with what he was allowed to do. He had always longed to explore the forest that abutted the bottom of the garden, but never been brave enough before. He had on occasion hopped over the fence for a little exploration of the dense undergrowth for anything interesting, perhaps some long-forgotten pirate treasure (Even though Winkleford was a good hour by car from any kind of coastline, and any pirate wishing to bury their treasure this far inland would almost certainly have had no sense of direction and would have been too lost to find their way back). All he had discovered so far was an oyster shell that had no earthy right being there, a vintage can of a pop drink that no longer existed called 'Sprunt' and what looked like an old track which didn't look to lead anywhere and had almost certainly been developed over when Wobble Lane was built.

The early morning sun was shining, and Bongo was particularly uninterested in any of Timmy's games today, so he looked mischievously at the spot of the fence he could scale to hop over and continue his exploring. He made one more attempt to play with Bongo, who looked at him very unimpressed. So, with a sigh that seemed to sound more like 'Well, I tried' he stood up and walked with a bounce in his step that made it more of a skip towards the shortest point of the fence. He placed both hands on the top of the fence and skilfully bounced over it with the precision and accuracy of a well-trained, triage winning show jumping horse. The ground he landed on was becoming well-trodden from the number of times he had already scaled the fence. He stood up straight and looked at the unused beaten track that lay before him. He started to wonder forward, tentatively with the awe of exploring somewhere that's potentially never been discovered before. After a few minutes he got to the point along the route he reached last time, he had never ventured any further than this before, this was the exciting part. His footsteps forged a new path through the undergrowth between the trees that lined the old track. A particularly thick bush lay ahead of him flanked by two old oak trees, with his hands, he managed to excavate an opening a little smaller than he could comfortably fit through, and before he could take his first step through, the startling sound of pigeons bursting out of the hedge, as two birds flew over him, and gave Timmy a fright so shocking, he stumbled backwards.

The incident with the pigeons had startled Timmy, but not enough to dissuade him from his adventure. He stepped off with his left foot though the opening to what looked like a clearing, untouched and undiscovered. In the middle of the clearing and immediately in front of him was a bush, standing prominently beneath the only beam of sunlight able to make it through the canopy above. It was off centre from the track, but this was no average bush, it seemed to stand proudly full of life and happy to exist, clearly well established, and been present for many years. All the vegetation looked to grow in a fashion that revered the perfectly formed, perfectly shaped plant, and with lighting that would adorn a famous artwork, the bush stood proudly.

The bush wasn't naked, it was adorned with fruit of some kind, large berries, very large berries, abnormally large berries, with the colour of a blueberry, but the shape and proportions of a blackberry. But there was something wrong, all the berries on the bush were lifeless and barely clasping the branch or had fallen to the ground to form a brown/blue mulch. This was true of all the blue jewels the bush wore, except for one. Hanging proudly to the side, bright, strong, healthy, juicy, and despite glowing in the dew dusted sunlight, Timmy had not noticed it immediately. Timmy's instinct was to approach it cautiously, still very conscious of the unfamiliar surroundings which could house any manor of creature.

As Timmy approached the lone berry, his hands reached up to support it from the bottom as he took the strain off the branch and started to lift it. As he did, a pair of eyes appeared on the berry and opened looking him straight in the eye. Starring at each other a few feet apart, Timmy froze, terrified, confused and wasn't sure exactly what was happening. The now opened eyelids blended in with the rest of the spherical protrusions from the berry and had simply appeared out of nowhere. Neither of them dared move first, not even to blink, taking in the sight that neither of them had seen before. Eventually Timmy had to blink to refresh his view of what he held in his hands, and the berry followed suit, relieved not to be the first to break.

Timmy was speechless, gasp less, and couldn't move, what exactly was this in his hands? His mouth slowly opened as if to force out some kind of inquisition… 'Wha….' was all he could muster. Before he could attempt it again, a slit in the berry beneath the eyes started to open and a fully formed mouth uttered the words 'Wha. Wha wha wha?' confidently with the tone and pace of an overly dramatic gameshow host. 'Wha, wha wha wha wha, wha wha?' it spoke awaiting an answer to the question it had clearly asked. Timmy didn't know what to do or say, couldn't move, and unable to complete the word 'what' he attempted something else. 'How…. Err… Wha?' The berry in his hands started to look frustrated, but after what seemed like an exasperated exhale, looked intently back at him. 'Wha wha how, wha how how err how. How wha err how??' the berry uttered softly. Timmy's mouth closed, as he tried to assemble his brain to think of what to do next.

The two faces starred at each other in the same way a turtle would look at a dog, neither knowing what the other is thinking, or what to do, but each too scared to move first. Timmy had no idea what was happening and what to do next, subconsciously he muttered out loud 'Oh for goodness' sake, I wish I could understand you' which was quickly met with the response 'You can!' Timmy didn't know how to feel more confused than he was, but here we were. Had he misheard that? It may be time to regroup and vocalise exactly what was happening. He closed his eyes 'I'm in a forest, holding a fruit that has a face and can talk to me?.' He opened his eyes again and was greeted by everything he had just uttered, save for the fact that the berry was now looking at him with a smile that wouldn't have looked out of place on a middle-aged gentleman looking across a bar at a woman clearly out of his league.

'Hi there! That's all true, and may I say, what a charming face too. I know I've been around a few years, and don't do as many stretches as I probably should do for a berry my age, but you know, *berries gotta berry!*' Timmy slowly took his hands away from supporting the berry to return the weight and strain to the stalk connecting to the branch. The berries face winced as he did, and before he could utter something to express his discomfort, Timmy interjected 'You can understand me?' The berry looked at him, 'Are we still on that? Yes, I can. You're that clever, are you? I'm so please to have been discovered by such a learned traveller. Oh, the nights I hang awake hoping that our first meeting would be…' Timmy could sense the sarcasm in the tone, so cut him off mid-sentence 'Ok, I get it. So, what exactly is happening here?' trying to calm the confusion in the air.

'Listen my good man, I am as in the dark on this as you. It's been a very lonely existence for me. I have been hanging around here for a long time, and the creatures I encounter are, let's face it, not very good conversationalists. Despite my best efforts…' The berry was distracted mid-sentence when he noticed something walking along the branch above him 'Oh look, here he come, here's one now' as he gestured to a caterpillar minding its own business. 'I say, how are things with you? The air is particularly crisp this morning, don't you think?' The caterpillar completely ignored the questions and carried on about its business. 'See, nothing.' Stated the disgruntled face of the berry. 'This is all too weird, I wish I knew what was going on…' then Timmy stopped, frozen as if a long-forgotten memory had surfaced and completely took over his chain of thought. 'You're a Quibbleberry.' Perplexed the berry replied, 'Excuse me, I'm a what?'

'You're a Quibbleberry!' Timmy repeated. 'And this is the Quibbleberry bush. It's the only one in existence and came into being some 227 years ago by a fluke accident, when some potions and rare ingredients were accidently mixed and cooked together where this bush now stands. They fell off the back of the cart of a wizard escaping capture from… well, all I know is it was someone, and the ingredients were heated by a burning branch of a lightning strike. The bush then became fully formed after 76 years of growing, before starting to fruit. Over 1,380 of your brothers and sisters have come before you, and you are the first to be found.' The look of sheer shock and confusion had now transferred from Timmy to the Berry. 'Have they really, well I say' Timmy continued to explore his memory as he looked closer at all the lifeless berries on the bush, and on the floor 'Quibbleberry are very special you see, they can grant wishes to the discoverer, and only the discoverer of the berry, unless they wish to transfer the power to someone else.' The berry then looked at the bush too, as much as he was able to turn 'Well I never. Would you look at that. So, I'm the first to fulfil its purpose?' The look of confusion was slowly replaced with a hint of pride. 'It would appear so, yes' Timmy replied.

Timmy looked sad as the memory continues 'But you see, you are probably to be the last one, as the Quibbleberry bush has almost completed its life cycle, and now that you have been found, it will cease fruiting' Both looked at the bush, and with a sombre tone the berry replied 'Oh how sad. How truly sad to be the last.' A moment of silence passed between them. 'So, what happens now?' the berry asked Timmy 'I don't know, shall we try it out? Officially I mean, not by accident' The berry looked back at him with excitement, 'Oh good show old boy, so how does this work?' Timmy consulted his memory again 'Well, I think maybe I should hold you and say *I wish*, and you grant it.' The berry looked confused 'Seems a little archaic and a bit *Genie of the lamp*, but let's give it ago... grab a hold like you did before.'

Timmy started to reach up to the berry but paused as he noticed something. One of the sacks of berry juice was ever so slightly faded compared to the others. This observation was quickly met with the feeling that this isn't the most important thing to have noticed today, and so Timmy placed his hands on the lower sides of the berry where he had before and lifted him slightly to take the strain of the berry from the branch... and then stopped. He was faced the opportunity to have anything, absolutely anything he wanted, and his mind went blank. 'What shall I wish for?' The Berry shot him a side glance, still half looking at the caterpillar above him, and still reeling from the relief of not being hung by his head on the branch. 'Oh, well is there anything you want?' Timmy looked around desperate for inspiration for something to come to mind 'There is lots I want, but nothing springs to mind. As this is only a test wish, we should probably make it a small simple one.' Overcome with his feeling of kindness, Timmy pondered the needs of the berry in his hands. 'Is there anything you want?' He asked. 'Wow, that's very considerate of you, how very kind. Let me think...' Instantly the berry thought of his location, how relieved he is when Timmy lifts him up, and how liberating it must be to walk around freely and pick things up.

'You know young.... Actually, my friend, I don't believe I know your name!' Timmy looked on with a smile, 'I'm Timmy, I'm a human boy, and it's very nice to meet you um...' The berry replied with a grin, 'Ah yes, hello young Timmy, it's very nice to make your acquaintance, I'm... I'm... err... a Quibbleberry' The berry looked deflated 'That's what I am, I don't think I have a name' Timmy felt sorry for him 'That's really sad, everybody should have a name, what would you like to be called?' deep in thought he replied 'Well, I have no idea. Any suggestions?' Timmy pondered for a moment and thought back to his English teacher from year 4 that the berry very much reminded him of, from the way he spoke. 'I had a teacher who sounded a lot like you, his name was Mr Kibble... Alan Kibble... Kibble... Quibbleberry... How about Kibble?' The berry then looked back at Timmy with distain 'Kibble Quibbleberry... it's a bit of a mouthful! Oh no, that won't do, it won't do at all. No, no, Alan would be much, much better.' Timmy then smiled with a grin of a first meeting 'Its lovely to meet you, Alan! Now what about this wish, what did you have in mind?' Alan's thoughts were still reeling at his newfound name, he had completely forgotten about his earlier desire.

'Do you know young Timmy, I would very much like to not be-so-berry, to not be bound to this bush. Perhaps some arms and legs, and possibly to be a little larger. It's very intimidating being so small and defenceless with all manner of creatures out there tempted to swallow you up... What do you say?' Timmy agreed and started to formulate the sentence to cover Alan's request. 'I wish for Alan to have all the things he needs to feel less berry-like' And with that, two spindly arms emerged from the sides of the berry, which sprouted some small fingers and thumbs at each end. No sooner had they appeared, he was already exercising stretching and bending them in amazement. Then, completely unnoticed were two long thin legs dripping from under Timmy's hands, which then seemed to bend at the end to form feet. As soon as they were noticed, the testing procedure commenced to make sure they bent and moved the way he would undoubtedly need them too.

Still holding and bearing all the weight of the berry in his hands, Timmy was so distracted with the orchestra of movement that was being performed in front of him, he didn't notice that the weight had started to increase. Not only had the green stalk that was connecting the berry to the branch been severed like and umbilical cord, allowing Timmy to carry Alan entirely, but he had started to grow, and grow, and grow in size. Timmy had no choice but to let go, with the same motion as launching a small boat into a lake.

The previously scrawny legs that were doing a little dance were now called to action to bare the increasing weight of the blue fruit. Alan's eyes were a collage of fear, intrigue and confusion tinged with excitement. The whole ordeal lasted less than a minute, and by the time the pair of them could gather their thoughts to realise what had transpired, the transformation was complete.

There they stood, an average height, average build 11 and $5/8^{th}$'s year old, standing in a clearing, looking up at an 8ft tall, 6ft wide, blue… blackberry, with eyes so bright and a grin so wide, no child on Christmas morning seeing all the presents they ever wanted could compete. One of them had to speak first, each waiting for the other to add some sense of order to this unfamiliar situation. The silence was palpable, and finally Alan uttered the first words to remind them both that time was still moving, despite what had just happened. 'I say, that's turned out ok don't you think? Yes, that will be perfectly acceptable' Timmy couldn't do anything else but take in the intimidating size of the being in front of him, framed by the beam of sunlight that seemed to illuminate everything around him.

Timmy had started to feel a degree of regret and intimidation at the size the berry had become. If he had wished, there would be nothing to stop him from picking little Timmy up and catapulting him over the trees, even though he was comfortable that would be unlikely. As Timmy surveyed the results of his wish, and as his eyes scanned the oversized body, they were drawn to the small area that had previously looked a little faded, to find it had faded a little more. He did some quick thoughts and wondered to himself, was something happening every time a wish was made, that was causing the colour to slowly disperse. Perhaps there was something in the memory he had been given to explain, and indeed there was. It would seem that Quibbleberries and their wishes are not everlasting. Each wish, cost the Quibbleberry some of its life. Alan was clearly blissfully unaware of this, standing in front of Timmy doing what could best be described as an awkward Rumba of excitement at the new gifts he had been given.

Before Timmy could broach the subject with Alan, his intake of air was interrupted by 'Thank you young Timmy, this is more than acceptable. I can dance, I can walk, I can defend myself from those hungry looking birds floating overhead, yes, I am a very happy berry indeed. So, what's next? You are a man with the world at his feet, anything you desire will now be yours, what shall we do, where shall we go, and what do I need to pack if we go there' he said with a comedic grin. Timmy only had one thing on his mind, and that was that the wishes he had left should not be squandered. He was also reluctant to tell Alan this yet, as he was clearly euphoric at being given such freedom. 'I must say Timmy, I have seen this small area of green for my entire life, and very satisfied that I've seen it all. Would you mind awfully if we leave? I want to try out my new pins!' Timmy completely understood his desire to leave. 'Oh yes of course… Come and meet my friend Bongo.' Alans eyes lit up wider, the thought of meeting someone new, and potentially showing off not only his new limbs, but, well everything. His excitement was euphoric and very infectious. Timmy nodded and reached for Alan's hand, and they turned to leave.

'Lead the way young Timmy, I'm ready to see the world. Now which way do we go? Alan uttered in excitement. Timmy started to move in the direction of the opening he had formed moments earlier. 'Come with me Alan' as he pulled Alan's new hand along with him to leave the clearing, and head back to the house.

Chapter 2:
I Feel all Fizzy

The track back seemed a lot shorter than the way to the clearing, Timmy thought to himself as he walked side by side with an 8ft tall blackberry shaped body with spindly stick like arms and legs. The silence was filled with thoughts of trying to grasp what was actually happening, how would he conceal his new friend from his parents, or how could he explain where Alan had come from? The garden fence was starting to come into view, as Alan broke the silence. 'So, you're a human boy… I don't know much more about you then that I'm afraid. Do you have a similar life to a Berry? How big is the bush you would have sprouted from? Are you all the same colour, and indeed do you all taste the same to foragers? Are you even on someone's dietary requirements?' Timmy could sense this was going to go on, and on, and contemplated the risk of wishing him all the knowledge he needed against the effect it would have on him? '…Do you eat berries? Do you forage for your own kind? What do berries taste like? What do you taste like? Do you plan to eat me? What's a Bongo? Do you eat them?' Timmy sighed an exasperated sigh… he had to give him what he wanted, so he lifted his hand and placed it on Alan's shoulder and, while watching the noticeably faded part of Alan's side, 'I wish you had all the answers and knowledge you needed to answer all these questions' and with that, Alan stopped talking with a 'Ooooooh'. The faded area on his side had indeed faded a little more. 'Well, that all makes perfect sense… yes I understand now, thank you my boy.'

They had arrived at the base of the garden fence, and Timmy was ready to climb over before pausing to look at Alan. He was an exceptional size now, could the fence take his weight? 'Do you know what Alan, let me go get Bongo and bring him to you.' This would also eliminate any risk of anyone seeing a massive blue blackberry with a smiling face and dangly arms and legs that would happen to see into the garden from the road. 'That sounds spiffing, thank you kind sir.' Timmy then scaled the fence and hoped over the top and into the garden. Alan had nothing to do now but whistle, look around, and bend and straighten his newly acquired arms and legs. Timmy landed on the partly trodden flower bed, nothing was damaged, but it was clear from his shoe prints that someone had been standing on it. His first duty was to find Bongo, who was not sitting where he had left him. The lettuce leaf had been devoured, and there was only a small area of flattened grass where he had sat. Timmy had adopted Bongo as a pet nearly a year ago. His parents finally gave in to his repeated requests for a pet but compromised with him not being responsible enough to have a dog, but to have a rabbit instead. Bongo had brown fur, floppy ears, and a collar with a blue pendant on that had inscribed in gold, the initial 'B.'

The flattened area of grass where the lettuce leaf was, had a path of trodden grass leading away from it to the vegetable patch. Timmy followed the track and intercepted Bongo seconds before reaching the patch of his dad's prize-winning carrots, lettuce, cucumbers, and potatoes. 'Oh no you don't, I can tell what you were after' He picked him up and started to walk back to the spot of the fence to scale over. Bongo was small enough to fit into Timmy's oversized coat pocket, so he lowered him in, and climbed the fence. As he landed the other side, Alan was sat on a tree stump, legs crossed in deep thought. If he had had a glass of port, a monocle, and was sat next to an open fire, he would have looked very civilised. His eyes scanned the area and landed on Timmy. 'Ahh dear boy, good to see you again' in a voice as if at an audience with the king. Timmy didn't know how to answer this, so moved swiftly on. As he walked up to Alan, he reached into his pocket to raise Bongo from his seat and present him the big blue berry.

As soon as Bongo was raised aloft for presentation, he jumped out of Timmy's hand and fell to the floor, a significant drop for a creature of his size. As soon as he landed, he limped into the nearest hedgerow. Timmy was hot on his tail and managed to again intercept him before getting to an out of reach position. Bongo had clearly given up with another escape attempt now in Timmy's grasp. He held him close to his chest this time as he would a new born child. Alan leaned in to have a closer look 'Fascinating… Hello Bongo, it's a real pleasure to make your acquaintance' He held out a hand for a handshake, to be met with a sniff and a shrug off. 'Well, how very rude. Are all your friends this impolite?' Timmy chuckled 'He's a rabbit, and he doesn't talk much, I just wish I could understand him and do for him what I did for you.' Timmy instantly realised and regretted slipping in the 'W' word into the sentence without realising what he may have done. He looked down at Bongo who was laying completely still, but then… He started to get heavier, and heavier, as he increased in size. Timmy had no choice but to lower him to the ground softly and take a step back. Bongo sat up on his back legs, no bigger in size than a Labrador before he stopped growing. Bongo looked around at them both. His collar had fortunately also proportionally increased in size, as had the pendant, and suddenly his face bore a range of facial expressions that were very clearly conveying absolute confusion and fear.

He turned his head to look directly at Timmy, who clearly knew what he wanted to ask. Timmy intercepted the question before Bongo could ask it. 'Bongo, now remain calm, everything is ok, can you understand me?' Bongo nodded slowly looking too scared to utter a word, he then turned to look at Alan 'Hi Bongo, my name is Alan, I am Alan the Quibbleberry, but I would be grateful if you just called me Alan. I can grant Timmy's wishes, which is how you became like this… We are both frightfully sorry for the slip of the tongue which has caused this, how do you feel?' Bongo looked back at Timmy for further information. Alan looked confused and asked Timmy 'Is he ok, isn't he supposed to show some signs of intelligence. He's not saying anything?' Timmy looked a little closer and said, 'Do you remember me Bongo, I'm your friend.' Bongo nodded again. 'Are you ok' Timmy asked again. Bongo drew a deep breath and uttered a sentence which confused Timmy and Alan just as much as Bongo had been perplexed to be in the conundrum he was in. In a delicate, well-spoken lady's voice 'I remember you Timmy, but please know I'm not a boy, I'm a girl' stated Bongo. 'He's a girl!' Alan exclaimed in shock 'He's, she!' he continued, 'She's not a boy!' stating the obvious, 'He's not a….' Timmy cut him off there for repeating the same facts repeatedly. 'She is… Its lovely to meet you madam, I apologise for the confusion' as he slightly bowed his head. Bongo smiled and accepted Timmy's apology.

Timmy asked again 'How do you feel Bongo, I can imagine how strange this must all be for you' Alan interjected 'I'm inclined to sympathise with you, young lady, I myself have been through quite…' Timmy cut him off again with a swift 'Shhh, let her speak.' Bongo looked up at Timmy and stated, 'I feel... good, but I feel… Fizzy' Timmy smiled, and forgetfully muttered 'Aww I wish you didn't' and closed his eyes with a disappointing sigh. After a few seconds, Bongo noticed the fizzy feeling had completely gone 'I feel good, the fizz has now gone. Its lovely to meet you both' As Bongo looked at Timmy, and then Alan who had a warming smile on his face, she glanced down at Alans side, and saw the clearly faded juice sack. 'Oh, my dear Alan, you have something on your side there, here let me wipe it off' as she hoped closer toward him to wipe his side, Timmy exclaimed 'Oh, no, it's ok, its nothing, I'm sure he's fine' but it was too late, Bongo was already trying to wipe the grey surface off the dark blue berry. Alan could do nothing but watch and expect it to wipe off. 'Oh' Said Bongo 'It looks like you've lost some colour, how peculiar' Alan observed with concern 'That's new, it wasn't like that this morning. I've, I've lost the feeling to that area, that's… why would it do that?' His voice progressed to mild panic. Timmy mustered up his most soothing voice to put Alan at ease. 'Listen Alan, everything is alright, I think that every time you grant a wish, it takes its toll on you, and will ultimately be the end of you. We need to be careful with the wishes now, and not waste any. Does it hurt?' Alan exclaimed 'It will be the end of me…' he sighed 'How disappointing. It tickles a bit, it feels… fizzy' he smirked as he shot a glance at Bongo, and she smiled back.

'Perhaps you could wish it better?' Bongo asked Timmy. He checked his memory and was sure that wouldn't work. 'It won't work, it's the juice within the berry that is able to grant

the wishes, and depending on the size of the wish, will cause the level of damage to Alan.' Bongo looked at Timmy with a confused look, Timmy replied 'Like, if I said I wish for an oversized piece of lettuce for you, that would be a small, easy wish' He immediately stopped and looked at Alan, who had a look like he had just been elbowed in the side. Bongo looked down at the floor in front of her, to see the biggest lettuce leaf she'd ever seen, green and juicy, laying at her feet. 'Be careful Timmy, look what you've done!' Bongo exclaimed. They both looked at Alan, who was clearly in pain, but managing to put a brave face on it. 'My dear boy, I am absolutely tickety-boo, I have plenty more juice in me yet. Don't you worry about good old Alan Quibbleberry the 1,381st. I added that last bit myself, quite sporting don't you think?' he said proudly. Timmy noticed he was clasping his side while speaking and vowed not to be so frivolous with his future wishes. 'So where did you come from, and how did you meet our dear friend Timmy?' Timmy looked at Alan and shouted 'The Quibbleberry bush! Perhaps that can heal you?' They both smiled at each other and turned to follow the track to the clearing where the berry had been born. Timmy led the way, and Alan followed behind. Not wanting to be left out, Bongo hastily followed with a limp she had gained from trying to escape Timmy's earlier grasp. 'Excuse me, wait for me chaps' She stopped, quickly turned around and smiled before reaching down to pick up the lettuce leaf, she had just been granted and returned to follow chase with the leaf in her mouth. Timmy approached the thick undergrowth first that led to the clearing. With both hands he forged an opening large enough for Alan to squeeze through and held it open for Bongo to hop through after Alan. As he let the opening close, he turned to see Alan frozen still, and Bongo by his side, staring straight ahead. The sun had moved across the sky, and the beam of light which had previously shone solely on the Quibbleberry bush was no longer visible.

Timmy tentatively approached Alan's side and realised why he was frozen still. There lay before them, a large patch of dark blue and brown mulch, scattered with the lifeless berries which were clutching onto the bush earlier that morning, and in the centre was a lifeless, pitiful stick poking out of the ground. All the leaves had blown away, the bush had fulfilled its purpose and given up. 'It's gone' Alan gasped 'She's gone, my mother, she's gone' he whimpered with a tear forming in each eye. Bongo approached and reached for Alan's hand. 'Oh Alan, I'm so sorry' Timmy approached the bush and looked down at what remained. A mournful silence fell across the trio for a few seconds. Timmy broke the silence, 'I'm so sorry Alan, I understand how hard this may be' Alan stood tall and gathered himself up, 'Its ok, she did her duty and grew me, I'm just a little sad.' Timmy pondered 'We could see if I can wish her back for you, but I don't think it would work, and only cause more damage to you' Alan took a second to think already knowing the answer 'No no Timmy, these wishes are becoming increasingly scarce, and are starting to take a noticeable effect on me. Besides, she has had a long life, I should let her go.'

Bongo thought the best thing to do would be to leave and tried to think of a sensitive way to suggest it 'It's getting late now, perhaps we should head back?' Her soothing voice was comforting, and the pair silently turned to leave and follow Bongo who was taking the lead back through the gap in the hedge. They all walked in silence, only interrupted by the crunch of Bongo eating her oversized lettuce leaf. Timmy turned to Alan and asked, 'Have you always been alone Alan, or did you meet any of your brothers and sisters?' Alan looked Timmy 'I have been alone most of my life. When I was a budding flower, I could hear others talking, but they had shrivelled away and died by the time I was old enough to recognise them. They have also fallen victim to foragers after a bite to eat. I recall several of my siblings were eaten by a fox of some description not so long ago. I'm pleased their demise can sustain life for others. It's been a rather lonely existence since, and I had accepted my fate until you came along and freed me' Timmy didn't know what to say, so Bongo responded, 'That must have been so hard for you, I'm sure your fellow berries were just as funny, charming and interesting as you, and I bet none of them were your size, and certainly didn't have arms and legs!' Alan smiled, Bongo seemed to have a talent for making people feel better 'Here we are, what shall we do now? I don't think you turning up with a giant berry and an oversize rabbit will be very easy to explain to your parents Timmy.' Bongo stated. That was a very good point, there was still a few hours before Timmy's parents got home from work, where they would expect to see Timmy alone playing with an average sized rabbit.

'We should make the most of the time we have together, I'm sure we can think of something before they get back!' Alan and Bongo looked at each other 'Very well my boy, the world is your oyster, what would you like to do?' Timmy knew what he wanted to do, he wanted to go visit the lake and see all the boats floating around, but suddenly remembered the list of things his mum had asked him to do before she came, home. Could he wish for them to be done? Was this being too frivolous? Timmy tried to recall the list.

> Timmy's Chore's
> 1. Take Out the Bins
> 2. Tidy Your Room
> 3. Hoover Downstairs
> 4. Do All Your Homework
> 5. Mow The Garden
> 6. Feed Bongo
>   Love Mum x

That's a simple enough list, it would barely have an impact on the berry, surely. 'Alan, I'd like to go to the lake, and see the boats, but I have a list of chores to do first, and don't think we will have time to do both' Alans eyes lit up, 'Boats? How frightfully wonderful. I shall join you' Bongo looked on casually nibbling on what was left of her lettuce leaf. 'Would you like to wish all your chores to be completed young sir?' Timmy glanced at Bongo for approval before looking back at Alan 'I don't want to cause you any more damage, I mean it would only be a little wish, and probably wouldn't take too much out of you?' Timmy looked down at the area which had taken all the brunt of his wishes. Now three of the little juice filled capsules had drained and hung grey and lifeless at his side, and a fourth was already starting to look like a partially deflated balloon. 'Its fine little man, it would only be a small wish, and I suspect would hardly impact me at all, you go right ahead' replied Alan, reassuringly. 'Okay, only if you're sure' Bongo remained impartial and now having finished her leaf, offered no expression in her face for what was being agreed.

Timmy assembled the list in his head and started to recite it. 'I wish the bins were taken out, I wish my room was tidied, I wish downstairs was hovered, I wish I'd done all my homework, I wish the garden was mowed and I wish Bongo was fed' Both Bongo and Timmy watched Alan intently to see what impact this would have. Alan winced, put his hand on his side, and took a sharp breath as the wish was granted. Alan exhaled and opened his eyes. 'Bang' There was a slam as the back door of the house over the fence was flung open, and two neatly tied bin bags floated down the path to the wheelie bins, patiently waiting with open lids. Once the bags had landed, the bins closed along with the door to the kitchen. Timmy started to smile, as it was one less job for him to do, but something was wrong. 'Oh, oh dear' Alan exclaimed, bent over in pain as another wish was granted, his eyes scrunched up as he put his other hand on the hand that was already clutching his side. There was a sound of clothes and toys whooshing around the room, the curtains fluttered to the open window of Timmy's bedroom. Timmy could see shadows of things being tidied away; bed covers briefly came into view as the bed was presumably being made. Dusters flew from one side to the other, and the few toys that were on his window cill suddenly jumped up and disappeared into the room. Then finally the windows closed and silence. Timmy was happy to know his room was cleaned, but what about Alan, he only made one wish, what was happening?

'Oh, that's not nice, not nice at all!' Alan bent over in pain, eyes streaming and scrunched up as he clutched his side tighter with both hands. 'There was the familiar sound of a vacuum firing up in the house, but instead of the usual sound of forwards, and backwards, there was the noise of things being knocked over, glasses smashing and some very painful crashing noises coming from the open window of the downstairs toilet. Timmy's face dropped, as he looked at Bongo for an explanation. 'I think something is wrong, it was only one wish, I just wanted the chore list done' Bongo replied, but without the comforting tone she had previously used 'But you made six separate wishes sweetheart, and I don't think they were very detailed.' Timmy recounted the sentence in his head and suddenly realized the multiple wishes he had made. The crashing and banging were relentless, as the vacuum whizzed around the house smashing into things and seemingly causing a lot of damage to the, not clean, but lived in property. The sound of the hoovering was still going on, in and out of every room. Timmy could hear and potentially workout the path it was taking through the house, and what specifically was being damaged in its wake. Then Timmy heard the vacuum return to the cupboard under the stairs, reconnect itself to the charging station and shutdown, and then… silence. However, Timmy was also well aware that there were still three further wishes to come, and desperately tried to recount them in his head and confirm exactly what he had said… Bins taken out, that was easy, room tidied, it would appear that was done, and he was really looking forward to seeing it, hoover downstairs, that was clearly done, although from the noises he heard, there was a lot more damage done than good, but that was a problem to look at after… what was next… Homework! All his homework was done, that would be an easy one, wouldn't it? Before he could continue to recite what was next on the list, his chain of thought was interrupted by a chilling yelp!

By this time, Bongo had made her way to Alan to comfort him. Alan had dropped to his knees in pain. His hands were no longer able to completely cover the area of dead looking berries, as it had now taken up most of his side. 'Oh, ooooooooh….' Alan trailed off with his exasperation as his lungs emptied with air. Before Timmy could turn to go and comfort Alan, his movement was interrupted by the sound of a window smashing, he turned back to look at the house, and glass was raining down from his bedroom window as his

Timmy and the Quibbleberry

school backpack had flown through it and was making a beeline for where the trio were standing, flying like a Timmy-seeking-missile locked on his location. As the bag hurtled towards him, it started to empty itself of contents, the zip opened and books started to disembark the vessel, along with a pen and a calculator. The pen accelerated from the bag targeting Timmy's hand, flew straight passed it and circled back to land itself in a writing position. The notebook followed shortly after, but before reaching Timmy, he felt a force pushing him to the ground, crossed legged in a seating position as the notebook landed, open on his lap. The bag then landed beside him as the calculator then landed on his leg. He looked at Alan and Bongo in shock, and they both looked back at him, Alan with eyes watering from the pain, and Bongo concerned that she had two people she wanted to comfort but couldn't reach both, and her maternal instinct was to sit with Alan who needed her most. Before any of them could utter a word, Timmy's had was forced, as if by some unruly bouncer, to put the pen to paper and it started writing the answers to the questions.

Question 1: Jason buys 9 pairs of laces for his hiking boots, it cost £19.26 altogether. How much would 3 pairs of laces cost? The pen in his hand wrote effortlessly £6.42 in the space provided next to the 'A' with no input from Timmy. *Question 2: Matthew's van can carry 192 boxes. Matthew has 6,240 boxes to move from Norwich to Cambridge. How many journeys must this van make to transport all the boxes from Norwich to Cambridge? Show your method and workings.* The pen then started to squiggle in the space provided next to the 'A' all the workings out and calculations to reach the answer of 33 Journeys, adding the caveat that the return journey would mean double. The workings and calculations were exactly as they would have been if written by him, including the fact that a half load would still need a full journey. *Question 3: Hannah has 34...* This went on for some time for over forty questions in Math's, all answers and workings scribbled down.

And then to English and science. 25 minutes had passed before it was all complete with no conscious input from Timmy. Once the last question in science had been answered, the books closed and returned to the open bag, which dutifully zipped closed as it launched off the ground to return to Timmy's room through the smashed window. Timmy's hand was sore from being clasped and forced to write continually for twenty-five minutes, but he was relieved to have finished. Alan was grateful for the short respite, and Bongo had her arm around his back to comfort him. But they were all very aware that there were a couple more wishes to be granted. Timmy frantically tried to recall what was next... The Garden!

Alan had enjoyed a moment of rest whilst Timmy was doing his homework, so the next wish caught him by surprise, like a punch to the ribs, Alan yelped out 'Oh my goodness, this one is going to sting a little. Ooh, oooooh...' and as Bongo and Timmy looked on in concern at Alan, a massive crash of wood broke the silence, as the lawnmower, fully active, burst through the shed door, ripping it off its hinges and smashing it to a thousand pieces. The petrol-powered lawnmower landed, it immediately raced in a predetermined route, engine at maximum revs as it careered around the garden. Cutting the grass as it went round, and round, and round, collecting all the grass cuttings and spitting them out as it went. The whole orchestra was hypnotic in its dance and was gracious to watch. Once it reached the last piece of grass to be cut, Timmy, Alan and Bongo breathed a sigh of relief that the ordeal was almost over, but the problem was that the lawnmower didn't go back to the remains of the shed, it was still circling, and heading towards the flower beds, Timmy cried out 'NO! Not mum's flowers!' but it was too late, bits of Petunia's, Sunflowers and Roses were already airborne as the mower made short work of the flowerbed. Without even stopping, it completed a U-turn and returned to what remained of its former home.

All three froze and starred at the freshly mowed garden with a trail of cut grass, sprinkled with the remains of flowers. The smell of the grass wafted through the air and made Timmy think of the wonderful summer evenings. Even the remains of the flowers added their individual flavours to the aroma. Timmy couldn't think of that right now though, he couldn't move, but had to, he had to remember what the last wish was. Bins, Tidy room, Hoover, Homework, cut the grass and… and, what was the last one, what was the last important job his mum had… A look of fear washed over his face and a cold shiver rushed through his body, he shouted… 'Oh no, BONGO!'

Chapter 3:
Slice, Swoosh, Slice, Swoosh, Slice

Bongo looked at Timmy and the surprise of him calling out her name. She hadn't been thinking about what the wishes were, she was more concerned with Alan and the toll this was all taking on him. Her paw suddenly felt him tense up, the berries crunched closer together and felt like they were firming up. Alan's eyes shot across at Bongo as he held his breath to prepare for what was about to happen. A surge of pain raced through Alans body as he felt yet more life force escape him, but this one was different, it wasn't from the same place, this was refreshing to start with, it seemed to come from his other side. The relief was quickly extinguished as the familiar pain from one side, now surged through his other side. 'Oh, Oh I say, that's… that's… oh dear…' Alan uttered. He closed his eyes and leaned into Bongo's paw as he endured the pain until it finally started to subside. When he opened his eyes, Timmy was standing right in front of him in panic. Before they both looked at Bongo. There was a faint rumble in the air, and the earth beneath their feet very faintly started to vibrate. Bongo suddenly sat bolt upright as if standing to attention at the arrival of a superior officer. She turned to face the fence as her mouth started to slowly open. Just over the fence, Timmy could see all his father's vegetables floating as they were ripped from the ground. Dirt was still falling off them as they float motionless suspended in the air.

An almighty smash of glass came from the house, it couldn't have been Timmy's bedroom window again, no, it was the kitchen window. A squadron of kitchen knives were making their way through the air to the vegetables. Synchronized in a perfectly formed flying V formation. If they had started to emit multi-coloured smoke in flight as the famous British Red Arrows would have, it would not have looked out of place at all. The floating vegetables realigned themselves for dissection. All the carrots moved to the front of the pack in a floating straight line, and the lead knife sliced through them all in one swoosh. It immediately stopped once the last carrot had been severed and flipped round for a return severing flight slightly lower down to create multiple floating disks. This manoeuvre repeated back and forth until the line of rods, became a cloud of disks. Meanwhile, to the back of the carrot massacre, a handful of around a dozen lettuce heads waited patiently for the next knife. It was a larger knife, and perfectly suitable for the job. It sliced through the first head creating an explosion of floating lettuce debris. Instead of immediately stopping, this knifes flight path looked more orchestrated to most effectively use its angles and come in for a second attack in one continuous motion. Slice, swoosh, slice, swoosh, slice… it went on.

The cucumbers floated in a line like soldiers being reprimanded. Six long, firm, green cucumbers of varying sizes and shapes patiently awaited their fate. Cucumbers were always Bongo's favourite, and only ever got them as a treat. A slightly smaller knife bringing up the rear of the formation swooped to the side on a planned trajectory to take out all six in as least moves as possible to efficiently slice them into disks. The whole ordeal could have been barbaric if it were anything other than vegetables. The remaining two knives seemed to serve as support knives, nipping between massacres to assist as needed. Before long, there was a cloud of salad floating in the air… and all of a sudden, the knives stopped, resumed the V formation, and hurtled to the smashed kitchen window to resume their space in the block on the worktop. As the trio watch the aeronautical display of flying knives return to the kitchen, they were unaware that the fresh salad had formed a line and flowing like a string of ants, flying directly to Bongo's open mouth. Bongo had no choice but to chew and swallow the food. The line of food was flowing faster and faster than Bongo could cope with, it just kept going on and on and on, it was only the start of the endless spiral of freshly cut salad, and already Bongo was showing signs of discomfort as she started to flag under the relentless flow of food.

Timmy and Alan looked on helplessly. She wasn't going to last long being force fed at this rate, Timmy had to do something, he had to help. He jumped to his feed and rushed over to try and obstruct and push the bits of salad out of the way, but it was no good, every piece he tried to stop, just floated back to its orderly place in the line, like trying to stop the flow of water using only your hands. Timmy stopped, ran into the woodland, and returned with a large piece of bark to use as a makeshift shield and stop the food from entering the paralyzed rabbit's open mouth. But the food just built up and found a new way passed the obstruction. Timmy tried to think again, and tried to push Bongo out of the way, but it was not use, whether he wasn't strong enough, or there was no way to budge her. He only had one more idea in his head but had tried to avoid thinking it. He looked over at Alan who was still doubled up enjoying the relief from the pain. But then he had to do something to help Bongo, tears were starting to form in her eyes at being force-fed the salad she would have normally enjoyed. He looked back at Alan and rushed over to him. 'Alan, we need to do something, Bongo can't cope much longer' Alan knew what Timmy was about to say, and although he was still in pain from the last wishes, he agreed that he had to help Bongo. 'I understand dear boy, make your wish, but do it quickly please.' Alan took a deep breath and held it. 'I wish to stop the last wish, now!' Timmy cried out. Alan looked at him with a smile of recognition for the way he phrased the wish, 'Good work young Ti…' before he could finish complimenting him, the inevitable pain started again, the same side as the last, a stronger stabbing pain. It seemed to last longer than the last, but it was a pain he was willing to endure to rescue Bongo.

Suddenly, the march of various pieces of salad stopped their dance and paused for a moment. Then gravity got the better of them, and all the pieces of food fell to the floor. Dropping and bouncing on the ground. Bongo fell to her knees beside them both, gasping for air with tears streaming down her face, coughing, and spluttering. 'Little miss Bongo, are you ok? Gasped Alan on the floor next to her. 'Cough, cough, I'm fine, I'm ok, cough, cough, but I never want to see another piece of cucumber again!' Bongo gathered herself up and managed to get to her feet. Her first though was to go for Alan, who had endured another wish to rescue her. 'My dear Alan, what did you do?' Alan looked at her, 'It was a pleasure to rescue you madam… Well, not entirely a pleasure, but still, it was my privilege' Timmy looked at Alan, and feared the worst. 'Alan, perhaps we should assess the damage, stand up so we can see how you are' Alan mustered up the energy to get to his feet, and stood upright, like a hero, proudly displaying his battle scars, wearing them like medals. Timmy and Bongo looked at him, his drained and greyed juice capsules to each side of him were evenly coloured. Against the dark blue, they gave a distinguished look to him, like a grey dusting to the side of a middle-aged man's head. 'Well, aren't you becoming a silver fox' Bongo said with a smile. This made Alan feel himself again. Although still tender, he felt 'Berry' again.

Timmy looked at Alans eyes, they'd stopped watering and he was reminded of the first time they opened in front of him. Full of life and excitement of what the world was to hold before him. That hope was still there, and long may it last. Timmy's mind then returned to the carnage that awaited him over the fence. He hopped over the fence with Alan and after a little more effort, Bongo followed. The garden was a state, there was scattered Salad everywhere, bits of wood scattered over the piles of cut grass from the exploded shed door, remains of the mutilated flower heads, the vegetable patch which looked like it had just been ploughed, and broken glass everywhere from the kitchen and bedroom window. Timmy looked down at his Casio calculator watch, it read in an exceedingly small faded digital display 14:27. He had a few hours before mum and dad would be home, there was no way he was going to make this right before they got back. 'Little bit of a state here young sir, it occurs to me we have two choices. We rally together to tidy up and repair what we can. Or…' pausing for effect before announcing granting another wish '…we could run away' he said with a smile. Bongo turned to look at him, 'I do hope you're joking Alan' he smirked with a wink 'Of course I am madam, we all know the second option' Timmy ignored both of them while he tried to think what to do. 'Young sir, I am here to assist you, but you need to wish for it' Bongo stepped forward and put her paw on Timmy's back 'Don't Timmy, we will find another way, poor Alan has been through enough.' Timmy sighed, and walked slowly towards the back door, and opened it. The inside was a bomb site. Everything had either been knocked, damaged, shifted, broken, cracked, or shattered. The only thing which looked presentable was the small bits of the floor which were rigorously hoovered.

Timmy felt a hand on his shoulder 'Young man, there's a solution here you're not seeing, it's an easy solution, and can clear everything up in one sentence' Timmy turned to look at Alan 'But I can't do that to you again, it would be a big wish, and will hurt you' Alan glanced around at the mess. 'I'm afraid young sir, it's the only way to clear everything up' Timmy was slowly starting to realise the implications of each wish. As he started to muster up the courage to think of a wish that would return everything back to normal, in the easiest way possible, he felt something in his pocket vibrate… and then again… and then again…. His phone was ringing. He had placed it on silent a few days back when he visited the cinema and forgotten to turn off the silent mode. It was a gift from his parents for his 11th birthday, mostly so he could keep in touch with them while they were at work. All his friends at school were also demonstrating the latest phones, and although his was by no means the latest model, it was more than sufficient for what he needed, which was mostly to message his friends in the class group chat. But people hardly ever actually called him, it was only ever message alerts, so who could this be? He reached into his jacket pocket, and pulled out his phone which was vibrating, flashing, doing all it could other than making a noise to get the owners attention. Timmy looked at the screen, which displayed in big letters 'JACKSON MOBILE CALLING.'

Jackson was his friend at school, the only one he really got on with. They messaged a lot and were normally found together in the school playground. Timmy slid his finger across the screen to answer the call. 'Hi Timmy!' the speaker said, 'Hey Jackson, you doing, ok?' Timmy hated talking on the phone, what was wrong with messaging? 'Yeah man, are you coming down the lake? A group of us are now heading down there, wondered if you wanted to come?' Timmy looked up at Alan, who was staring back in awe at this little playful device that Timmy had stuck to the side of his face and talking to. 'I'm not sure, I'll try. When are you going down there?' Timmy surveyed the damage again trying to determine how long it would take to tidy up. 'Now leaving mate, come on! Message me when you're on your way' Timmy now looked at Bongo who had the same expression on her face 'Okay, will do' Timmy could sense the need for another wish, despite his best efforts to resist. 'Cool see you later' and the line went dead. Timmy took the phone from his face and looked at the screen to make sure the call had ended before sliding it back into his inside jacket pocket.

Bongo and Alan were standing in front of him like two of the oddest-looking school children, waiting for their instructions. 'Right then, how shall we do this?' Timmy said looking at Alan. 'Might I suggest a smaller wish, perhaps wishing for a servant to clean up the mess from all the wishes, or perhaps a small army of workers?' Timmy thought about it and looked at Bongo 'That would work, I think if you wished to reverse the wish, it would be a large one. Getting a small assistant to carry out all the repairs would be less damage to our big berry friend here' Bongo said as she gestured to Alan. Timmy looked at them both 'Could I wish that all the damage to the house and garden to be repaired, and just get a little helper to assist if I need help later?' Alan looked at

Timmy 'A wish like that would be huge…' but Alan was cut off mid-sentence. He dropped to the floor in agony as the wish was about to be granted. 'Alan… Timmy what did you do, did you wish for it?' Timmy tried to recall his sentence, 'Could I wish…' Timmy felt a wave of guilt wash over him as the responsibility for what Alan was about to endure was entirely his fault.

Alan was clutching his belly on the floor this time, as he could feel the juice drain from some of the capsules appropriate to the size of the wish. Timmy could see the shed door out of the corner of his eye. The fragmented pieces were starting to assemble themselves and move back into position as a door to the shed. Bongo was now by Alan's side on the floor but couldn't help but notice all the pieces of freshly cut Salad scattering the garden float up into the air and reassemble themselves as fresh vegetables, then dance their way back to the vegetable garden before replanting themselves back into the ground. The remains of all the flowers jumped up into the air and one by one headed back to their original place in the flower beds. None of them noticed the rustling from inside the house as order was completely restored. The only sign that the house was being repaired was when the bits of broken glass around their feet lifted off the ground to re assemble themselves as windows panes. Alan was gasping for air at this point, with Bongo's comforting paw on his back, and Timmy on his knees beside him. None of them noticed the triangular shard of glass at Alan's feet which lifted off the ground to join its other fragments and reassemble in the form of a beautiful pane of glass. But its flightpath was too close to Alan, and as it lifted, caught a juice capsule on Alan's side, slicing it open, draining the contents on the floor. 'Ahhhhhhhhh, my goodness that hurt' His hands reaching to clasp the juice that was oozing out. Timmy and Bongo quickly rushed to help, but it was too late.

The small puddle of dark purple fluid on the grass beneath them had already started to seep into the ground. Alan was clasping the remains of the capsule, Timmy trying to put his hands over Alan's while Bongo tried unsuccessfully to scoop up as much of the juice in her paws as possible, but it was too late, the damage had been done.

Chapter 4:
That Wasn't Me, Was It?

The shard of glass, blissfully unaware of the damage it had caused, had returned to its rightful place in the window, and the whole tidying up ballet was now complete. Timmy sat back to look at Alan and assess the overall damage that had been done. His whole lower half had was a collection of grey drained capsules. If the situation hadn't been so serious, it would have looked like Alan was a very top-heavy orb wearing an inadequate grass skirt, but this was definitely not the time to bring something like that up. Bongo looked at Timmy 'Now Timmy, you know I love you dearly, but you need to be so careful with what you say. We need to start treating the phase 'I wish' with the same strict caution as an offensive swear word or an obscenity. Please be careful from now on sweetheart' Timmy had to agree. The repercussions of not being careful with his wording were on its knees in front of him. Alan was coming round, opened his eyes, looked at Timmy and smiled a smile of joy that hid his pain well. He then felt the loving paw on his back and looked at the owner, continuing his smile. His attention was then drawn to the remains of a small purple puddle on the grass beneath him. He looked up, and with a tone of embarrassed humility 'Oh how embarrassing, that wasn't me, was it?' Timmy stifled a smirk and looked at Bongo who was doing the same.

They were all looking at the puddle to avoid making eye contact with each other, as the mood would have sparked a laughing fit. Bongo looked up at Alan and then to Timmy and froze, stuck in a gaze at Timmy's shoulder. Alan was the next to look up at Bongo who was in a trance, frozen looking at Timmy 'Are you alright my dear? What's wr…' Alan turned to see what Bongo was looking at and stopped mid-sentence trying to understand what he was seeing. Timmy had noticed that Alan had stopped mid flow and looked up at him to see what was wrong. Confused he noticed that they were both looking intently at his right shoulder. He could not feel anything, or could he? He had only just noticed some weight on there. Two points, as if someone small was standing there. He did not dare turn his head to look, instead slowly moved his eyes to see what was there so as not to shock something so close to his face. A figure, leaning against Timmy's scarf, about eight inches tall in dirty dark blue overalls, a worn out brown flat cap and a miniature pipe beneath his oversized thick glasses, which hung in his mouth. Would not have looked out of place having just come up from a coal mine. He was standing minding his own business looking at the puddle the trio had been trying to distract themselves with seconds earlier.

'I'm lookin,' and I'm lookin' but I give up, it's a puddle of purple stuff. You gonna tell me what's so interesting 'bout it?' the little man uttered. He reached up and put the pipe back in his mouth, then looked up at Alan and Bongo, before turning to his left to see the face as big as him gawping back less than a few inches away. 'What you all looking at? Ain't you not never seen a Task-Miner before? I don't know, I come 'ere to be of 'elp to ya, and not even get offer'd a brew for me efforts' Timmy broke his gaze to look at Alan and Bongo for an answer, but they were doing the same thing to each other. Bongo was the first to enquire 'You must forgive us; you have us at a dis-advantage. Can you tell us where you came from and why you are here?' The three looked intently at the little man for an answer. 'Why I'm 'ere? Well to 'elp you lot of course, that's what a Task-miner does. We mine and help with problems for ya. Someone 'ere must've wished for 'elp with something, and 'ere I am. Names Pob,' He held out his dirt covered hand to shake. 'Not 'and shakers 'eh, never mind.' He looked at Bongo disapprovingly 'You're not one of them Fist-Bumpers are ya? Heard of you lot. Can't see the appeal meself, too American for my likin.' Naa-then, has that shipped sailed on getting' me a cuppa before we start work? Whole British empire was built on cups of tea, can't start me work without one'

Pob looked around to get his baring's, looked at Alan and said 'Cor you're a big fella aren't ya? Are you alright mate, you look like you've been in the wars there, you need some 'elp with something?' he said with a tone of genuine concern. Alan finally mustered up the energy to reply. 'I do apologise sir, I've been under the weather you see, and not… as you might say… running on four cylinders' Pob chuckled to himself 'Ah, an engine joke, I like you pal' He then turned to Timmy 'And what 'bout you lofty? Something you need some 'elp with?' Timmy didn't know what to say, he just stared back at Pob 'Come on boy, cat got ya tongue or something? Me old man used to say that to me all the time when I was shut up as a nipper. Never understood it, wot's a cat want wiv ya tongue?'

Alan was trying to work out why he was here? 'Timmy, your last wish, I believe it was finished with *just get a little helper too* if you needed help for anything' Timmy broke his gaze at Pob to look at Alan in realisation. Pob chirped in 'And there ya have it ya see, you wished for 'elp, and a task-miner was discharged to you, so 'ere's your old mate Pob to 'elp!' he put the pipe back in his mouth and blew out a cloud of smoke. 'Can't help with your problems without a brew mind, nope' With that he jumped off Timmy's shoulder, and landed on the ground at his feet, took two steps backwards, held his hands apart to smack them together, and looked around 'Right then, where's the kettle' clapped his hands together and in a flash of light disappeared. Timmy, Alan, and Bongo all looked at each other in amazement. Before anyone could utter a word, the noise of the kettle boiling from the kitchen broke the silence, followed by the sound of cups and cutlery rattling. They could hear indecipherable muttering of a cockney talking to himself.

Then with a flash, Pob appeared in the middle of the three with his hands open 'Any of you want one?' Nobody said anything, not to be rude, but couldn't get the words out 'No? I don't know, try and be nice and…' Pob took a step and clapped his hands together, and in a flash of light he disappeared again, the same muttering was heard with clattering in the kitchen. The kettle had now finished boiling and the clattering had stopped but replaced with the sound of water being poured. Before Timmy could get up and look in the kitchen window to see what was happening, a flash of light and Pob reappeared with a normal sized, half filled, mug of tea. 'Right then' he said taking a sip of tea from the mug 'Who are ya then, I'm Pob the Task-miner, what's your handle' he said looking at Timmy. 'I'm Timmy' he said trying to keep up with the conversation. 'Happy to meet ya Timmy, knew a chap named Timmy once, helped me with building a wall, ain't seen him since. How about you princess?' Bongo looked at him flattered 'My name is Bongo, and I'm a rabbit, Timmy's pet rabbit in fact' Pob looked up from his mug 'An a pretty lookin' one too'! Happy to be acquainted.'

'What about you, big fella?' he said turning to look at the Berry. 'Pleasure to make your acquaintance, my name is Alan, and I'm a Quibbleberry' Pob looked down at his tea, 'A Quibbleberry eh, not heard of one of you before, funny lookin' fella, do you all look like that?' Alan looked down at himself

'I grant wishes you see, and every time I do, I lose some of my juice. It's really starting to take its toll on me you see' Pob looked at the lower half of Alan 'Cor you ain't kiddin' might be able to help with that. Hold me mug Tim' Pob held his mug up to Timmy, which he reached out to take. Pob then clapped his hand together and walked over to Alan to assess him closer. 'Got a nasty cut there 'un all, need to sort that first' he reached into his overalls and pulled out a tube of super glue. Squeezed a dollop out onto his finger and applied it to the cut. Held it there for a few seconds while everyone watched inquisitively, and finally let the empty capsule go. Pob took a few steps back and looked at Alan. 'Yeah, I recon I can help make you look better… give me a sec.'

Pob clapped his hands together again and paused before turning to the other two onlookers 'You guys may want to give me a little room for this' Pob said to Bongo and Timmy. They both took several steps back until they had their backs to the house. 'Much obliged' said Pob to them. He turned back to Alan who was now on his feet. 'Brace yourself big fella, this is gonna feel right funny' He clapped his hands together again and started walking around him. The walk became a sprint, then a run, faster, faster, faster, until he was just a blue blur forming a ring around Alan. Then the ring started to get smaller around him and started to lift off the ground till it was level with the stalk at the top of his head. It then got smaller till it was inches away from Alan, and starter to move down, as if in a massaging motion from top to bottom. When the ring reached bottom it would expand again, rise to the top and repeat the motion, massaging the juice capsules downward. Timmy and Bongo could do nothing but spectate in wonder at the event before them. Alan could feel what was happening, the juice from the berries to his top half were being forced down to inflate the dead capsules below. He felt invigorated but the motions, and before long the actions of the ring slowed down, and slowly descended to the ground. As soon as it landed, Pob slowed down and eventually became a small man running in a circle at Alan's feet before coming to a complete stop. Not even out of breath he wondered over to Timmy and calmy held his hand out to receive his mug of tea. 'Yep, that ought to do it' Pob said calmy as he took a sip of tea.

Alan stood proud, all the same colour again, his dark blue berries had now turned a slightly lighter blue, and all the juice capsules that circled his body were now inflated. They were not as firm as they once were, but they were all equally inflated. Alan felt normal again. 'Now listen big fella, nowt has changed you understand, I've just equally spread your juice out to all of them ya see, bit of redistribution if ya like' Alan was gazing at himself in the reflection of the kitchen window. 'Oh Pob, you are a gentleman. I have to say I look rather striking now. I am in debited to you' Pob took another sip of his tea 'Ahh, it ain't no bother son, now then, how can I be of assistance to you rag tag bunch, I'm 'ere now, what's the situation?' Timmy was watching Alan admiring himself in his reflection, whilst Bongo had already made her way to Alan for a closer inspection. He couldn't think of how to answer Pob. 'Well, you see, you were wished for by accident, we have solved the problem we had, and I think all is back to normal.

We were going to take a trek down to the lake to see the boats, you are more than welcome to join us?' Pob had fixated on one word 'An ACCIDENT? Gordon Bennet, you can't go and wish for things by accident, wishes are extremely valuable things. Why I'd give my right arm fer a wish or two' Timmy looked back to Pob who was drinking the last of his tea from the mug. 'So, I rushed all the way 'ere and you don't need me now? *Sigh* Ne'er you mind, I'll be alright. I tell you what I'll do for ya. As you lot are such lovely folk and trust me you meet some real humdingers in this line o' work, as you're such nice folk, I'll let ye 'ave a freebie. If the suit wearers over at TM-HQ got wind of it though, they'd 'ave me license, so don't you go spreading the word about this y' hear? Keep it under yer hat' Pob reached into his dirty overall pocket and pulled out a small black box, with a big red button on top, protected by a plastic cover, similar to that on a plane that could launch a missile.

On the side of the box in red letters were the words 'Stay Calm' & 'Task Miner Direct Link' Pob handed it to Timmy. 'Ere you go mate, this is my Task Miner Direct Link… It's my own personal TM-DL, them suits up at TM-HQ won't know about it. You push that there button, and it'll summon me from wherever I am' Pob took the last sip from his mug 'Cracking brew that' as he handed the empty cup to Timmy. 'Now it's on the house now, so you just hit that button and I'll come running. I think that concludes our business for today, so I'll be headin' on now if thas alroit?' Timmy couldn't think what to say, so he simply nodded. Pob turned to face Alan and Bongo, 'You mind how you go big fella' he gestured to Alan, then reached to tip his flat cap at Bongo 'Princess.' Then he took two steps backwards, clapped his hands and Flash, he was gone.

Timmy looked down at the little box. The big red button had a plastic guard over the top of it so it couldn't be accidentally pressed. He took his handkerchief from his pocket, and wrapped the box in it, then slid it into his side jacket pocket. Alan was still admiring his reflection, while Bongo was admiring how much better Alan now looked. 'So young sir, what now? Shall we head to the lake to see boats, and so you can see your friend Jason?' Timmy looked at Alan and corrected him 'Its Jackson' he said looking at his watch 'We have a few hours left, that's plenty of time' Timmy went through everything in his head, did we have everything we needed, was the house ok to be left, which would be the best route to take? Timmy had visited the lake lots of times with his parents, but never on his own. 'I think the best way to go would be cutting through Quibbleton Forest, but we will need to go through the village to get to the entrance.

Before Timmy could turn to start to leave, he suddenly looked at the pair 'I can't just walk through the village with you two, we're going to need a disguise. 'I'm an amazingly fast runner Timmy, we could risk it if you want to climb on my back. I would happily take the lovely Mrs Bongo too, but suspect she would be faster than me on her own? We only need to make it to the entrance to the Forest' Timmy pondered the proposal, it wasn't that far, down the road, passed the corner shop and the pub, round the corner and over the

Timmy and the Quibbleberry

fence. It would be easier than a disguise, and certainly better than accidentally wishing for something. Timmy looked at Bongo for her thoughts 'What do you think Bongo?' She looked up at him and said 'If we are to head to the lake on foot, I am happy to keep up with you' Timmy looked at Alan, and wondered how he could possibly climb on for him to carry him? 'Ok, let's go then, but we need to be quick if we go through town' Alan walked towards Timmy, and knelt down beside him and picked him up to put him on his shoulder. 'Up you get young man. Are you comfortable up there, sir?' Timmy didn't have any issues with height, but knew when Alan started running, he'd have to hold on tight 'I'm alright, let's go' Alan prepared to leave, he turned to face Bongo 'And you little miss, can you keep up?' Bongo hoped up beside Alan, like getting ready at the starting line of a race 'Don't you worry about me Alan, I'll be hot on your tail' Alan turned to face the garden gate 'Then, start your engines, and let's go!'

Alan started to run for the gate, swung it open and bound his way down the driveway, Bongo running closely behind him. They got to the bottom of the driveway, and quickly tuned right onto the footpath to run down Wobble Lane onto The Street. This would normally take Timmy a couple of minutes to reach the end of the road, but with the speed and strides Alan was making, it would only be a few seconds. Timmy was keeping an eye out for anyone who may accidentally catch sight of this strange trio running down his street. Everything was ok. Alan was running as fast as he could with his new legs, which were only a few hours old, and he had never seen civilization before. It was all so wonderful. As they approached the end of Wobble Lane, Timmy warned Alan 'You'll need to turn left here Alan, but be careful, this is the main road though the village' Alan understood and barrelled round the corner onto the street. Timmy checked both ways, aside from a car travelling the opposite direction out of the village, the coast was clear. He checked on Bongo, she was keeping up hot on Alan's heals. They raced down the road, they just needed to get passed the corner shop, and the pub, and then it's onto the carpark for the woodland and we're safe. Alan ran as fast as he could, passed the corner shop, hoping nobody inside would notice him running passed the window. Alan didn't look, he just kept running. Timmy scanned the window trying to see if anyone would notice. A couple of customers were too engrossed in the contents of the frozen ready meals, and just having a natter with each other about the price of fuel down the road. They were safe, one more obstacle and they were home free. The corner shop was a couple of buildings away from The Stoat car park. They ran in full view of the car park, it was too early for anyone to be sitting on the benches outside the pub, the smoking shed looked empty, so Timmy shouted to Alan 'It's safe, we can go' Alan acknowledged with a nod and carried on running. There would be people inside propping up the bar, day drinkers, but they would not notice, or care to look out the window. The goal was in sight, there it was, the entrance to Quibbleton forest carpark, a few more seconds and they would be there, safe. Timmy took one last look at The Stoat to make sure they hadn't been seen, but then, as they were halfway across the car park, the front door opened…

Timmy panicked… what should they do, run faster, and ignore it, slow down, and try and hide or give up and embrace being caught? No, Alan was a fast runner, perhaps they wouldn't be seen? Timmy shouted to Alan 'Don't look, just run as fast as you can!' Alan and Bongo both understood and just… ran. From the open door of the pub emerged 'Old Chris', a local resident whose life was split between work and the pub, that was it! Half his time was earning money at the local garage, the second half was spending it all in the pub. Timmy didn't look, just focused on the target. Chris was completely though the door now, freshly rolled cigarette in his hand while he was frantically checking his pockets for a lighter. He looked up to see, in full view, Timmy Tumble-whisk (The little boy from down Wobble Lane) riding an eight-foot blackberry with arms and legs, being followed closely by an oversized brown rabbit. Bongo looked across at Chris, and gave him a wink, then carried on the chase. Chris froze in place, rolled up cigarette an inch from his mouth, as his eyes watched the spectacle in front of him. As they disappeared out of sight beyond the carpark entrance. Chris could do nothing else then stay frozen in place, take this as a sign, he thought to himself, that he had reached the limit of an acceptable number of beers for the day. He simply dropped the cigarette, finished putting on his coat and walked home to sleep in the hope that when he woke, he would be sane again, and this would all just be a funny memory he would NEVER TELL ANYONE!

They had done it, they had reached the car park in broad daylight in full view, almost entirely unseen. Alan ran round the corner, and into the undergrowth, out of sight. Out of breath he sat on the ground, trying to reassemble himself. Bongo, unphased by the run, joined a couple of seconds later. 'That was truly wonderful, so exhilarating to be able to run and be free like that' elated Bongo. Alan, struggle to respond while trying to catch his breath. 'Indeed… it… was… young… little… miss…' Timmy scaled down the side of Alan and onto the ground, allowing him to breathe deeper. Timmy was trying to remember the way to the lake from here, he found a sign showing a map of the forest, clearly indicating a 'You Are Here' arrow to signify their position. Timmy wondered over to it to have closer look, leaving the other two to have a quick rest. He was familiar with the woodland having visited it with his parents several times, and there it was, a pale blue splodge in the middle of a sea of green, with numerous red dashed lines indicating the paths leading to it.

The route was fairly simple, in fact it was even signposted from the car park. Timmy knew the route to take and returned to the duo to show them the way. Alan was standing taking in the surroundings, Bongo saw this as the perfect opportunity to have a bath and clean herself. 'You know young sir, I know this is the same forest as the one I was born into, but it's amazing how different it looks here. The colours and the smells, all very refreshing to see' Timmy looked around, it all looked the same to him. 'Are you both rested, shall we head off to the lake, its truly magical down there' Bongo looked up 'Ready when you are Timmy' Alan looked at her, and then to Timmy 'Let's not diddle-daddle around here young man, lead the way!' They headed to the footpath entrance to the woodland, blissfully unaware that a few feet away in the hedge, a set of eyes was watching them intently, ready to follow.

Chapter 5:
Bluey, Purpley, Greeny, Brown Mulch

It was a spring morning, just like the 1,000's that had come before it, and more than likely, the 1,000's that would come after it. The earth was damp with dew, and the sound of the rustling trees was only interrupted by the morning chorus of a bird song. Walking through the bushes, quietly on the hunt, was a golden-brown fox. She had been up all night looking for food, but the night before wielded very slim pickings. The frog she had caught the night before had sustained her for last night's hunt, but there was very little food to be had. She leaped through a gap in the hedge to a clearing she not been to before. As she landed, she paused to get her bearings and take in her surroundings. The first thing she familiarised herself with was the best vantage points, and any potential threats in the area. The next was to calculate the best exit points of the clearing in the event of an emergency. After all her calculations were complete, she assessed the food situation of the area, nothing of note. A snail was slowly making its way up the tree, not worth the energy, a Finch had landed seconds earlier, but just as quickly escaped when he clocked the fox looking at it, and a bush with some pitiful looking berries hanging off it.

Her primary instinct was to feed, then hunt, and the bush offered the best and most easily accessible solution. She tentatively moved closer to the bush. She knew the berries wouldn't offer much in the way of sustenance, but there were plenty hanging in reach to give her the energy to find something more fulfilling. As she arrived at the bush, on closer inspection she could see that some of the berries were all dried up, and well past their prime. A few were semi fruitful, and one was just coming into flower and far too ripe. She sniffed the first berry she could reach; it didn't really smell of anything, so she took her first bite of the most appetizing looking one, squeezed it to the roof of her mouth, and swallowed what juice it had. It was bitter but refreshing, she then proceeded to the next one, then the next. She'd had nine berries, but the remaining ones on the bush looked too shrivelled and dried up to be worth the effort, so she moved on to scout the area for anything else that could offer sustenance. She left the clearing which could offer nothing more, to look elsewhere. As she made her way through the woodland, when she heard running water from a stream. These were normally excellent hunting grounds for food, so she cautiously moved towards the sound.

Her nose was the first thing to poke through the hedge, constantly sniffing and taking in all the various scents and smells. She had an excellent sense of smell. She edged closer to the stream, no signs of life yet, so she took the opportunity to have a quick drink. The berries had made her mouth dry, and the juices had dried up in her throat. She lowered her head to the water and lapped it up with her tongue. It was very refreshing, and she was much thirstier than she thought. She drank and drank, and drank, this wasn't normal. It was never enough water. She drank and drank and drank. The dried berries in her mouth and throat had mixed with the water and turned to a tar like substance clinging to the inside of her, and impenetrable to the water she was trying to wash it away with. She drank and drank, more and more, she was becoming uncomfortable, what was happening? She gingerly backed away from the stream, panicking, what could she do? The nausea was setting in now, she backed up some more until she was up against a tree. The sound of the flowing stream was now muted by the deafening sound of her whining. Her eyes closed firmly, crying for what was happening to her, it was becoming dizzying, and she couldn't think straight, her primal instincts were fading to clasp onto consciousness, but it was too late. She lowered herself to the floor, with tears streaming down the fur on her cheeks until she could fight it no longer. She passed out in a frightened state, exposed against any of her better instincts, and vulnerable.

'What's happening? Where am I? Is this my voice I can hear? Its dark. Why am I so cold?' She opened her eyes to see grass. Beyond the grass was woodland, trees and trees and tress. She could see hedges and hear running water. These were all familiar things, but she didn't know why. She lay motionless for what seemed like an eternity as she tried to come to terms with what was happening. She lifted her head up, slowly to get a better view of her surrounds. 'Why does my head hurt… and WHAT is this awful taste I have in my mouth?' she tried to make more saliva to take the taste away, but it wasn't working. She needed a drink, so she instinctively edged back towards the stream to take a sip. 'What's the last thing I can remember? It's all a blur' She thought back to the last thing she could remember. 'The stream' she was just here drinking. She immediately stopped and backed off. She could remember approaching the stream on the hunt, but that was a totally different attitude to life. She wasn't a hunter, was she?' She had never been able to have thoughts about how, or why she was there, everything suddenly had more meaning and depth. She was more aware of everything, more self-aware. 'But how did this happen? Was it something in the water?' she furiously tried to remember what happened before that. She remembered seeing a snail climbing a tree, she remembered where her burrow was, but there was something else. Something her subconscious mind was trying to remind her of. She sat down, distracted briefly by all the noises, and smells she was exposed to.

She turned to look at the path which she remembers approaching the stream from. 'Did I come from through there? Yes, I remember now, I was hunting for food by the stream, that was it' she stood up to go and look at the gap in the hedge she had emerged from. Her legs were still a little shaky, but she got to the opening. She needed to get back to her burrow to rest, that was her safe space. It was easy for her to track her way back to her burrow. The scents and features were easy to follow. 'I really don't feel right, not right at all. That's what I need, I just need sleep' she approached the opening in the bank she was very familiar with. A wave of relief spread through her as it came into sight. She crawled inside, and curled up, using her big bushy tail as comfort for additional warmth. She nuzzled her nose under her back legs, and no sooner had her tail wrapped round her face, she was asleep.

The hours turned to days, then to weeks. It was only the intense hunger that pulled her from her sleep. She opened her eyes wide, fully refreshed and wanting to eat. She lifted her head up, but she hadn't moved for… 'How long was I asleep for?' and it ached to move. She tentatively positioned herself to emerge from her den. As always, nose first, slowly, smelling, followed by the rest of her. She was hungry, she had never been this hungry before, and needed to eat something. 'What was that?' she heard the sound of something landing. Immediately she turned to fully face the toad that had landed close to her. 'Hello!' she thought, and pounced, it didn't stand a chance. It was just what she needed. As she finished the meal that had landed in her lap, her mind was drawn to the events of the last day she could remember. Where was she before the river? The snail was climbing a tree, the tree was in a clearing she had discovered 'There was a berry bush there, and one of the berries hadn't ripened yet, perhaps it was still there and was ready to eat now?' she finished off the last of the toad, and full of energy set off to find the bush. As she sniffed her way through the Forest for the familiar scent she had previously followed. Her mind was alive with a thousand thoughts of what was happening to her. She wanted more, more than just food. She wanted to explore and have new experiences; she wanted to learn and live life. Perhaps if she had that berry that was full of juice, it would make her stronger and more intelligent. Was it the berries that had done this to her? She needed to find out.

As she approached the clearing, there was an unfamiliar sound. Immediately she went into self-defence mode. She stopped and lowered her body to the ground to crawl closer. Her ears were on high alert, as the new sound got louder as she approached... voices. It was the voice of a well-spoken lady, a smooth and comforting voice 'Oh Alan, I'm so sorry' She could understand it. She wasn't close enough to see what was going on and didn't want to risk breaking cover. Then a second voice, it sounded like a small child 'I'm so sorry Alan, I understand how hard this may be' She has heard voices like this before from when she was a cub and ventured too close to the edge of the forest. She knew very well to be extremely weary of these voices. Then a third, voice, a posh well-spoken voice, but not the same as the first one she heard, this sounded like a man, a big man 'Its ok, she did her duty and grew me, I'm just a little sad..' She was now able to slowly raise her head from behind a fallen tree. She would be obstructed from view by the hedge in front of it, as she was able to get a glimpse of where the voices were coming from.

Three silhouettes stood facing what was left of the bush, two smaller ones, and a large round one. One of the smaller one reached for the hand of the large one 'We could see if I can wish her back for you, but I don't think it would work, and only cause more damage to you' then a pause before the larger one answered 'No no Timmy, these wishes are becoming increasingly scarce, and are starting to take a noticeable effect on me. Besides, she has had a long life, I should let her go' What were these wishes they kept speaking of? She waited patiently for them to leave so she could go get the berry that had no doubt fruited now. Once they were out of sight, she gingerly approached the bush.

Where was it, it was on that branch, she was sure it was. There was nothing left, no leaves, no old berries, no life at all, just a sorry looking stick poking out of a pile of bluey, purpley, greeney, brown mulch. Had they done this? What did it all mean, she needed to follow them to see what was going on. But which way did they go 'Was it through that hedge there?' she approached it, but she had spent so long inspecting and sniffing the bush that she had lost the voices. All she could hear was the leaves rustling on the trees and the singing of the birds. She approached the bush she thought was the way they had exited, which was the opposite side to where she had come from. The grass was well trodden, a large foot, a smaller foot, and some long feet. Was this them, they looked fresh. She picked up the scent and poke her nose through the hedge to see where it went. There was the strong aroma of berries, the smell of lettuce, and the faint smell of a human child. She continued through.

There was what looked like a path forging its way to the hedge she had emerged from, and the flattened grass clearly showing the footprints was leading down it. As she emerged further, she could pick up the smell of the trio, but she couldn't risk being seen by walking down the middle of the path, she had to find a route down the side. She climbed through the opening and crawled tightly to one side before she could sneak in behind the bushes that flanked the path to go undetected. She could slowly start to hear the voices again as she slowly approached what looked like an opening. She was very familiar with this area, as a cub she was warned by her mother not to approach here as it was where the humans lived. They were destructive, evil monsters who destroyed our natural habitat to make way for their dens. This was not something she wanted to interfere with and knew only too well to stay away. The last time she saw her mother was when she had left to find food for her, and never came back. She believed she had ventured too close to the human world and suffered her fate at their hands. 'Should I turn back, or should I follow?' She could very easily go back to carry on with her day to day, but she had conscience now, and her curiosity was overwhelming.

She moved closer and was able to get a perfect vantage point to remain unseen and get a clear view of the three. It was indeed a human boy, quite short with a brown coat on, and a red scarf. He was accompanied by a delicious looking rabbit, but this was huge, almost the same size as the boy. Was this a new breed of rabbit? This could keep her fed for weeks. Surly they didn't grow this big normally, perhaps it was a wish that had caused this, it seemed to be all the three were speaking of and her curiosity surged. But where was the third silhouette, the big well-spoken one? Then she saw him… 'That looks like… that can't be… it looks like a berry! A big berry, a massive berry! Was it the same berry that was hanging from the bush? Had it grown that much? She thought to herself 'And why is he speaking, walking, talking? Is that what had happened to her?' She needed to know more.

The hours seemed to fly by as she sat observing the events of the three. The arrival of a smaller man, and his swift departure. The whole event was almost entertaining from her perch overlooking the garden. But then, the small boy, they kept referring to as 'Timmy' climbed onto the shoulder of the large berry they were calling 'Alan' and they headed for the gate, followed closely by the delicious looking rabbit they were calling 'Bongo.' She had to spring into action and follow them. The toad she had eaten earlier wasn't very filling and she was getting hungry. She leaped into action, over the fence and through the gate before it swung shut. She raced behind them as they sprinted down the street, always out of sight, but always aware of where they were. She raced round the corner and passed a very confused looking human walking along the footpath in a dazed and intoxicated state, almost knocking him over, and stopped before turning the corner of the entrance to another part of the forest where the trio had stopped for a rest. She found refuge in a small bush behind them and watched. She was getting hungrier. Little Timmy had now disembarked from Alan and had wondered off to look at a sign. This could be her moment, to attack Bongo, to leap from the bushes and strike. Or would Alan be a better target? She had seen what had happened with the little man, and how he managed to make him one colour again, this could have made him weaker and more vulnerable. She now had a taste for the juice he was made of and what it had done to her, she was hungry.

As she calculated her next move, Timmy had returned to them, excited to know the way to go from here, she would have to wait. Maybe striking from the back while they were travelling, she could be quick, so quick the other two would be unaware they had been attacked. But for now, she would have to wait. Alan was up on his feet, and Bongo had finished preening herself and was ready to leave. If she were going to strike, now would be the time, but she knew she couldn't overpower all three of them, one would be easy, two would be possible but not without its risks, but three, the odds were not in her favour. She watched patiently as they headed towards the footpath. Patience, it's what foxes do best, patience.

Chapter 6:
The Snarl Had Turned to A Smile

The path was well worn that calved its way through the woodland from the carpark. At some point, the council had laid some wood chippings to make the route more clearly defined, but this was some years ago now, and the wood chippings had turned to mulch, but still managed to serve its purpose of defining the route. Timmy and Alan were walking in front, side by side. Alan in wonderment and the sights and sounds of this new and exciting world around him The smell of the trees, the sound of the creatures, even the breeze on his face somehow felt different, whereas Timmy was on high alert looking out for anyone who they may accidentally bump into in such a public space. He hadn't really had the time to give much thought to what would happen when they got to the lake. The fact is he was accompanied by an 8ft blackberry and a brown rabbit the size of a dog, be a tough one to explain… but he was trying his hardest to think of any way he could make it work without resorting to a wish. Bongo was hopping behind the pair, her limp had gone after the run, and she was feeling back on top form again… but something was wrong, she had a feeling she just couldn't shake they she was being watched / followed / observed. These feelings are heightened in rabbits, they need to be, as they are bait for many creatures. It's something she couldn't do anything about, and she hadn't had this feeling for a very long time, the sanctuary of Timmy's home never made her feel threatened. Although the feeling was refreshing and new, it was nevertheless very worrying.

Bongo paused briefly when she thought she heard something behind them 'Did you hear that?' she called to the others with a sense of urgency. She jumped round 180 degrees and stared at the path behind them on full alert, eyes frozen looking for the smallest sign to justify her fears. Timmy and Alan stopped in their tracks and turned around to look at Bongo. Seeing how scared she was, they too scanned the path behind them for any signs of movement. A few seconds passed 'Are you ok little miss? What do you see?' Alan asked. Bongo was still frozen, poised ready to leap to retreat 'I'm sure I heard something. Do you feel like we are being followed?' Timmy scanned the area again with a higher degree of panic. 'I don't see anything' Timmy was far more scared of being seen by someone, than being followed by someone, the trio were hardly conspicuous. Alan walked closer to Bongo to comfort her 'Are you sure you heard something? I'm no expect my dear, but I do know that forests are always full of noises and things moving you see, it would be strange if it didn't' Bongo trusted her instincts, and this was one to trust. 'We are being followed, I know we are' Bongo reiterated, still frozen and on high alert. Alan looked back at Timmy 'You know dear boy, there is a way…' Timmy replied before Alan could finish 'No, I am not wishing to find out. We don't know how it will affect you now your berries have been refilled, you are now more vulnerable to wishes' Alan understood 'But we might be in danger, I trust Mrs Bongo's instincts' Although Timmy felt the same way, he didn't want to jump into wasting a wish just yet… especially when it could all be for nothing.

'I tell you what, let's keep walking, and if Bongo hears anything else, we will stop again and have a proper look' Alan reluctantly smiled back at Timmy 'As you wish Chief. Little miss, are you happy with that?' Bongo was still frozen, ready to run, desperately scanning the area for the smallest sign that her fears were justified. She didn't answer. Alan put his hand reassuringly on her back, in her heightened alert the contact made her jump slightly, but she was comforted by the gesture. She slowly started to calm down and began to stand up straight. 'Oh Alan, perhaps you're right, we should keep moving' her guard was clearly dropping. Alan gestured to turn her round and walk beside him as they walked up to Timmy, and all set off again.

Bongo was walking in the middle of the pair, still on high alert, but comforted by the protection of the two of them. Alan kept his hand on Bongo's back to reassure her she was safe but had quickly returned to the awe and wonderment of his surroundings. Timmy seemed to be on high alert looking for any unsuspecting passers-by who would stumble upon them, perhaps this wasn't such a good idea, should he find an alternative route, a less exposed path to the lake? Should they even be going to the lake at all? What would happen when they get there? Avoiding the need for any further wishes was becoming increasingly unlikely.

Bongo stopped and jumped around again; this startled Alan who still had his hand on her back whilst looking at the canopy in awe. Bongo's ability to see 180 degrees was keeping her on high alert 'There! You must have heard that!' Timmy stopped and looked at Bongo, she was shaking in fear. He then looked at Alan who was fiercely scanning the path behind them for any signs of unnatural movement. Timmy walked back along the path very, very slowly to investigate further. Anything he could do to avoid making another wish would help. One step, two step and scan the bushes either side. Three steps, four step and scan the undergrowth. Nothing. Timmy then took two further steps back to investigate further, focusing all his attention on the surroundings to find what could be making the noises Bongo kept hearing. Two further steps and he was blissfully unaware of what had stepped out of the undergrowth into the path between him and his friends.

He was still searching 'Timmy' Alan said calmly. Timmy wasn't listening 'Timmy' he said again with a slighter increase in urgency. No response from Timmy who was focusing all his attention on his investigation. Then a completely new voice that resonated correctly with Timmy, one he hadn't heard before, it was deeper, huskier, and gravellier than he had ever heard. An evil voice with a tone of clear intentions. 'Timmy' it said. He froze and slowly turned round only expecting to see a large blackberry with a rabbit by his side, but there was something else, something between them walking slowly to a point centrally on the path. If pure intimidation were a physical form, this was how it would look. Her eyes fixated on Timmy, her tail swaying so slowly as if only to demonstrate her readiness to move at any second, like a race car at the start line, engine running, ready and waiting for the green light.

'Who are you, what do you want?' Timmy uttered, his voice shaking with the severity of the situation he now found himself in. 'You're a fox' Timmy astutely pointing out the obvious. 'I am a Vixen' she replied 'I am hungry, and you have something I want' she demanded as she turned her head to look at the duo standing in fear behind her. 'What do you want?' Timmy said to draw her attention back to him. 'Your friends. I am hungry and have an appetite for rabbit, and yours looks delicious. And your berry friend, I found it first, and you stole it from me, now I want it back' Alan then interjected 'Madam, how rude of you, I am not an 'It,' I am a Quibbleberry, and I am a gentleman. I will thank you to refer to me as such' Vixen then turned her head quickly to Alan and bore her fangs at him. 'It doesn't matter if you're an 'It' or a gentleman, you will still taste the same' she said in a sultry voice. Her attention was then taken to Bongo, who was frozen trembling in fear.

'And speaking of taste…' she turned her body to move closer to the pair. 'Wait!' shouted Timmy. 'I didn't know the berry was yours, I found him in a clearing in the Forest, there was no indication that he belonged to anyone else' Vixen stopped in her tracks and turned her head back to Timmy. 'I found him as a flower, and waited till he was ripe to eat him. I ate his brothers and sisters, who gave me the ability to think and speak, and now I want more of what's rightfully mine' Alan exclaimed 'Good grief, it was you! You're the one who ate my brothers and sisters. I saw you' Timmy panicked as he was losing control of the conversation. Vixen was licking her lips looking intently back at Alan. 'And look at you now, look how big you've grown. I'm salivating at the thought of the powers you could give me' she said, but then stopped and turned her head to look square on to Bongo, teeth showing, big black eyes frowned 'But first…' she creeped closer to Bongo. Alan could feel her muscles clenching up as she prepared to run. 'STOP!' shouted Timmy. 'I won't let you do this. You must know enough about the Quibbleberry to know that I can easily wish for something to stop you' Vixen paused in her steps, the snarl had turned to a smile. She turned her head back to Timmy 'I've been watching you long enough to know that your berry is running out of juice. The damages your wishes are causing are killing him, and I want the juice while there is still some left.'

Bongo wasn't going to wait anymore, she was clearly Vixen's first target and her primal instincts of flight more than fight, kicked in. She took the opportunity of the distraction. She jumped, ran in the opposite direction, and into the undergrowth. Vixen was caught off guard looking at Timmy, and in a second, she quickly leaped into action. Hot pursuit of her food. Timmy and Alan were helpless, the two had completely disappeared before they realised what was happening, left standing staring at each other. 'Bongo!' Timmy shouted, but they had gone. Timmy ran up to Alan, we need to do something, we need to help. 'I agree young sir, but what?' They both scanned the area looking for some signs of the direction they had both run off in. 'BONGO, COME BACK!' Timmy shouted, knowing full well that she wouldn't while being pursued. Alan, having the benefit of height and a better vantage point, was able to see further than Timmy, and although was able to see the undergrowth move to follow the line Bongo had taken, despite her size, she was still agile, but her visibility didn't last long. He was also able to see the route Vixen had taken in the chase, but they had both disappeared now. Timmy was clambering up the side of Alan, to take hold and rest on his shoulder. 'Let's go, after her!' Alan obliged and leaped into the undergrowth following the route of the pair, for as long as he remembered it.

Before long, he had lost them completely, and was just running. They had travelled so far that he couldn't even remember the way back to the track they were on. They were both lost. Alan stopped, and lowered Timmy to the ground. 'I'm sorry my boy, I fear we have lost them' Timmy frantically searched the area around them, in complete denial of the facts. 'BONGO!' he continued to shout, but his voice was becoming horse from screaming as loud as he could. 'They've gone' Alan said trying to calm Timmy down putting his hand on his shoulder. 'But...' Timmy was interrupted by Alan 'My dear boy, she is a resourceful young lady I have every faith she will be safe and be able to evade her predator. There is nothing we can do now. Might I suggest that we continue to head down to the lake? She knew that's where we were heading, and when she feels safe enough, I'm sure that's where she will go to find us' Timmy felt a tear running down his face, which Alan reached down to wipe away. 'It's the most sensible thing to do' Timmy wasn't thinking straight, overcome with emotions, and didn't think about what he was saying 'I know Alan, I wish I believed you' Alan dropped to his knees and clutched his side in pain. This was only a small wish, but the berry capsules were less full. Three berries on Alans side proceeded to drain away, as Timmy suddenly realised what he had done.

Timmy's face was awash with the realisation that they needed to head to the lake, but quickly followed by the remorse of what he had just done. 'I'm afraid dear boy, I don't think that was a very clever thing to wish for, given our current predicament' Alan said finally able to speak. Timmy's remorse hit harder being reminded by Alan of what he had just done. 'We need to head to the lake... but... which way is the lake?' Timmy said looking around. They had only run for a few minutes, but neither of them paid any attention to the direction they were running in, and certainly didn't consider the many changes in direction they had to make to avoid trees and thick impassable vegetation. Timmy tried to visualise the map he had inspected before they left, he knew the direction he had come from, and sure that if they back track, it was very likely they would find the path again eventually. So, he had no choice but to try 'This way, we need to try and find the path again' he said. Alan kept close to him, as they started to make their way back.

As they both walked along the unfamiliar route to find the path again, Timmy asked Alan 'Do you remember seeing Vixen before? You never mentioned her' Alan looked at Timmy 'I was young and didn't realize what was happening. I saw her eat the other berries and assumed she had had her fill. There was very little I could actually do then. I'm just glad you found me before she came back for more' Timmy understood. 'Were there any other animals that discovered you before me, that you can remember?' Alan looked perplexed by the question. 'None that found me specifically, aside from Vixen who I didn't think would return, and that uninterested caterpillar we saw when we met, I was alone for all my life' Timmy nodded 'That was a very uninterested caterpillar wasn't it!' he said with a smile. Alan looked back at him and grinned before they continued their hike through the undergrowth looking for the path. 'I don't recognize anything here, I'm sure we have lost the route now' Timmy said, Alan nodded and reluctantly agreed 'Well my boy, I welcome any options and suggestions for what we should do now?' Alan said in his reassuringly posh voice.

Timmy pointed forward and confidently replied 'This way.' There was silence between the two, Timmy was replaying the look of fear on Bong's face, and Alan was visualising Vixen's face, and how terrifying it must have been for Bongo. Timmy was very conscious of the time it was taking to get back to the path, what if they couldn't find it before sunset? What if his parents get home and see that Timmy wasn't there? But the bigger question was, where was Bongo, is she alright? He was so distracted by it, that he had completely missed the fact that the large 8 ft blackberry that was close behind him had stopped walking. Timmy stopped and turned around to see Alan stood looking at a small bush. 'Are you ok Alan, what's wrong?' Alan was motionless gazing at some juicy blackberries hanging from a small bush, wondering to himself, thinking about his future, his past, his mum. 'My boy, my time is slowly running dry, would you be ever so kind, as to promise me something my boy?' Timmy didn't like where this conversation was going, but humoured him 'Of course Alan, anything. What would you like?' Alan didn't break his gaze of the berries, one specific berry hanging alone, ripe, and lonesome 'When I have granted my last wish to you, and my days are done, would you please… I have to say I'm incredibly embarrassed by all this… but would you be so kind, as to plant me?'

Timmy had to take a moment to digest the question. 'Plant you?' he uttered 'You see, I think my purpose was to become a bush, to carry on the Quibbleberry dynasty, and provide fruit for future generations. I would very much dislike to be the last' Timmy still struggled to understand the request 'You see, I am covered in seeds, and hope that, with your permission and assistance of course, at least one of them will take, and in time will grow into a wonderful bush. All it would take is a little juice, the seeds, and to be nurtured to become a seedling for something more.' Timmy felt humbled by the request 'It would be an honour, Alan; I will do all I can' Alan then turned to Timmy with a face of happiness that he had a destiny he was able to fulfil. 'But enough of that now, you have many years left in you... we need to find Bongo' Alan smiled and although didn't challenge the 'many years left' statement knowing full well that neither of them would believe that, they pressed on.

Alan was following Timmy closely, and his attention had already returned to the wonderment of his surroundings. Timmy pushed his way through a dense bush ahead of him, to burst out into the track they had previously evaded. 'We found it!' Timmy shouted with glee. Alan was elated 'Well done young man, am I proud of you!' They both enjoyed their brief celebration, which was inevitably overshadowed by the fact that there were still bigger issues to address. 'This way, we need to hurry' Timmy said already heading in the direction they needed to go. Alan followed closely behind; they were back on track.

Walking faster, boarding on a gentle jog, they hurried along the path to get to the lake. 'I say young man, is it a lot further?' Timmy was unsure how much of the track they had either lost, or gained during their brief excursion, but before he could answer, the sight of a beautiful shimmering lake came into view on the horizon. The sun reflecting off the water like a light shining on 1,000's of disco balls, blinding in its beauty. 'There it is!' Timmy said with happiness.

Alan had never seen anything so beautiful, he never imagined anything so enticing, it was more wonderful than he had ever hoped. 'Oh, I say, that's absolutely first class. Colour me impressed' Alan said. It was a gentle downhill slope to the shore of the late, neither of them had noticed the gradual incline beneath their feet. Timmy looked up at Alan, who was hypnotised by the view. 'Come on Alan, let's go take a closer look. Despite the gradient of the hill, and the urgency, their pace had subsided, and they stare in disbelief at the spectacle before them. Alan could start to see that the little non reflective dots were in fact floating objects, boats, scattered over the shimmering canvas. 'Are those the boats you were talking of?' Alan asked Timmy. 'That's right, I told you they were pretty' Alan wholeheartedly agreed. They got closer and closer to the shores edge, Timmy suddenly put his hand in front of Alan and said 'Wait here Alan, I need to go and see if anyone is down there' Alan reluctantly understood, stopped, and dutifully waited for Timmy to investigate. Alan stood there, watching Timmy run to the shoreline, taking in the view, and thought of what it would be like to float on a boat into the lake. When suddenly, a noise came from the undergrowth to the side, like a branch snapping, Alan quickly moved to the side out of view, and watched, and waited to see what it was.

Chapter 7:
Looked Like the Number '8'

Timmy reached the bottom of the hill and slowed down the run he had unconsciously drifted into as he approached the shoreline. When he stopped, he looked left (The most common place to hang out by the lake, there was an open sandy grassy space, along with several tree stumps for sitting. Some years ago, the tourist board installed half a dozen permanent BBQ's which were well used through the summer months, but this year's season had passed for that. The picnic benches which were scattered around the area were vacant, quite a rare sight for a picturesque evening like this. Timmy then stole a quick glance back up the hill to check on Alan, but he was out of sight, Timmy repositioned himself for a better look back up the path to see if he could see him, but nothing. It was fine, Timmy thought to himself, he would check it out further once he had a better understanding of where his friends were. He checked out the other direction, and sure enough, he could see a few children playing football on the grassland near the lake. He then started to walkover, assessing the figures to see which one Jackson was. He had a very distinctive way of running, like a strut you would expect a pimp to have, but faster. He was very easy to spot, so he headed toward the group.

Jackson was so busy playing; he didn't notice Timmy approaching. The ball was passed to most of the other players, as Jackson couldn't get to it in time. The ball raced around, before being kicked by one of the lads towards the makeshift goal, which was being very poorly defended by someone who really didn't want to be in goal. Although they appeared to try and save the attack, it was unsuccessful, and the ball flew passed him into the goal. A cheer erupted from half the crowd playing, and all the running and urgency seemed to stop. Jackson noticed the figure walking towards them and smiled. 'Just a second, Timmy's here' he shouted to the group before running towards him. It wasn't a big distance before Jackson said 'You made it, I didn't think you would. Where are your parents?' looking round. 'They are at work' Jackson looked at him impressed 'That's a first, you came down here on your own?' Timmy thought for a second before replying 'Yes, well no, not really. I need to show you something' Jackson looked back at the football game which had just started again. 'Huh, oh. Who are you with? James? Adam? they would need to be with their parents because they don't live in the village like us' Both more acquaintances than friends from school. Timmy was thinking of the best way to explain the situation.

'No, not them, I've made a new friend' Jackson looked back at Timmy, 'Oh that's cool. Where are they from? Bring them along, we need another couple of players, not having much luck at the moment, Gareth doesn't want to be in goal, he's not very…' Timmy interrupted him 'It's kind of a new situation, I sort of… I… well I kind of found him' Jackson looked back at him 'Oh did you? Where did you… find him?' I was exploring the woods behind my house, and I…' This wasn't working 'Probably better if I show you' Jacksons attention was then drawn back to the football game behind him 'You found him in the woods? Was he lost?' Timmy could tell he was already losing Jacksons attention 'He was hanging from a branch and took him home because he was lonely you see, and now he's here with me. But we are in trouble because my rabbit Bongo is now in trouble and we need to find her because she is being chased by an evil fox named Vixen who is trying to eat her, and my new friend' Jackson was listening to every other word, and none of the important ones registered 'I thought you had a boy rabbit. Lots of foxes in the woods round here at the moment' Gathering more interest in the facts that had landed Jackson continued 'I saw a fox last week walking across the road near my nans house…' Timmy raised his voice with a clear and concise request 'We need your help to find my rabbit, come and meet my new friend' Jackson turned to look back at Timmy 'Don't you want to play football?' Timmy reached up to gesture him to follow him 'I need your help first, but you need to come and meet my friend' Jackson nodded 'Ok mate, where are they?' Timmy tuned around and started to walk, 'This way' and the pair started to walk back along the coastline to the track back into the woods.

'Have you done your homework yet? I haven't, can I borrow yours?' Timmy wasn't really listening and was more concerned about how he would introduce him to an over-sized blackberry with a face. 'Yeah sure, he's just up here' The pair walked a little faster up the hill to where Timmy had asked Alan to wait for him. No sign of him yet, perhaps he was hiding. The pair approached the spot that he stopped at. 'Alan!' Timmy shouted 'Alan, you can come out now, where are you?' It had been quite an afternoon for Timmy, lost both friends in the space of 20 minutes. 'Alan! Where are you?' Jackson was looking round, not a clue who he was looking for, but trying the help. The sooner they found Timmy's friend, the sooner they had a new goalie! 'Aaaaalaaaaan!' Timmy shouted again, to be met with the same silence as the previous attempts. Buzz, buzz! Timmy's pocket had started to vibrate, with the familiar feeling of his phone ringing. He reached into his pocket to pull out the phone, 'MUM MOBILE CALLING' Timmy's phone has never rung more than once in one day, why were people not messaging anymore? 'It's my mum' Timmy said as he slid his finger across the screen to answer the call.

'Hello' Timmy said as he placed the phone to the side of his head. 'Hi sweetheart, its mum' the voice on the other end said. 'Hi mum, is everything ok?' Timmy replied 'Yes sweetie, we're going to be around an hour late, your dad is stuck at work, and he's my lift back so you're going to have to find something for tea. There is fresh loaf in the bread bin, are you able to make a sandwich? I'd prefer if you didn't make a crisp sandwich, but just something small. Or if you can wait, I will bring Pizza home?' Timmy loved a crisp sandwich, lots of butter, non-brand cheese and onion flavoured crisps, preferably freshly cut bread, but he wasn't allowed to use a knife like that, so any sliced bread would also do. 'It's ok mum, I'll wait for Pizza' Timmy replied 'Ok sweetheart, have you done your chore list? Is everything alright at home?' Timmy relived what it took to complete his chore list and tried to think of the most conservative answer he could give to avoid any further questions 'Yes mum, all chores complete. I was invited down to the lake to meet Jackson, so I've just walked here.'

There was a pause while the news sunk into the caller 'You walked there, on your own? I wish you'd have asked me first, that's very naughty but I'm pleased you got there safely. If you're still there when we get back, we will pick you up on the way' Timmy had hoped to be home before they got back but thought it was best to tell the truth about at least one thing 'Ok mum, I'm sorry. Give me a call when you are in the car park and I'll come up and meet you' 'Ok sweetheart, please be safe, and ring me if anything happens. I love you' the voice replied on the phone. Timmy was very hesitant to reply out loud in front of his friend 'Love you too mum, I'll see you later' Timmy could tell that his mum wouldn't hang up first, so he took the opportunity of ending the conversation to hang up the phone. He took the phone from his ear and slid his finger across the screen to end the call.

Jackson was still looking round for any sign of a person he was supposed to be here to meet. Timmy put his phone back in his pocket and resumed his search. 'Alan, you can come out now!' he shouted, 'Are you sure you have a friend here, and you just didn't want to get out of me asking you to be in goal?' Jackson asked sarcastically. Timmy wasn't a particular fan of football, and the thought of standing alone, away from all the action as a last line of defence against a group of players intent of getting passed him, didn't appetize him at all. 'He was here, I left him right here!' Timmy exclaimed desperately looking around to find a glimpse of blue. He was massive, how could he just disappear? 'Well, shall we keep walking along the path to see if he has made his way back?' Jackson suggested. Timmy was impressed by his ingenuity and not only interested in returning to play football. Perhaps that was a promising idea, but before Timmy could reply 'Oh look Timmy, is that a fox over there?'

Jackson was pointing back up the path as a fox sat in the path staring intently at them, her tail still slowly swirling back and forth, unphased, staring. Timmy recognised her immediately, and goosebumps appeared on his neck. 'Be still Timmy, don't scare her away' Timmy knew she wouldn't get scared away, but took the opportunity to look as closely as he could at her from the distance he was away from her, no blood on her, no purple juice, she didn't look out of breath, nor satisfied. She just stared at them motionless aside from her tail.

Jackson started to creep closer to her, but she wasn't looking at him, her eyes fixed solely on Timmy. 'Jackson, stop. You don't want to make her feel threatened' but he wasn't listening. He crept closer and closer to Vixen 'Shhh, I've never seen one this close before' Jackson replied. His arms out in an attempt to make himself look bigger, but actually looking like he was about to start flapping to take off. He was still some distance away, and the speed he was approaching her would give Timmy a little longer to think of something to do. Vixen stood up which startled Jackson and made him freeze in place, like playing a rea life 'What's the time Mr Wolf' and the wolf had just turned around, a game the pair had played a lot during playtime at school.

Jackson froze, Timmy didn't know what to do. Vixen's tail was still softly swinging from side to side, still locked onto Timmy, poised and ready to pounce. Jackson could start to tell that he was not a factor in the equation, and that she was only focused on Timmy. He looked round to see the look on Timmy's face, his friend was worried. Jackson then turned back to Vixen who had started to bare her teeth. Without thinking, Jackson raised his arms and screamed at the top of his lungs before running towards her, waving his arms up and down screaming 'Ahhhhhhhh.' This startled her, and instinctively Vixen looked at Jackson and darted into the hedge to the side of the path running as fast as she could to escape the threat.

Timmy didn't know what to say, 'What are you doing Jackson, that was so dangerous, she could have attacked you!' Jackson had stopped his little dance by this point and was starting to walk back to Timmy 'It's only a fox, they are usually more scared of us than we are of them' Timmy looked back at him knowing full well that this was not an ordinary fox, she was on the hunt for him and his friends, so this was a lucky escape. Next time, he wouldn't have been so lucky. 'Maybe, but that was still dangerous' Timmy said. 'Its fine, it's gone now, besides, I think it had already eaten something anyway, did you see what it had in its mouth?' Timmy wasn't close enough to notice anything in her mouth 'No, what was it?' Timmy asked with a hint of concern 'It looks like she already had a bit out of someone's poor dog, it had a little dog collar in its mouth, light blue with a little pendant on it, blue with something written in gold in the middle of it.

'No idea what that meant, poor little thing though. Didn't look like a big collar' Timmy was trying to work out what that would be… but then realised. He frantically thought of a question to ask Jackson that wouldn't confirm what he was thinking. 'Something in the middle, do you know what it said?' Jackson looked back at Timmy 'Looked like the number '8', seemed a bit random. '8' or could have been a 'B' not sure, couldn't really see. Why would you name your dog '8'… strange people out there' Timmy knew exactly what it was, Bongo's collar, she had Bongo's collar, she had caught her. His bottom lip started to shake, and tears started to build as the reality sank in.

'Oh mate, are you ok? That fox proper shook you up?' Jackson could see the look on Timmy's face. He didn't have any compassion at all, it had been pointed out to him before, but he simply didn't know how to deal with anyone crying. 'You need a minute mate? You want to come play football with us?' was the only thing he could think of saying to comfort his distressed friend. He approached Timmy and forcefully patted him on the back 'Come join the kick about, you can go in goal?' Timmy was grieving hard 'I'll… I'll be down in a little while. You go play; I want to keep looking for my friend' he said with a shaky voice. Jackson was grateful for an escape plan for trying to comfort his friend. It's not that he didn't care, not at all. He just panicked in the face of emotions, and didn't know what to do 'Alright mate, come join us when you're ready' Jackson said softly before slowly walking off down the hill to the lake. Timmy stared forward at the spot Vixen had just escaped from, there was something blue on the ground, was that her collar? He walked towards it to confirm it was, Vixen had dropped it in her haste to escape. He approached it not taking his eyes off it. It had chew marks all over it and covered in mud. He bent down to pick it up. It was indeed her collar, slightly larger than he remember it, but it had grown when she did. He held it in his hand a moment longer feeling the full gravity of the situation. Vixen had got her. He had to find Alan, because he was most likely her next target, and much easier considering his size.

Timmy lowered the collar into his pocket. Before letting go, he felt his hanker chief, and pulled it out to dry his eyes. As it left his pocket, something fell out of it and landed on the floor to the side of him. A little black box which landed on the ground on its side, revealing plainly on one side 'Stay Calm' in striking red letters. Pob's box! Timmy finished wiping his eyes and managed to sneak in a cheeky nose-blow, before returning the hanker chief to his pocket. As he did, he reached down and picked up the box. Looked closely at it and lifted open the plastic button protector. Timmy was alone, worried about his friends and didn't know what to do, surely this was a suitable time to need a Task-Miner? He pressed the button firmly with his thumb until it clicked. The bright red letters on all sides of the box glowed as the box was brought to life to fulfil its purpose, then silence. The lights extinguished, and the box was returned to its dormant state. Timmy looked around at the silence, surely the instructions were not more complicated than 'push the button' and Pob did say he would be summoned from wherever he was to come and help. Timmy looked around again, only to confirm he was still on his own. He looked down at the box again. There was a Flash, and a reassuring voice from his shoulder said 'Alright me 'ol mucka, long time, no see. What 'ave I missed?'

Chapter 8:
Survival of The Fittest

Bongo ran, and she ran, she ran for her life. It was a reflex action to just escape, she didn't even know she had done it, her legs just suddenly sprang into life, as fast as they could, instantly propelling her away from danger, right now in the form of a hungry Fox. She knew that if she sprang into action without any warning, it would give her a precious few seconds' head start. Her hind legs started before she could even turn her head to see where she was going to go. Since her increase in size, she noticed while trying to follow Alan and Timmy earlier that day, that her larger feet were able to propel her further, and her larger front paws had more traction to steer her precious cargo, sharper turns, with a softer impact while running. She was more agile, nimbler, and certainly a lot faster than she had ever been before.

The incident with the food earlier that morning was also providing her with all the fuel she needed to sustain this speed for as long as she needed. She knew that Vixen would be hot on her tail, and in pursuit as soon as she realized what was happening, so she just did what she needed to, and ran, hard. From her viewpoint a couple of feet off the ground, she couldn't see through the undergrowth, not very far into the distance, but she could see far enough to avoid obstacles. She didn't think about Timmy, Alan, Vixen, food, her life up to this point, how wonderful the lake must have looked, she just primally needed to escape. Everything seemed to rush passed her grazing her cheeks. If there was a cliff edge less than 10ft in front of her, she would not have had time to stop and would have propelled herself off. She knew Vixen was behind her, but how far, was she about to pounce at any second and pin her to the ground? She couldn't think of it, she just needed to not be where she was.

Seconds turned to minutes, feet turned to yards, time and distance were inconsequential. The vegetation was relentless, a tree trunk could be anywhere, and she could career straight into it, knocking her out, and offering herself on a plate to her predator. Vixen was indeed in pursuit, but not as close as she should have been. Average sized rabbits were fast, Bongo was no longer an average sized rabbit, she had faster feet. Vixen wasn't used to having to give this kind of chase for a rabbit, but the prize was worth the effort. She instinctively followed her nose, she had her scent, and was being guided by it. But as the distance between them increased, her guide was fading, she had to rely on noise and sight next, she could hear the grass being trampled on a few feet ahead of her and could occasionally see bushes move as they were being pushed out of the way, but all these indicators were slowly getting further and further away. She couldn't sustain this pace a lot longer, and unfortunately neither could Bongo. But they both had to try, push for the survival of the fittest.

The minutes raced by, and the chase started to show signs of slowing. Vixen could no longer see any signs of movement ahead of her, and the scent had all but disappeared into the wind. Vixen had no choice but to slow to a walking pace. She knew Bongo couldn't have lasted a lot longer, so she scanned the area ahead of her. 'Bongo!' vixen called intimidatingly 'Bongo! You can't run from me forever! You must be so exhausted, come to me so we can talk' A line that they both know would never work, but Vixen needed to keep Bongo aware that she was near 'I've been watching you for a while now, I know the way you think, I know the way you move. I'm coming for you' Vixen was walking slowly now, sniffing the ground, looking for clues, ears up and pointing at anything that made a noise 'Bongo, come here to me my delicious friend. You are I are the same you see; we were both touched by the magic of the Quibbleberry. It granted us both our intelligence.

There is no sense in running from me, I am the dominant predator, and I will find you' Vixen yelled out. She continued her hunt; she couldn't have been far. Every few seconds the wind would drop a hint of her smell for Bongo to react to. She was getting closer, and her hunger raged. 'Bongo, stop playing now, time to show yourself. You are mine and I'm getting closer!' she cried with a hint of frustration in her tone. She scanned left, and right, sniffing the air.

Intently listening for any signs of life. *CRUNCH* Instantly Vixen turned to the noise and launched herself like a cheater instantly springing into action towards it. She didn't see what it was, didn't have time to think, charged in headfirst to where the noise came from, less than a second and she was there. A field mouse had fallen of a branch and landed on some leaves, Vixen didn't care, she grabbed the mouse in her mouth, and made very short work of it. It didn't stand a chance.

Bongo could hear Vixen's voice faintly in the distance. She had stopped to take shelter at the base of a fallen tree. Her breathing was regulated, as quiet as it could possibly be, her heartbeat slowed, and a few seconds rest was all she needed. She knew she couldn't stay here long; Vixen was close. She managed to see Vixen jump to devour something that made a noise, and saw she was close, she needed to go. She Backed up slowly, something was getting tighter round her neck, what was happening. She knew she wouldn't have time to find out what it was, so she pulled, and pulled, it was choking her, and she couldn't breathe. She pulled harder until something must have given way, she was released of whatever was restraining her, and she was free to escape. She didn't care what it was or what had happened, but she ran. The noise of the snack Vixen had been given obstructed the faint sound of Bongo escaping in the distance. After a minute or two, Vixen was back on the hunt.

She moved slowly forward scrutinizing every noise and movement she saw. She creeped slowly forward so as not to startle anything. She picked up a scent close to a fallen tree, it was Bongo. She approached the tree from the top and slowly walked along it as the scent got stronger and stronger the closer, she got to the base. Her creep turned to a tip toe, slowly ready to pounce into the crater at the base and feed the food she had waited for so patiently and hunted for so intently. Closer, closer, ready, ready, and…. She leaped over the tree, through the air expecting to land face first into succulent rabbit flesh, but there was nothing. She landed gracefully, like a cat would. After the surge of disappointment, she was thrilled to see the chase was still on. She turned to look for a possible escape route, but as she did, her attention was drawn to something hung on one of the routes of the tree stump, it was what was giving off Bongo's scent. It was blue, round and didn't belong there. She reached to take it with her mouth. She was salivating at the aroma of Bongo and how she would taste. Where did she go? She could see some flattened grass leading away from the crater, which had to be her. Vixen, refreshed from her break and the snack, carried chase.

Bongo continued to run, throwing all caution to the wind, not thinking of obstructions, smells, sounds, just needed to run. Vixen was almost certainly back in pursuit of her, and every second counted. She continued to push the branches and undergrowth out of the way completely oblivious to the river that lay ahead. The river Winkle was at its highest, following a recent rainfall, and capturing all the surface water runoff from the fields, Bongo had no idea it was directly in front of her. Grass, grass, branch, grass, leaves, branch, bush, bush, branch, grass, reeds… Straight into the water. Launching her some several feet into the river. She had no chance to stop. Splash, straight under the water. It wasn't a deep river, but deep enough to carry her away with the current. She couldn't swim, she knew she couldn't swim, but she also knew that if she filled her lungs with air for as long as possible, she could at least float and be taken away with the flow, and down the river she went. It was far from ideal but safer than being in Vixen's grasp.

Vixen ploughed forward, the fresh scent had completely gone, and all she could smell was the collar in her mouth. All she had left was the path of flattened grass that laid before her. But then her ears picked up the familiar sound of water flowing. A stream or a river lay ahead, and she was running straight toward it. She slowed and managed to approach with a pace that would not have run the risk of running into it. She stopped at the water's edge, was this where Bongo met her demise? The path of flattened grass would appear to suggest so. She scanned the river for any further signs of life, signs of disturbance, something to show that there was still hope of food, but nothing was there. 'What a waste' she thought to herself. She waited there for a few minutes to see if she was hiding, or if there was any sign that she had managed to get across the river to the other side but noting new happened. She was understandably extremely demoralized by the result of her chase, and slowly got to her feet and returned along the path she had forged back to Timmy and Alan. It wasn't what she wanted, but the Quibbleberry now looked twice as appetizing. Her walk had become a gentle trot, as her hunger was starting to resurge. The path was just ahead of her, seconds away, and she could smell something, the Quibbleberry juice now filled her nostrils, Alan must be getting closer, she would feed shortly. She leaped forward with the hunger to pounce and devour the berry, through and over the hedge until she reached the path. She stopped and checked her surroundings, but there was nothing to be seen. She could still smell the Quibbleberry, but the scent was faint. She took a moment to analyse smells and sounds, then she noticed the sound of voices coming up the hill, human voices, one she didn't recognize, and one she very much did. She sat in the middle of the track, watching for the voices to approach, when suddenly the talking stopped, and they noticed her.

Chapter 9:
I Don't Think It Is, I'm Afraid

Alan stood patiently watching Timmy walk hastily down the hill to the lake. He was happy that Timmy would finally see his friend Jason… or was it Jackson, he couldn't remember, but it had been quite a day for everyone, and he was sure that Timmy seeing his friend would be good for him. His attention was then drawn to the beauty of the lake. And the boats, how wonderful they looked floating peacefully on the water. He would love to know what it would be like to just drift around on a boat… maybe one day he would, providing he could find a boat big enough for him. He was blissfully unaware of his surroundings when a noise from the woodland to the side of him startled him. Could it be Bongo? Oh, how he hoped it was… but could it be Vixen, returning to feast on him like she had threatened to earlier?

He weighed out the odds, and although he had hoped more than anything that Bongo had escaped, it was just as likely that Vixen had caught her, and she was coming back for him. He didn't want to hang around to find out. He couldn't run down the hill to see Timmy, he had specifically told him not to, and he didn't want to walk back down the path, where could he go? He looked at the verge the other side of the path to the noise, it was very thick scrubland, but he had no choice. He would almost certainly get scratched or maybe even worse in there, so he looked for the safest spot and he tentatively climbed inside, careful not to catch or scratch himself on anything. He managed to crawl deeper and deeper into the woodland, it was starting to thin out, to allow him more space to move. He didn't want to venture too far, but it was too late, he had lost the path. He carried on walking and climbing over, under, and through the vegetation. If it had been a different situation, he would have gazed in wonder at all the smells and colours, but he needed to get safe first. He arrived at a clearing, just large enough to see the lake again, but it was closer, and he was still at the same height. No matter, if he could head towards the lake, perhaps he could somehow catch Timmy's attention? 'It's definitely worth a try' he thought to himself. So, he started to make his way towards the lake.

The woodland started to get denser, and the thicket was causing several scratches to his berries. He had to be careful. Finally, he reached a clearing, the floor had turned to rock, and he had somehow stumbled upon a cliff edge, not too high from the surface of the water, but a sheer drop. The view was truly <u>spectacular</u>. He had a two-hundred-and-seventy-degree panoramic view of the lake in its entirety. The boats were so close he could almost touch them, he could see the picnic area, and a little further on where a group of children were playing football. They were too far away to be able to work out if Timmy was one of them, but Alan was sure he must have been there. In the distance he could see where the river fed the lake and had a bird's eye view of all the trees. The sun was fast approaching the lake giving it a reflection just as bright. Alan didn't know what they would be, but he would very much appreciate glasses to protect his eyes from the glare of the sun at this point, some king of sun-protecting-glasses… he must remember to ask Timmy about them when he next saw him.

This was truly wonderful. He took a step closer to the cliff edge, to peer over the side, and down to the water. 'I say, quite a drop' Alan said out loud, 'You could really hurt yourself falling from a height like that' said a familiar voice coming from behind him. A wave of fear washed over Alan as he suddenly realised who the voice belonged to, it was Vixen, she had found him. He turned round slowly to see her sat on at the edge of the woodland looking back at him, mouth drooling, eyes looking hungry, blocking any escape opportunities. 'Hello, Alan' she said calmly. 'I would say it's a pleasure to see you again Vixen, but I don't think it is I'm afraid' said Alan sarcastically.

This was the first time Alan had been alone since his discovery, he wasn't thrilled that the first person to find him, wanted to eat him. He was even more disturbed by the fact that they were alone, he had no form of protection from the predator that sat before him. He knew what she wanted, and if she had just fed on Bongo, she would have enough energy to get it. He had to think, he had to survive, and find Timmy, find out if Bongo was safe, he wanted to go home.

As the pair stood facing each other, Alan assessed the area for any possibility of escape, but he was big, and awkward at running, he wouldn't stand a chance of escape against her. She had a look of hunger in her eyes, not to satisfy her hunger for food, but her need for the berry juice that her given these gifts she now had. If this is what happens when she consumed older dried-up berries, she wanted to find out what fresh juice would do for her, the possibilities were endless. She got to her feet, and slowly walked towards Alan, prepared to circle him backing him up to the cliff edge. Alan could sense what was about to happen, and frantically tried to think of what he could do to stall her till he could think of something, some way of getting away. 'Vixen my dear, would you mind if I asked, what do you want with me? Surely you would get more energy from some fresh meat, my berries are not very full anymore, and this would surely be a waste of your energy?' Alan was backing closer and closer to the edge of the cliff. He saw the opportunity to enquire 'Are you not satisfied with your recent kill? Did you catch the lovely Mrs Bongo and feed?' Vixen could sense what he was trying to do 'Bongo is gone, and you don't need to worry about her anymore' She didn't want to startle Alan, as he was getting perilously close to the edge, so she stopped and sat down, still obstructing any chance of escape 'When I ate your brothers and sisters, they changed me from a wild animal to a fierce predator with intelligence, and now I want more. The berries

I had were old and dried up, but you… you could make me into so much more, and I want to try. I want to explore the potential' Alan started to sidestep, to get further away from her, but still smiling so as not to agitate or upset her.

He had the advantage of size, but that was it. She was faster, stronger and from what she was saying, smarter. Alan tried to assess the options on what he could do next 'But how do you know my berry juice would do anything for you? You don't, it may harm you, I remember some time ago, long before Timmy arrived, I would offer some to a small caterpillar who would visit me regularly, they drank some and nothing happened to them, wouldn't even talk to me, very rude little chap. So, you see my dear, I don't think it would do you any good at all, so let's stop all this foolishness, go and find young Timmy and head home' Alan gestured to Vixen to back up and move on 'Vixen looked at the lake behind Alan 'I want to know, and I'm going to find out what your berry juice will do for me' She stared intently at Alan's body, assessing the best place to attack and bite.

'I remember seeing you as a ripe young seedling flower' Vixen said 'I considered eating you as a seedling, young and helpless, but wanted to save you to be at your best, I never imagined the feast you would become' Alan looked back at her, still smiling so as not to show any fear, he had no intention of feeling sorry or sympathetic for her. His thoughts turned to Timmy, was he safe, where had he gone to, and had he come back to look for him? He had only known him for a few hours, but he was very much at the forefront of his concerns. And what of poor young Mrs Bongo?

Where had she gone? Surely Vixen hadn't caught her, she would have signs of a fight, or blood on her somewhere surely. Had she escaped to safety? She was a fighter, and oh so very fast, surely, she had gotten to safety in time, she just had to have done. Vixen got to her feet and started to circle the other side of Alan the direction he was moving to 'There's nowhere to go Alan, now give me what I want' She leaped forward, taking a bite out of Alan's side, the opposite side the capsule that had taken the brunt of Timmy's recent wish, puncturing the capsule that Pob had fixed earlier. The juice started to erupt into Vixens mouth. It tasted sweet, sweeter than she imagined, this was what she wanted. She could already feel something changing in her, she was getting bigger, smarter, her muscles were tensing. Her mind was suddenly open to a world of possibilities. Even the taste of the Quibbleberry juice was suddenly amplified. The textures and viscosity of the juice as she extracted it, comparisons with other berries, meats, fruits, each wave of flavour ignited a memory of something within her. She pursed what she could of her canine lips against it to extract more. All the new experiences above became vastly accelerated with the more juice she extracted. Alan could feel his life force draining as she claimed her prize. She was concentrating so much on the prize; she lost her balanced and leaned further forward that she had planned.

The shock of the bite made Alan crouch in pain, losing his balance, and dropping to the floor. As the pair were intertwined, Alan's foot gave way and the duo as one, fell backwards over the edge of the cliff, and then silence. They plummeted toward the water, Alan couldn't scream from the pain he was in, and Vixen was still locked onto Alan's side, devouring the juice she had wanted for what felt like forever. The mass of fruit, meat, fur, and juice plummeted down the cliff face, in silence, then *SPLASH* as they both hit the water at terminal velocity. They both went under, as the water settled, and the bubbles dissipated, and then, silence.

Chapter 10:
A Hint of Blue... BLUE!

The water was flowing faster and faster, over rocks and branches, forming eddies and whirlpools as it flowed. Bongo's head briefly emerged from the water every few seconds to give her the much-needed air she sought. She had never been anywhere near water before, certainly never submerged in it, it wasn't exciting for her, she was terrified. Where was she heading? Where would it take her? How would she get out when she got there? At least she had evaded Vixen to a slightly higher degree of safety, but she needed to think, paddle, swim, and float. She was not going to be beaten by a river. She watched as the trees and bushes rushed by, could she reach one? She raised her paw out of the water, but they were too high. She tried again but missed it. She attempted a third time, completely unaware of the rock poking out of the water the current was hurtling her towards. It smacked her in the side, briefly winding her, but not enough to cause any long-term damage. She needed to do something quickly, she had already depleted her energy supplies running from Vixen, 'Stay Calm' she kept telling herself.

Completely out of the blue, the thought of Pob's box that he had handed to Timmy popped into her head with the words 'Stay Calm' written on the side, quite a moment for a thought like this to enter her head, but the thought distracted and calmed her. She floated and floated down the river, trying to think of something she could do… but what was happening, she was slowing down, yes, she was sure she was slowing down. Was that even possible? The fight to stay afloat was getting easier. She could briefly see where the river was taking her as she bobbed up and down with the current, it was opening out, the horizon briefly opened out to a vast lake. This must have been the lake they were heading to. It was huge, certainly from her perspective.

As she approached the lake, her eyes were drawn to all the boats floating ahead of her, and the birds flying overhead. As she was discharged into the open water, her attention was drawn to the sound of children playing on the bank near to where she was. She noticed a figure that looked like young Timmy walking up to them. There was no way she had any anergy to shout anything out, and even more unlikely that he would hear her. She tried to paddle to the bank, but the current was far too strong for her. She tried to call out, but only managed a muffled and spluttered 'Tiiiii…. Tiiiimmm….' She tried again to swim in the direction of the shore, but it was no use. She must conserve her energy until she could attempt to fight the current. She was carried further and further out into the lake, but always kept a vigilant eye on the figure that looked like Timmy now talking to another figure. She was getting further and further away to be able to see any more detail of what they were doing.

They were specks on in the distant shoreline by the time the current had a grasp on her that she could start to fight. Then the figures started to move away from the crowd, what was happening? Why were they leaving? She started to paddle in their direction, but not really knowing much more about the water than how to stay afloat, this became a harder operation that she had thought. She eventually figured out what movements, and which directions to move her paws to propel her in the direction that she needed to go, but by this time the figures had gone. She still needed to try and get to him… as she paddled (In the loosest use of the term) she realised, there was only Timmy, she would have noticed if there was an oversized blackberry there too, where was Alan? Was he safe? She had to get back to the shoreline, which was still a very, very long way away. Despite her efforts, the current was still very strong, and she was still extremely fatigued by what she had just been though. She had nothing else to do but swim and get to Timmy.

As the time went on, and the minutes rolled by, she moved slowly towards the coastline. She was able to take in the stunning scenery of the Forest from this unique location. The trees seemed to step themselves up backwards, beautiful colours illuminated but the orange glow of the sun setting behind her, and the reflection of the sun on the lake giving an illumination from underneath. The trees were starting to dress for autumn, and the greens were tinted with a tarnish of oranges and browns, with a hint of blue…. BLUE! A lone spot of blue was placed centre stage to the painting before her, it was the unmistakable colour of Alan, standing very high up, with what looked like his back turned to her. She knew it would be no use, but she instinctively tried to call out his name… 'Aaaaaaaaaaaaaaaaa……. Aaaaaaaaaaaaalllllllaaaaaaaaaa….' The muffles from the water she kept swallowing were choking her. He was alive and safe. Maybe Timmy had taken his friend back to see him, and they were meeting up there to take in the view of the lake. This new revelation gave her added energy to paddle faster to get to them.

As she did the only thing she could, which was paddle, she never took her eyes off Alan. But then a figure walked back along the shoreline, in the same colours as the one that left to walk with Timmy. This wasn't Timmy, not with a strange walk like that! So, what had happened and where was Timmy? As she looked helplessly back at Alan, something was wrong, he was moving slowly to the side, he looked very uncomfortable with his movements, and if she didn't know any better would swear, he was talking to someone with the way he moved his hands. He must have found Timmy, but why were they talking and not taking in this amazing scenery. If they had, they surely would have noticed the splashing and noises she was trying to make to get some attention. She continued to watch him; something was happening that was making him agitated. She glanced down at the figure, which was now talking to the other children playing football, before returning to Alan, but he wasn't there, he wasn't standing on the ledge anymore, he was falling towards the water, with what looked like a brown, furry tag attached to him... She instantly recognised it as Vixen, she must have attacked.

Alan, and Vixen were now falling off the cliff. She couldn't do anything but helplessly watch and paddle for her life. She watched as the pair hit the water with an almighty splash. Instinctively she changed her destination from the shoreline to the point of impact to help Alan, if she even could? She splashed and swam as quickly as she could, but progress was slow. She couldn't see if anyone had surfaced, or if either of them survived the fall. She tried to make her way slowly in their direction when all of a sudden, she noticed shadow overcome her, and rope was flung into the water in front of her. Her first reaction was to reach for it to offer some sort of support to stop her from going under. She turned herself around to see where it had come from, when she got full view of a boat that she hadn't noticed before, floating over her, and offering her a lifeline. At the end of the rope was a figure holding a life ring before they flung it into the water, which splashed not too far from her. With her paw not clinging to the rope, she reached out for the orange ring and transferred as much weight to it as possible. She was wet, cold, tired, and exhausted.

And now she was experiencing a whirlwind of emotions form elation for the help she was now being granted, to curiosity as to who was helping her, was she in danger, was this kindness, and all overshadowed by the need to get to Alan. She was in the eye of the storm, but she needed to get out of the water first. She positioned herself firmly within the orange ring and pulled on the rope to signify that she was ready to be pulled out of the water, and the figure on the boat started to pull her to safety.

Chapter 11:
You Said a Mouthful

There was something reassuring about the cockney accent, and smell of pipe smoke, as Pob made himself comfortable on Timmy's shoulder. He was now sat on his shoulder to take in his surroundings having just been summoned there by the big red button on his Task Minor Direct Link box. 'You on yer own are ya little man? Had enough of the princess and the big fella already? Shame that, they both seemed like nice folk' Pob said still taking in his surroundings, putting his pipe back in his mouth. Alan had a lot to explain to Pob, but before he could utter a word of what had happened to Alan, Bongo, and about Vixen, Pob got back on his feet, clapped his hands together and took the pipe from his mouth 'Well now, you summoned me, and I'd wager me flat cap, it was fer a good reason. How can I help ya then? Whas goin on?' Pob looked around again 'This looks like a Forest! Not a lot of reliable places to get a brew in the Forest ya know, there's yer first problem. Need a brew before we get started. Let me have a think' He reached into his overalls front pocket and pulled out a medium sized silver flask. Unscrewed the cap and poured the contents into it. With the flask in one hand, and the lid/cup in the other, he looked at Timmy and said, 'Sorry mate, would offer you some of me tea, but only got enough for one' as he took a swig from the cup and downed the lot in one gulp 'See, all gone'. He replaced the cap and put the flask back into his overalls. 'Orrible and cold, but a brew is a brew. Still working out how to make tea from a flask taste decent, not done it yet ya see, but ya keep trying don't cha' Pob said reassuringly. 'Come on then, what's the task ya got in mind for your old mate Pob?'

Timmy took the opportunity of Pob's silence to start to explain what had been happening since they last saw each other 'It's good to see you again Pob. I think both Alan and Bongo are in trouble. You see, we have been followed by someone, a fox called Vixen. She has eaten some of the dried berries from the Quibbleberry bush, and now wants to eat Alan. She also wanted to eat Bongo and chased her into the woods. And now I don't know where either of them are' Pob took the pipe from his mouth 'That sounds like a dilly of a pickle, lots been 'appening since I went' Pob frowned, and he tried to think of a way to help. 'So, this vixen character, to be fair, she sounds like a wrong'un. Where is she now?' Timmy explained. 'First, she chased Bongo into the woods, we tried to follow but lost them because they were too fast. Then me and Alan thought it would be best to head to the lake, because that's where Bongo would go if she survived. But then I made Alan wait here while I went to go and see...' Pob took his pipe from his mouth 'Whoa whoa fella, hold onto your horses, you said a mouthful there! One thing at a time, do you know where the princess is now?' Timmy replied with a shake in his voice 'Vixen came back and had her collar in her mouth, I think she caught Bongo and ate her' Timmy reached into his pocket and pulled out the chewed-up collar with golden 'B' pendant shining in the evening sun. 'I see, that don't look good do it' Pob reached out to take the collar to inspect a little closer.

He put the pipe back in his mouth and adjusted his glasses to get a better look. Then, taking the pipe from his mouth again he said 'Foxes are quite messy eaters you see, reckon this should be covered in blood if she caught the princess. I knew a fox once, didn't 'ave no table manners. Made a right mess he did and left it to 'ol Pob to clean it all up... but thas' a story for another day. Which way'd they go?' he said looking round. Timmy pointed to the side of the track 'They ran off in that direction, but we couldn't find them' Pob looked at where Timmy was pointing 'Alrght mucka, gimmie a second' Pob got to his feet, took a step, and clapped his hands together, and in a flash completely vanished leaving Timmy alone in the woods. Timmy could only sit and listen to the trees rustling. What exactly was Pob going to do. Timmy knew very little about Task Miners, in fact nothing at all. He was very grateful to have met Pob, and wondered if they were all like him, assuming there were more? Timmy watched intently for what felt like an eternity at the woodland waiting for a sight or a sound that Pob would return.

He was still watching when a voice from behind him said 'I was right! Folk don't often listen to me, but I'm always right. Me 'ol man used to say *Pob, you can't be right all the time*, but I reckon I could count on me hand the number of times I ain't been bob on' Timmy turned round with a startle to see Pob standing leaning against a tree trunk, one hand on his pipe hovering just outside his mouth. 'Did you find her?' Timmy asked hopefully. 'Fraid not me 'ol fruit. Found the way they went, n' followed the path. Looks to me like she jumped into the river, before that fox could catch her. The princess must have lost her collar when hiding near a tree. I bet thas how she got the collar' Timmy's look of hope was slowly becoming deflated. 'So, she got away? But if she jumped into the river, she must have been washed to the lake.

Do you think she's alright?' Timmy had approached Pob and was on his knees in front of him probing for answers. 'I bet she's fine, them rabbits, good swimmers ya see! Big muscley back legs, keeps them moving. Knew a rabbit once called Taffy, think he was from Wales, loved to swim he did. I asked the same question then; *I didn't know you rabbits could swim?* He was very…' Timmy interrupted him 'So you think she's in the lake?' Pob was a little put out to be interrupted, but replied 'I reckon so, yeah. She may not have swum there, that rivers got quite a current to it, but she'll be in the lake I should think'

Timmy got to his feet and turned to run back down the path. 'Whoa whoa whoa chief, where are you running off to?' Timmy stopped and turned to reply with what he thought would have been obvious 'If she's in the lake, we need to go rescue her!' Pob looked back up at him with a smug look 'Thas an idea, and I reckon, a good one too! Thing is though, you have a Task Miner at your service' he said pointing to his chest 'An I'm here to help you. What do ya say we go and get on a boat to go get her? Them currents at the mouth of a river, strong as an ox some of them. She'll 'ave been washed out into the lake for sure by now. Probably swimming for her life too I reckon' Pob walked up to Timmy 'Put your mit, on my 'ead and I'll take us to a boat.'

Timmy wasn't really sure what Pob was suggesting. But stranger things had happened to him in the last 24 hours to be surprised by anything at that moment. He placed his hand on top of pobs hat, he could feel the worn-out tweed on his fingers. 'Okay, now what?' Pob looked back up at him 'Old on to your spare change…' Pob stood up perfectly straight and held his hands apart poised and ready to clap 'This is going to feel… a bit different!' Pob took a step back and clapped his hands together, and the flash of light that normally accompanied it was now all that Timmy could see. He felt as though he was hanging on for dear life while being spun on the outside of a children's roundabout at high speed. He imagined it would be the same feeling astronauts must feel just after a control tower reached '2… 1… Blast off' and before he could get his bearings, the light faded in a reverse flash When his eyes adjusted, he could see water against a green horizon. Before he could conclude what exactly he was looking at, his senses were overcome by the rocking motion of being on a boat. That's where he was, it was a boat! Much bigger than a rowing boat, but nowhere near a yacht status. He now had a few seconds to analyse his surroundings, he'd completely forgotten the fact that he was still resting his hand on Pob's head. 'You feelin' alright chief?' Pob said looking up at Timmy 'I... I feel fine. Really want a cup of tea though' This wasn't a feeling Timmy had ever had before, he never drank tea, but the thought of taking a swig of hot tea fresh from a teapot was heavenly.

Pob laughed and with a chuckle said 'Strange feeling int'it! Had the science bods over at TM-HQ looking at this fer years. Not been able to cure the after effects yet. Don't really bother me though, I like a good brew anyhow, now you 'ave an excuse to need one' Timmy looked around to work out his surroundings again. He was on a boat, on the lake. He could see the shoreline where Jacksons and the other kids were playing football. 'Sorry chief' Pob said 'It's up to you really, but d 'ya mind taking your hand off me head now? Plays with my claustrophobia if you leave it there too long. Not one for being constricted ya see. Think it came from my old mum, she was a tad claustrophobic too' Timmy didn't realise his hand was still on Pob's head, and removed it sharply 'Thanking you kindly bud, much obliged. Now then, do you reckon there's any tea on this here vessel?'

Timmy paused when he heard some splashing from the bow of the boat. Surprised it had only just registered, he moved towards the front of the boat to look in the water, it was Bongo paddling and splashing for her life. Instantly, Timmy's reflex was to throw her a line, so he reached for the first rope he could find. Making sure one end was secured, he threw the rope into the water near Bongo, and was relieved to see her reach for it. He then noticed a bright orange inflatable ring to his side, which he quickly jettisoned into the water near her. Once he saw she had secured herself, he started to pull her aboard. Timmy hadn't thought that since she had increased in size, how heavy she would be to pull out of the water but struggled through to bring her to safety 'BONGO!!! I'm so please to see you're alright. I knew you would be able to outrun Vixen, I just knew it. What happened then, tell me how you got away from her' Bongo was still gasping for air, out of breath, coughing up water and laying in a puddle on the deck 'Speak to me Bongo, do you need anything'?

She was barely moving, making the most of not having to swim, getting all the oxygen she needed. 'Give her some room fella. She's been through the wars and needs a second or three to get herself together again' Pob said rushing over after his unsuccessful tea hunt. Bongo had coughed up all the water and was panting heavily to try and get her breathing back in line. She tried to say something to Timmy but could barely get the words out. 'Alan… Alan… Got to save… Alan' Bongo gasped between breaths. Timmy looked confused 'Alan? Where is he?' Timmy replied impatiently, but Bongo was still gasping for air.

Pob sat next to Bongo to comfort her recovery. 'Now now princess, should think you've been through a lot. We will find Alan, never you mind… Just get yourself back to better' Pob said soothingly 'Need to get Alan… Into water… Vixen… Need to save Alan' Bongo managed to utter between breaths. Pob and Timmy looked at each other with a note of concern. 'What happened to the big fella?' Pob said looking at Timmy 'I left him on the track to the lake, and when I got back, he was gone' It was clear on Pob's face that his brain was working possibilities of what had happened to Alan. The urgency was increased with the word 'Vixen' from the clues Bongo had given them. 'Where'd you last see Alan, was it where we were standing before?' Pob asked Timmy which was responded to with a firm nod 'Right then, back in a tick!' Pob got to his feet, took a couple of steps back, and clapped his hands together, then a flash of light and he was gone.

Timmy was now able to give his full attention to Bongo 'You're doing great girl, good girl' he said soothingly 'Where did you see Alan, can you show me?' Bongo moved her paw to point to the coastline 'He was… on the cliff… fell into the water… Vixen attacked him… both in water' a cold shiver surged through Timmy as he jumped to his feet to look over the side of the boat to where Bongo was pointing. It was too far away; he couldn't see if Alan and Vixen had surfaced or not.

Pob still wasn't back yet, he hadn't taken this long to find Bongo. But he knew what he had to do. He found some ore's and tried to manoeuvre the boat to the shoreline under the cliff edge in the area Bongo had pointed, but it was a slow process. Then a flash of light and a familiar voice from the stern said 'Big fellas in trouble. I followed his tracks to the cliff edge, and that fox was there too. Looks like they had a bit of a to-do because there was berry juice on the floor. Most likely gone off the edge into the lake' Timmy, was already ahead of him 'I know Pob, we need to get to the cliff edge to see if they survived, but I can't row fast enough' Timmy exclaimed exasperated. 'I gotcha sport' Pob said rushing to the back of the boat. He stood at the stern and reached into his overalls pocket. Had a rummage around for a second 'Thought I had one somewhere. Didn't already use it I don't think, or was it when...' He stopped as he clearly found what he was looking for '...There you are, knew I had one left!' he pulled out his hands to reveal an outboard motorboat engine and propeller. It was white and had the letters 'TM-MB80' embossed on the side in red letters 'Task Miner Motor Boats. Very popular brand them. Tried to transfer to them a few years back but changed my mind. Not enough travelling, hate being stuck in one place for too long' Pob said as he lowered the outboard motor into the water 'This one's an 80hp engine, which should be enough for us I reckon.'

Pob secured the motor to the boat and pulled the chord rigorously to start the engine. Three attempts later and it roared into life. Instantly propelling the boat forward in the direction Timmy had been able to successfully orientate the boat to. Pob was able to maintain the direction the boat was moving by rotating the engine. Bongo was now on her feet, at the bow of the boat like a wooden mermaid you would normally find at the bow of a pirate ship. It only took a few moments to arrive at the impact site, and Pob was able to raise the motor out of the water and Timmy was able to use the ores to slow the boat down. They all rushed to the side of the boat to look for signs of life. Timmy and Bongo were looking intently at the water. 'There, what's that' exclaimed Timmy loudly pointing at the water. It looked like purple film floating on the water's surface 'That must be where Vixen attacked him, I think he must be bleeding juice' Bongo suggested in a remorseful tone. Timmy couldn't fault her conclusion 'We need to find him' he responded.

Chapter 12:
Here He Comes

Vixen's eyes opened slowly. She was drenched and laying on her side. She could feel sand on her cheek where her head was resting on the ground. She didn't feel the same, she felt smarter, or so much smarter than before. She still had her animalistic instincts, but they were very faint now. She was intelligent, still hungry, but was self-aware. She tried to recall the last thing that happened. She remembers attacking Alan, and the taste, the sweetness, and then falling. Had they both fallen into the lake? She felt a wave of guilt that it was all her fault. As a hunter, guilt from a kill was not something she had ever experienced before, but now she had a new feeling on taking life. Her barbaric instincts were now muffled. She had to find out where she was.

She lifted her head off the ground. She could still taste the juice that stuck to her fur she had extracted from Alan, it was a reminder of the killer she was, and it repulsed her. She managed to get to her feet. She lifted herself to her hind feet to stand up perfectly straight. Her tail was able to offer her a suitable counterbalance and she conducted herself with a posture of superiority and power. She was on the bank of the lake, not far from the cliff edge they had recently fallen from. She was able to see a boat there with some figures on but couldn't see clear enough because of the sand that was stuck in her eyes. She blinked a few more times to try and get a clearer view of the boat. It looked like Timmy and… was that Bongo? She felt a surge of relief that Bongo had survived her chase into the water, but this was then replaced with the wave of guilt her newfound intelligence had given her for being the one to chase her into it. She knew why she had to hunt her, but she wasn't proud of the fact she did. At least she was ok.

Timmy was now scanning the coastline for any signs of life, and then he spotted something standing on the shore looking directly at them. He instantly knew this wasn't Alan from the slenderness of the figure, and a few seconds later determined it to be Vixen from her colour. He could also see that she was looking directly at them in the boat. 'Bongo. Look' Timmy said to her. Bongo looked up from the surface of the water and locked her eyes on the figure, 'Vixen' she exclaimed in panic. Timmy put his hand on Bongos back and could feel her shaking 'We're safe on the boat, stay calm' he said as reassuringly as he could. Pob had now joined them looking at the shoreline at the figure looking back at them 'That the culprit? She looks like trouble to me. Let's head on over and I'll give her a piece of my mind' he said with authority starting to roll up his sleeve ready for a scrap. Timmy glanced at him 'Stand down soldier, she can't get to us here… we <u>need</u> to find Alan!' Pob glanced back at Timmy 'Right you are chief. Leave it with me' Pob took a step back and held his hands up ready to clap, but before completing the manoeuvre, he paused and said, 'I'm really gonna need a cuppa after this!' then he clapped his hands and promptly disappeared in a flash of light. The boat wobbled slightly from the different weight distribution following Pob's departure. Timmy and Bongo looked on and watched as Vixen stared back. Then she turned around and started to walk back up the beech to the trees and slowly out of sight.

Timmy and Bongo's attention was then drawn back to water to look for more signs of life, more juice floating on the surface, anything to give them a clue on what happened to Alan. Timmy was very aware that Pob had been gone for a lot longer than usual 'We will find him Timmy, he will be alright' Bongo said to Timmy sensing his concern in her comforting voice. Timmy was startled again by the flash of light, and the sudden rocking of the boat as Pob reappeared 'I'm gasping now, are you sure neither of you have any tea? I could murder a mug of Yorkshire now!' This would have previously aggravated Timmy, as finding Alan was far more important than a cup of tea, but he remembered the insatiable urge he had when he arrived on the boat, but was more concerned about Pob's news 'Well, did you find him?' Timmy exclaimed urgently 'Properly spitting feathers now! Yeah, I found the big fella, but he's in a very bad way I'm sorry to say. Not sure he'll pull through this one to be fair' Timmy's heart sank 'Take us to him' Timmy asked Pob, almost demanding 'Gordon Bennet! I can't take you <u>both</u>, what do you think I am, I'm a Task Miner, not a taxi service!' Pob scurried to the back of the boat to the engine and pulled the starter chord again, three times and then it roared into life before he lowered it into the water 'Captain Pob on the case, I'll 've you there in two shakes Kollop's Nimble' Pob said confidently, as though his audience would know what a Kollop was, and what their Nimble does.

The boat turned in a clockwise direction and was propelled at speed along the shoreline in the direction of where Vixen was standing, but at the speed they were going, they would rush straight passed. The makeshift speedboat careered round a corner on the coastline, to an alcove that was out of view, and there before them was a blue mound on the sand. It could very easily have been mistaken for a rock, or beached sea creature, but Timmy instantly recognized the colour. Pob slowed the boat down as they approached the shore, and before they could come to a complete stop, Timmy and Bongo launched themselves off the boat. They both landed in the water and ran up the sand bank along the trail of dark purple juice to the lifeless mound, and both slowed down as they approached, cautiously looking for his face.

Timmy dropped to his knees a foot or so from where Alan could look at him. He leaned forward to pick up his hand, and Alan's eyes opened 'Timmy my dear boy, what a wonderful thing it is to see you' Alan's eyes scanned the area and noticed a familiar, but very sorry looking Bongo to Alan's side 'Ahhhh, by dearest Bongo, you're safe and well! I'm so happy to see you my dear girl' Bongo leaned in and placed her paw on his head. A faint cloud of pipe smoke then rushed past them on the breeze as Pob approached with a sombre tone 'How are you doing big fella? Told you I wouldn't be long' Alan smiled an agreeable smile 'Thank you my dear friend, I had every faith in you.'

Alan's once dark blue berries were all but drained, and the capsules punctured over most of his body 'Is there anything I can do to help you?' asked Timmy, knowing the only exceptional measures he could offer would be to wish for something that could make him better, but also knowing full well that the wish in itself would only make matters worse. 'Is there anything you can do to help, Pob?' Timmy asked the Task Miner, Pob looked back at him and said 'Not much I can do I'm afraid chief, it looks like the big fella has lost a lot of his juice and being in the water would have washed a lot of it away. Not sure what we could do to help him at this stage?' Pob put the pipe back into his mouth as he pondered the options 'Perhaps if we could find something to replace the juice with, something that came from the magic caused by the Quibbleberry, it would be like a juice transfusion?' Bongo asked 'Hmmmmm, that could work m'dear, but not sure where you would get that sorta volume of juice? Reckoning even if we caught up with that scandalous fox, and if she were good enough to help, there's nowhere near enough in her to give to Alan' Pob said, as he put his pipe back into his mouth. 'He's right Timmy, I've lost too much juice to be able to survive with what's available. Just make a big wish for you and promise to fulfil what we spoke of in the woods, and I'll die a happy berry' Alan asked. Bongo was not able to fight back the tears by this point, and Pob quickly rushed round to Bongo, whilst reaching into his overall front pocket to pull out a tissue to hand to her 'Here you go princess, wipe away them tears' as she took the tissue.

'I would very much like to stand up though if any of you fine young men could oblige me?' Alan said gathering his strength. Timmy looked at Pob who was already rolling up his sleeves. 'C'mon lad, let's get the big fella to his feet' Timmy grabbed one shoulder, and Pob the other, as they attempted to guide him up and transfer all his weight to his feet. Their first attempt made Alan fall to his knees again. But the second attempt Timmy and Pob had an idea of the weights they were dealing with and managed to successfully raise Alan to his familiar standing stance. They were both able to return the weight to Alan and take a step back 'Happy, big fella? Can you stand?' Alan hid the pain he was in 'I'm on top of the world young Pob' he said with pride.

Bongo was watching with an impressed gaze as the 8ft tall berry rose to his feet before her, when out of the corner of her eye, beyond Alan was something moving in the distance along the shoreline, something large, but only small from this distance. Something green, moving up... and down, up… and down moving clearly in their direction. Both Timmy and Pob had their backs to it, and Alan was so focused on his spindly legs keeping him up. Bongo squinted her eyes, through the tears, to try and see what was heading their way. 'Err excuse me gentlemen, could I…' she was interrupted by Pob 'Now be careful big fella, take it easy on your pins. Don't want to bugger over and cause yourself more woes' Bongo tried again 'Sorry chaps, I think you should lo…' but she was interrupted again by Alan 'I'm good thanks young Pob, I feel better to be on my feet again now, I just might need to find a walking stick or something to maintain my balance.' Bongo could see that the green mass was gathering momentum and coming straight for them 'Listen guys, I really think you should loo…' she said louder but was cut off again 'Take it east Alan, if you fall I don't think we will be able to catch you' The frustration was peaking in Bongo when she finally yelled… 'Gents, look at that!!!!!!'

All three were started and a little scared of Bongo's interruption but turned to look where she was pointing before they could express any kind of frustration. All four of the beach dwellers stood in complete silence in shock and awe of the whatever it was that was galloping towards them 'What the devil is that?' Alan being the first to speak muttered 'Well thas a rumen, never seen one of them before' Pob followed with. The large green mass was itching towards them like a worm, a massive caterpillar, propelling itself forward by raising its mid-section, and pushing its face forwards towards them, a face that looked happy and innocent, almost welcoming if it wasn't for the size of the creature.

Closer and closer it crawled, creating a wake of sand as it slid. The creature was almost upon them now. It was large, had a face as tall as Alan, and simply smiled a smile of a new born baby looking at its mother. Alan had a face of utter confusion looking directly into the eyes of the face before him, when all of a sudden, like a bolt of lightning, his face changed to a smile of utter joy, filled with happiness and content of seeing an old friend 'OH MY DAYS!

How wonderful it is to see you again my friend, and my my, look how you've grown!' Alan said with glee. Timmy, Bongo and Pob looked at each other in shock… had they missed something? 'Alan, do you know this creature?' Timmy uttered in wonder at the face looking at them. 'But of course, my dear boy, this is… I'm so sorry my friend, what's your name?' The face looked back directly at Alan and said in a deep and booming voice 'You can call me Hericum' Alan looked back and accepted his name like he was greeting a long lost relative 'This is Hericum, I've known him all my life. He used to come and visit me on my branch as a baby caterpillar, and I would give him a drop of berry juice to try and get him to talk to me. He visited me for months, since I was a sapling' Alan turned back to the face to talk to him 'I'm sorry my friend, I didn't know your name was Hericum'.

The face looked lovingly at Alan 'You gave me this name. Every time I'd come and visit you, it's what you would call me' Alan looked perplexed and then laughed out loud a big joyful belly laugh 'Oooooh, I see, how very funny, I was saying *Here he comes*, but what a wonderful name, and suits you perfectly. It's very nice to meet you Hericum, my name is now Alan, Alan the Quibbleberry. This is my friend Timmy' as he turned to gesture to Timmy 'And this is the beautiful Mrs Bongo' he then gestured to Bongo who smiled back at the face 'And this is our friend Pob' Alan said as he turned to

Pob who was standing there smoking a pipe, admiring the face. 'Happy to make you acquaintance my big green friend, I'm a Task Miner, here to help and at your service' Hericum smiled at the three new friends 'It's a pleasure to meet you all.'

Alan looked back at the smiling face 'You look like you've put on a bit of timber my small friend, what has happened?' The face then looked back at Alan 'It have no idea, I was happy visiting you every so often, trying the juice you offered to me. And then when you left, and my lovely home wilted away, I started to grow, and get bigger and bigger till I was the size of our clearing. Without a home anymore, I made my way out and found a stream, which I followed, and it brought me to this very pretty lake, and I noticed you all standing here and recognized you Alan and came to say hello… Hello!' Alan looked back at him 'Well that makes sense. Do you have any other side effects?' Hericum thought for a second 'Well I can think and talk, does that count?' Timmy chuckled and said, 'I guess that counts too' Pob was still contemplating the situation 'I think I've got a cracker of an idea brewing here… BREW! I could destroy a lovely cuppa right now… That is to say, I 'ave me an idea that might work!' Alan looked at Pob 'Oh do share my boy, don't be shy!'

Pob put the pipe back in his mouth, and assessed Hericum's sheer size 'Well, with Mr Hericum's permission of course, we could borrow some of his juices to reinflate yours… he looks like he has ample, and it was your magic that made him this way' Pob said returning the pipe to his mouth. Hericum looked at Pob and smiled 'I'd be very happy to help Alan in any way I can' Alan looked at Hericum 'Well that's incredibly noble of you, but I would hate to cause such a nuisance to you, please don't feel like you have to my friend, my time is almost over' Bongo then said sternly to Alan 'Please Alan, take the offer, Its what's you need' Alan still reluctant said 'Even if I did agree to the incredibly generous gesture, how would we even do it?' Pob turned around and took the pipe out of his mouth and looked smugly at Alan and said with a smile 'Just you leave that to your Task Miner friend, Pob' as he breathed a puff of smoke out from under his moustache.

Chapter 13:
A Very Strange Looking Train

Timmy was trying to get clear in his head exactly what was going on, the berry that could grant him wishes, has made his pet rabbit, who is female, larger, and more intelligent, helped clean the house, this made things worse, so he got a small helper known as a task miner, called Pob. A fox accidentally fed on some berries and became smart and wanted to eat Bongo and the berry, and now a giant caterpillar has turned up named Haricum who also fed off the berry and is now able to save the berries life… Nope, it makes no more sense saying it out loud.

Alan was standing admiring the enormous caterpillar before him, barely mustering up the energy to stand up, while Pob was contemplating how he was going to carry out the procedure of transferring some of Hericum's mass to reinflate Alan. It wasn't a procedure he had ever attempted before but was convinced he would know how to do it. Bongo approached Pob 'So my dear, how do you suggest we go through with this? Is there anything I can assist with?' Pob turned to face Bongo 'It's alright princess, I never tried anything like this before, but I know a couple of TMs that 'ave. What do you reckon, should I just go for it, or nip off and 'ave a chin way with them, ya know, to make sure I can do it right?' Bongo looked at Pob 'Now I think you should just check with your friends that you can do this right. I have every faith in you that you can do this correctly but think it's probably best if you just check first, so we don't harm poor Alan. I think he has been through enough; don't you agree?' Pob returned his pipe to his mouth and stroked his moustache for a second 'Yeah, perhaps you're right, I'll nip back an 'ave a yarn with them at TM-HQ. Will be back in a jiffy' Pob took two paces back and clapped his hands together, and *FLASH* he was gone.

Timmy and Alan noticed the flash and saw that Pob had left. 'Is everything alright Bongo sweetie? Where has Pob gone?' Bongo didn't want to raise any doubts in Pob's abilities 'He's just gone back to TM-HQ to prepare for the procedure. He will be back soon though' Timmy, Alan and Hericum looked satisfied with her answer and carried on talking. 'I think it's wonderful how much you've grown since I last saw you. So, tell me, did you ever hear me all the times I tried to speak to you?' Alan asked the giant face 'Of course I did, I just wasn't able to answer you because, well, I am a caterpillar, and my only concern was food' Alan chucked and looked at Timmy who was still taking in the incredible spectacle before him. Alan felt a sharp rush of pain down his side, where vixen had attacked him earlier 'I wonder what became of Vixen, if she contracted any more powers once she had fed on me, or if she's even alive at all now?' Timmy had to tell him the truth 'She's alive and had escaped. Bongo and I saw her washed up on the beech just down there' Timmy gesture down the shoreline 'And she saw us in the boat, then she got up and walked away' Alan looked nervous at this news 'So she is still out there, right now?'

Bongo then tried to calm Alan before he would get upset 'Yes, but there was something stranger about her, she walked off on her back legs, like a human, more evolved, perhaps she has now lost her primal animal hunting instincts and become enlightened by a higher intelligence' Alan thought about it for a second 'You're probably right, young Mrs Bongo. Hopefully not a threat anymore. I wish her well wherever she is' Timmy didn't share his sympathy but respected his sentiment.

Timmy stood back for a moment to admire Hericum, he looked… somehow… bigger than when he first got there. Only slightly, but was he still growing? Timmy tried to stand in a specific spot and remember what he could see over the top of Hericum's head. Then maybe in a little while go back to the same spot and see if he could still see the same thing again. It was worth a try to give him a better idea. Timmy went to re-join Alan and Bongo 'How do you feel now Alan, does it still hurt?' He asked. Alan appreciated the concern 'Don't you worry about me young man, I'm a tough old berry. Let's just hope Pob can return soon before Mr Hericum here changes his mind!' He said with a grin. 'Hericum looked at Alan 'It's a pleasure to be able to be of service to you Mr Alan. My time on this earth grows short. We usually only live a few months, and I was approaching that the last time I saw you. So long as I don't get any bigger, it's becoming incredibly difficult to move around now, bit of a strain on the old Caterpillar ticker' Timmy's ears pricked up at the subject of Hericum growing bigger. He should casually step back to the spot he was on before to test and see if he could see the same things over his head. Timmy subtly took a few paces back and tried to look over Hericum's head… still the same, perhaps he wasn't growing, although it had only been a few minutes. Timmy casually re-joined the group.

'Oh my, I wonder where Pob could have got too' Bongo asked knowing full well what he was actually doing. 'He has been a little longer than I would have thought, I do hope the little chap is ok' No sooner had Alan replied, *FLASH* Pob appeared `next to him 'We were starting to get a little worried about you, are you all set?' Pob looked a little more nervous than normal 'Yes big Fella, I'm almost ready. It just looks likely we won't be able to do it here on the beach. Need to find somewhere a little less sandy, ya know. Any of you folk know anywhere?' Timmy thought 'There's a children's play park just up the hill. Its hidden away and not a lot of people know it's there. I bet that's empty' Pob looked at him and said, 'That sounds like a plan Batman! Let me go check it out and I'll be back in a tick!' Pob took two steps back and clapped his hands and then *FLASH*. A few seconds later *FLASH* as Pob returned coughing… '*Cough* Yes chief, that looks *Couch*, that looks *Cough*… Excuse me a second all' and Pob took two steps back and clapped his hands *FLASH*.

Timmy and Alan looked at each other concerned. 'What do you think all that was about? Do you think he's ok?' Timmy asked. Alan looked at the faint waft of smoke left in Pob's wake 'I really don't know my dear boy… It's all very strange' they all waited patiently not know what to say. Timmy decided to take the opportunity of the calm to return to the same spot to check on Hericum's growth… Didn't look like much, but it was close. Timmy stepped forward again unnoticed, or so he thought. Bongo looked at Timmy 'Are you alright my dear, you keep shuffling' Timmy, a little startled by the observation 'Yes, I'm fine. I'll explain a little later' Bongo sighed and before she could comment on the brushoff… *FLASH* Pob had reappeared looking refreshed, holding a big mug of tea 'Ahhhhhhhh, that's what I needed. Everything's always better with a decent brew! Ain't sure I could have gone on a lot longer without it, nope, don't reckon I could 'ave. I better remind myself to catch up with the science bods at TM-HQ, see if they've had any luck on the side effects… No bother if not, I love me a cuppa cha' Pob gulped down the contents of the mug, and very casually chucked the mug over his shoulder and approached the group.

'Right, my man 'ere is bob on with the play area, its hidden, and open. Problem now is getting Alan there; its proper steep and the track is now overgrown with all manner of stuff. I ain't got's the energy to jump you there, what with all the back and forth I been doin' today. Taking all offers and suggestions kindly!'

Hericum, who has remained very quiet through it all chirped in with his deep booming voice 'I can give Alan a lift, it's no bother to me.' Alan looked back at Hericum 'You're doing so much for me, but that's very kind of you' Pob removed the pipe from him mouth… 'Right then, we have a plan, let's not hang about, *Time, Time will be the crime, when the man with the offers has passed you by*. I'll take a hop, skip and a jump, and I'll meet you lovely people there!' Pob then took two paces back and clapped his hands and disappeared in the now familiar flash of light. Everyone always looked exhausted, especially when Pob seemed to have so much energy, which he clearly had after his dose of Tea. 'Right then, climb aboard Alan, and you Timmy, I need you to navigate me there' said Hericum to the Pair, and then looked at Bongo 'Do you mind following behind Bongo' and she gracefully nodded back at him. She had no intention of riding a caterpillar.

Timmy took his last opportunity to assess Hericum's size before helping Alan board the giant green caterpillar. He looked over the top of Hericum's head, and he had grown, a lot. A short burst of growth must have happened in the last few minutes. The tops of the trees he was using to gauge his size, which he had only just seen before, had now disappeared, completely. Even on tiptoes, Timmy couldn't see them, or anything near them His suspicions were correct. He needed to tell someone, but before he could 'Timmy my boy, would you mind helping me up?' Said Alan. Timmy's distraction hadn't gone unnoticed by Bongo, but for the moment, the priority was to get Alan in his weakened grey state, onto Hericum's back. They both helped him up, and made him comfortable, once he was aboard, Timmy scaled him to take a riding position to navigate them to the clearing. He held on tightly, and Hericum started to move into the woods with the pair on his back, following Timmy's direction.

The only route Timmy knew from the lake to the play area, was through a track that wasn't really a track, or at least it might have been at one point in history. It was a barely recognisable cut through the undergrowth, but Timmy directed Hericum along the route. Timmy was trying to look for the perfect opportunity to whisper to Alan about Hericum's growing, but now wasn't the time. Bongo was following closely behind them, as the giant caterpillar forged his way through the undergrowth and bushes, up the steeper and steeper path 'Is it much further little Timmy?' Hericum asked 'No, we're almost there. Just over this ridge and through the trees up ahead' Timmy gestured, but nobody was in a position to see his arm movements. Hericum continued to form a path of flattened vegetation through the woodland until he reached the trees Timmy was talking about. He burst through the trees and into the clearing like a locomotive bursting through a brick wall. Twigs, trees grass and branches bursting out everywhere as Hericum came to a stop just in front of the patiently waiting Pob. Bongo came running through right behind him, like a tender carriage to a very strange looking train. 'There you are, was starting to reckon you'd abandoned your 'ol mate Pob. Right then, bring the patient 'ere' 'He pointed to a large clearing in front of him 'And make yourself comfy. This shouldn't take too long, hopefully.'

Alan managed to gently lower himself off Hericum and went to sit down where Pob had directed him 'And you *Big Green*, come and plant yourself next to the big fella here' Hericum obliged as instructed 'Now then Timmy my boy, you must understand that there's a chance that polluting the Quibbleberry juice, will stop Alan being able to grant wishes anymore! It also means that, if his seed ever germinate, and a new bush grows, the berries they fruit may not be able to grant wishes either. Ya' see me boy, this is all a bit 'New Territory' for me, never been done before, never met a Quibbleberry before! Lots of never-before's for us all ya' see' he said looking at Alan, removing his flat cap and scratching the bald patch on the top of his head. Timmy looked at Alan, remembering his request he made in the Forest while looking for Bongo, is this what Alan would want? If he had the ability of granting wishes taken away, it would make him and the descendants he wanted, just normal berries 'Alan, you know if that's true, you and your offspring would just be normal berries, would you be happy with that?'

Alan looked back at Timmy from his seated position on the floor. 'Well, not really, I like how special I am, and how desired the berries from the bush I hope to grow into one day will be. Perhaps this procedure isn't a clever idea, perhaps I should just accept that my time is over and respectfully bow out to give another life a chance to spawn. Maybe we should reconsider this, and take time to think of alternatives?' Alan wondered. Timmy could see the hesitation in Alan, but he also knew that Hericum didn't have much time, he already looked a lot bigger than when he first arrived by the lake. 'There's something you should all know, it looks like Hericum is still grown, and I don't know how long he has left' Hericum looked at Timmy with a look of agreement 'I have noticed that too. I feel a lot bigger, and I'm not sure my heart can take a lot more. If we are to do this operation, I think it will need to be done soon' he said sorrowfully. Timmy watched and thought to himself, perhaps he had an idea...

Timmy looked at Pob, who was still mentally preparing himself 'Pob' he turned to look at Timmy 'Yes, young man' he replied, 'Would you just explain again what the risk is to Alan?' Pob looked a little frustrated 'Cor blimey, you need yer lugs clearing out? Starting to feel a little like a parrot now! You see, the thing is, nobodies never tried nothing like this before, never seen a Quibbleberry before. It's always possible that mixing Alans wishing juice, with Hericum's fluids, might dilute the wishing juice, and take his abilities to grant wishes away? That might also pass down to his descendants ya see? This is all a bit new to us all. Same thing happened to a friend o' mine, mixed a Saskimo's blood with a Vanwalla's juice… he was never the same again, always sat in the corner crying like a baby. Strange ol' do' Timmy looked back at Pob with a glint in his eye of an idea forming. 'So, what you're saying is, Alan may lose his power to grant wishes if he takes the juice of Hericum, and his descendants would also loose that power if his seeds spawn into a bush?' Pob rolled his eyes 'Gordon Bennet, you not right in the 'ead boy? There's a chance that is true!' Timmy looked at Alan and paused for a second to make sure what he was about to do was a good idea, and then he said something he had been trying to avoid 'I wish it wasn't true!'

Alan was slowly getting used to the pain of the accidental wishes, and the mass loss of juice, but the rug was pulled out from under him, as the wish hit him like a ton of bricks falling from a great height. His already drained and equally spread berries would have struggled to bare another wish but now he was cover in lacerations from losing so much juice after Vixen's attack. He screamed out in pain as what little colour he had left faded into almost obscurity. All his capsules deflated like slowly emptying balloons and hung from him like withered fruit from a dying tree. Alan fell back, and lay on his back, his eyes hardly open, barely conscious. Timmy's heart sank, had he gone too far with this one? He had to try, Hericum didn't have long left, and he didn't want Alan to lose his legacy that he clearly wanted. He rushed over to Alan's side.

'Speak to me Alan, tell me you're still there and can make it through the operation? I'm so sorry, I had to do it to save you.'

Chapter 14:
Strength & Honour

Alan's eyes were barely open, he wasn't moving. 'I understand Timmy' he whispered 'One last wish to gamble on either saving me…' He gasped what breath he could '…or letting me go to be planted' Bongo ran over as soon as Alan hit the ground 'My sweet Alan, please be strong, we are all here with you' Pob looked on in amazement of what had just happened. He knew that if he were to start the procedure, he would have to start it quick before Alan submitted to the pain. He also noticed that Hericum was getting lethargic and sleepy all of a sudden. Whatever he was going to do, he had to do it now, or he would lose them both. He loudly bellowed 'Stand back everyone, Pob's gotta work!' Timmy and Bongo reluctantly stepped back to give them space 'You gonna have to stand a lot further back then that this time, this is gonna get BIG!' Timmy and Bongo moved back as far as they could, their backs now against the trees at the furthest point of the clearing.

Pob reached into his overalls front pocket and pulled out a large yellow and red tube, on the side it read 'Task Miner *Super Strength* Ever Hold' Pob held out his hand and spaced his fingers apart. He then placed a dollop from the tube on the end of each of his fingers and thumb. Dropped the tube on the ground, and in a blue blur, ran circles around Alan.

Alan didn't, or most likely couldn't move at all while Pob was applying the glue to repair his capsules. Pob's blue haze retuned to the discarded tube, and he stopped to pick up the tube, and reapply a dollop to each finger, dropped the tube and disappeared in a blue line to circle Alan again in a blue haze. Hericum's eyes were now closed, Timmy tried to assess if he had grown anymore since he had been sat next to Alan, and he couldn't help but think he had. His time was definitely running short, but it was hard for him to keep his eyes off the spectacle that was happening to Alan. Again, Pob returned to the tube of glue, to reapply a dose to each finger, drop the tub and return to Alan, to repair his capsules. Timmy and Bongo could only watch in wonder.

After a few minutes of applying Alan's pre-procedure treatment, the blue haze of Pob's super-fast speed, made a bee line for a spot between the two patients, seemingly for a rest, but he didn't look out of breath or phased at all from what he had just done. He wondered over to the discarded glue tube, he was wiping his hands of excess glue with and oily towel he had picked up from somewhere, which he placed in his pocket. Bent down and picked up the tube, re-applied the cap, and returned it to the pocket of his blue overalls. He then returned the pipe to his mouth 'Gonna defo need a brew after this…' he said nonchalantly. He stood to assess what he was about to do, took the pipe from his mouth and placed it on the ground 'Right then, shall we begin' he said, walking casually around Alan, and then around Hericum. Then around Alan, then around Hericum. This repeated six of seven times in a figure of eight. Pob was constantly watching the patients, and muttering something to himself, like he was planning speed, trajectory, pressure, loadings, angles… the calculations were practically visible as Pob assessed what to do. Then whilst walking and calculating, he reached into his pocket and pulled out a pair of white surgical gloves and inflated each of them to stretch them out before putting them on.

'Right, you wonderful pair, let's do this… Task Miner - Strength and Honour' Pob said proudly, as the walk gathered momentum to a gentle jog, then a sprint, a full-on run… then faster and faster till he was indistinguishable as a figure, seemingly catching up with himself in a figure of eight that seemed to encapsulate Alan and Hericum. Before long a blue haze, much faster than he had gone before. Bits of debris on the ground, started to move with the breeze generated by Pob. The breeze became a gentle wind emanating from them, then a full-blown storm, trees all swayed away from the event. Timmy and Bongo made use of the trees they were up against for bracing support. Alan and Hericum seemed to both become weightless and slowly elevated off the floor, equally raising as the blue figure of eight lifted them up. There seemed to be lightning bolts flashing as the intensity of what was happening increased. Alan and Hericum were no longer visible through the dust, debris, and blue glow. Timmy could be sure, but there was the faint sound of screaming coming from Alan… there was too much noise to tell. Timmy checked on Bongo to make sure she was ok, she had her eyes closed from all the dust, he pulled her closer to him to protect her, which she was clearly grateful for as she buried herself into his side.

The storm started to intensify, as they raised higher. The blue glow was becoming blinding, Timmy couldn't look directly at it anymore. This went on and on for what felt like an eternity, the noises of the storm occasionally hinting at screams from Alan and what he assumed was Hericum. Timmy could occasionally catch a glimpse of Hericum, who had drastically reduced in size. It must be working. The wind that was blowing in Timmy's face was dispersed with rain drops, or at least that's what he assumed they were, not thinking about what was actually happening before them. Timmy began to worry about the attention something like this would start to cause, it was bright, loud, and tempestuous. It would be clearly visible to anyone in the vicinity, and now was not the time to be calling attention to themselves. His chain of thought then led him to Vixen, she had just walked off, was she still watching them? Was this the perfect time for her to attack again? Timmy scanned the woodland around them for any signs of the vicious spectator, but there was nothing of note to be seen, there was too much dust and debris flying around to get a conclusive view of the surroundings. He then returned his gaze to the floating storm before him.

The tornado had raged on forever, when only 15 minutes had passed, surely this couldn't go on for a lot longer. The faint screams were consistent, but Timmy could no longer hear Hericum. Then all of a sudden, the lightening seemed to stop, and the wind dissipated quickly, and the blue glow dimmed. The mass lowered itself to the floor gently landing and the blue glow quickly slowed down until Pob was clearly visible running to a complete stop and collapsing into a heap, unconscious on the floor. Bongo and Timmy, paused for a second trying to work out if it was safe to move to help. Then silence as all the debris and dust settled on the ground. It was an eerie silence that whatever had just happened had finished.

Pob had collapsed into a heap at Alan's feet. Alan had been restored to his fully plumb, deep dark blue, original self at the moment Timmy first found him once he had increased in size, but he was also unconscious in a mound on the floor. Timmy's eyes were then drawn to what remained of Hericum. He had clearly taken a beating, covered in lacerations and scars, presumably where Pob had been able to extract what he needed to for Alan, shrivelled and a quarter of his former size. Completely lifeless. Timmy didn't know who to run to first, Pob, Alan or Hericum, all of them lay lifeless on the floor. Bongo was in no doubt where she was going, and she ran forward, propelled by her giant back legs, just as fast as escaping Vixen to head straight to Alan. She ran to his side to try and see his face. He was covered in scars from Pob's repair works to his capsules, but his eyes were closed. His face was facing Pob, so Bongo had the ability to turn and check on Pob too from this position. Timmy made a bee line for what was left of Hericum, while bongo attended to the other two.

Timmy ran to Hericum and sat near his face. His luscious green colour was now pasty grey. Covered in scars and still bleeding. Timmy reached down and cradled his head to face him. To his surprise, his eyes opened, and locked onto Timmy 'Did it work?' Did it work, Is Alan better?' he whispered to Timmy, he didn't know what to say yet, but tried to reassure him with positive news 'We think so, you have done an amazing thing for him, and we are all eternally grateful to you' Hericum managed a faint smile 'I'm pleased. Now I can rest' he said looking up at the sky 'Timmy?' he said looking at him 'Yes Hericum?' he replied welling up 'It was lovely to meet you. Be good' as the last of his breath left his body and his eyes gently shut. He was gone. 'Good night Hericum' he whispered as he returned his head to the ground. He sat in reverence of his new friend for a moment, very grateful to have met him, even briefly. He then got to his feet to go and see Alan & Pob.

'Alan, Alan, speak to me Alan' Bongo urged to Alan to show some signs of life. Timmy headed to Pob to try and bring him round. 'Pob, are you there? Pob, come back Pob, can I get you anything?' Timmy gently rocked Pob's shoulder. 'Pob, wake up Pob' He was breathing gently. Resting, and almost… snoring. Timmy tried to be as gentle as he could before becoming a busy parent, trying to wake a sleeping child up who is late for school. 'Pob, wake up Pob, rise and shine!' Timmy kept nudging him to wake him from his slumber. 'Mmmmmmmm, 5 more minutes' Pob mumbled. Timmy couldn't help but smile, reassured that he was ok. 'You did it Pob, wakey wakey, rise and shine' Timmy said in full parent mode 'I don't wanna go to school, go away!' Pob groaned back at Timmy. Timmy continued to rock him to wake him up, trying to think what he could say, then it came to him 'Pob, your brew is ready, come and get it!' Pobs eyes opened 'Brew?' he sat upright, checking his location and trying to recall what had just happened. 'Cor, I could murder a brew, two ticks…' Pob jumped to his feet, took two steps back, clapped his hands, and disappeared in a flash.

Timmy could now give his full attention to Alan who still lay lifeless to his other side. Bongo had her paw on Alan's face, stroking it trying to elicit some sparks of life. Alan lay unconscious, seemingly not breathing, and unresponsive. 'Do you think he's going to be ok?' Bongo said gently to Timmy who replied 'It looks like Pob has done everything he could. We just need to wait, and hope.'

The familiar flash of light returned behind them, although neither of them turned around to see what it was, they both knew, which was then confirmed by the sound of a large slurp of tea, and a satisfying exhale. Pob then joined the two kneeling down 'I should think he needs to rest fer a bit now, been in the wars a bit' then he took another loud slurp of his tea 'Now that… Is a cracking brew' he said, before looking at the sad looking green over Alan's shoulder 'And what of Hericum?' Pob asked Timmy, who simply shook his head.

Pob then sighed 'What a shame, he was a proper strong one, he gave his all, thought he would pull through to be honest, but his time was almost over. An honourable death for a strong soul' He placed his mug on the floor, and slowly walked over to Hericum, and removed his hat and placed it into his overalls pocket 'Well done big green' he then dropped on one knee and rested the top of his head against Hericum's side, clapped his hands, and they both vanished in a flash. Timmy and Bongo hardly noticed, focusing all their attention for some signs of life on Alan.

After a few minutes, another flash from behind them, as Pob returned and picked up his mug and put his flat cap back on from his pocket. *Slurp-Sigh* 'Proper trooper, both of them. Just give Big Green a proper burial, happy he's laid to rest now. Right thing to do' Pob moved closer to Alan and stood between them both. Leaned in to inspect closer, and adjusted his glasses, before reaching into his pocket to pull out his pipe to place in his mouth. 'Big Fella! You in there? Big Fella?' Pob then stood back a bit. 'Did all I could, in a bit of a state he was, lookin' better, but I reckon he just needs time to rest. Not too long mind, knew a guy, laid down for weeks, eventually sank into the ground! Nobody knew where he went, reckon he's still there' Pob took a final sip of his tea, and put the empty mug in his pocked. 'You still got my TM-DL box in yer pocket young man? Should think I've fulfilled my promise to you now ain't I?' Timmy replied a little flustered 'Oh, yes of course' he reached into his pocket and pulled out the little black box wrapped in the hanker chief. 'Here you go, thank you for all your help Pob, you have been wonderful' Pob took the box and put it in his pocket 'Thank you young man, it's what we do. Been a privilege helping you. If it's alright with you though, I'll be off. Plenty more tasks to mine ya see' he said with a reassuring grin.

'You may get a message in a few days rating my service, I know it's silly, but your feedback helps ol' Pob reach his dream' Timmy looked back at him a little confused 'I didn't know you had a dream Pob, what is it?' Timmy enquired. Caught a little off guard 'Wow, nobody's ever ask what my dream is? It's always *we need this* or *these needs doing*, not used to 'avin my needs heard. I'm saving up for a little house. A little cottage by a lake, where I don't 'ave to keep helping folk, and there is always a pot of tea on. That's Pob's dream, and your feedback gets me a bonus and helps me save ya see' Timmy looked back surprised at Pob 'That's lovely, if I can do anything to help with that on top of positive feedback, let me know' Pob winked at Timmy 'Will do little fella. Will check in on you again soon, it's all part of the customer care after service, but I'll be off now' Pob took two steps back, 'Be lucky!' he said with glee and clapped his hands, gone.

Then silence, it was the three of them again. Alan had barely moved, faintly breathing, but breathing. Bongo looked over him, trying to think of was she could comfort him. Unable to tell if he was asleep, or in a comma? She just wanted to make him comfortable and keep him safe. Timmy put his arm around Bongo, to reassure her that everything was going to be alright, even though he didn't know it would be. Timmy felt something in his pocket, unable to remember what it was he reached inside, and instantly knew when he touched it. 'Bongo, I think you should have this back' He pulled out the collar she had lost and had been chewed a little by Vixen. She looked up at it, unable to fathom how, or why Timmy had it, but really pleased to see it again. The blue pendant shining, and the golden 'B' looked pristine against the dirty and chewed collar.

She bowed her head enabling Timmy to undo the clasp and place it around her neck. Once he had secured the metal clasp, he turned it round to show the pendant hanging just beneath her chin. She was so pleased to have it back, it felt like a little piece of home finally being restored to her. She looked back at Timmy 'Thank you my dear, I've really missed this' Timmy sat back down, it's good to see you wearing it again, back where it belongs' Then from behind her a muffled but very familiar voice filled the silence 'I don't want to be rude madam, but I have to say, you looked ever so strange without it on' They both turned round and smiled the biggest smile 'ALAN!' they said in chorus, 'You're alive!' Timmy said with absolutely happiness. 'Welcome back, how do you feel?' Alan looked at him with one eye and said with a smirk 'I feel… Fizzy!'

Chapter 15:
It's your Gra…

Alan hadn't moved a muscle other than the ones on his face, he lay there motionless on his side where he had landed moments earlier. What little energy he did have was used to keep his eyes semi open and muster the occasional sentence. Timmy had suggested to Bongo to go and find some water for Alan, and she had only just hopped off to find some, and some kind of container to carry it back to Alan, so it was just Timmy and Alan in the centre of the clearing. 'I'm so sorry for making that last wish Alan, I should have spoken to you about it first. But I knew we were running out of time, Hericum didn't have long left, and I wanted to make sure you maintained your legacy' Alan managed to open both eyes in realisation 'Hericum, did he make it?' His eyes attempting to scan the area in front of him without having to move his body to look around. Timmy closed his eyes and gently shook his head 'He put in a brave fight, I managed to speak to him before the end, but his time would have been up anyway. If anything, I think we may have given his heart a few moments longer when he reduced in size' Alan closed his eyes again to conserve his energy 'Oh no, how truly heartbreaking' Timmy tried to reassure Alan 'His demise wont have been in vane if you manage to pull through, you have all your capsules replenished, your colour bluer than ever and you look as good as the day I met you. Pob did a wonderful job' Alan opened his eyes again 'Ahhh Mr Pob. Where is he, I'd very much like to thank him' Timmy looked back at Alan 'I'm afraid he has left too, he took his TM-DL and left a little while ago' Alan closed his eyes again 'Oh how disappointing. I do hope to be able to thank him one day' Timmy nodded 'He also gave Hericum a proper burial, although it would be nice to know where' Alan nodded in agreement as Bongo came hopping through the hedges, holding a bottle of water.

Bongo unscrewed the lid, a little clumsily as they were not designed to be opened by rabbit paws, and held the bottle close to Alan's lips, before slowly starting to pour the water in 'Here you go Alan, drink this' Alan drank the water, not realising just how thirsty he was. Before long the bottle was completely empty 'Thank you my dearest Bongo, I feel much better now, I think I could even attempt to stand' Timmy cradled him trying to offer support to him, but if Alan had have actually needed it, there is no way Timmy could have borne the weight of Alan. It was mainly for Timmy's piece of mind that he was helping 'Slowly Alan, slowly… be careful… no rush!' Timmy tried to warn him. Alan raised himself to his knees, and in one burst of energy, pushed himself up to a standing position 'There we are, good as new' Alan said proudly standing over Timmy and Bongo. All his weight now transferring to his spindly legs. He turned around to have a proper look at the area 'So, what have I missed, what would you like to do now?' Timmy had an idea in his head, mainly to test a theory, but didn't think it was the right time to raise it given Alan's delicate state. Bongo returned the bottle lid to the empty bottle, and held it in her paw looking round for a bin to place it in. Alan noticed her holding it, and asked 'Bongo, where did you find a bottle of water in the forest?' Bongo then looked back at Alan 'There were some children playing by the lake. The bottle was with a pile of their jumpers. There were several bottles there, so I managed to take one without being seen' Timmy looked at Bongo 'You really shouldn't have taken that from them Bongo, that wasn't yours to take' Bongo then lowered her head 'Sorry Timmy, I know it was wrong, but I thought Alan would need it more' Timmy started to have sympathy for her and tried to avoid becoming a parent telling off her child 'I understand Bongo, but steeling is wrong. We should find a way of returning it' Bongo nodded her head.

'Look, I told you it wasn't a dog, it's a rabbit that took it!' a voice came from the track leading out of the clearing. It was a boy's voice, not one that any of them recognised. Timmy bolted round to look; it was a pair of children that Timmy had kind of recognised playing football with Jackson earlier. One of them was tall, dark brown hair with a blue t-shirt and khaki shorts on, the other was half a foot shorter, bright ginger hair and glasses with a beige t-shirt on and blue shorts. The combination of them standing side by side in stark contrasting colours was striking If they had had swapped tops, they would be dressed in entirely the same colour. Timmy panicked as they crept into the clearing, about to see Alan in full view. 'We should try and catch it Kieran, to show the others, they will never believe us' the shorter one said to the taller in a whispered voice. 'Alright you go that way, and I'll circle round the back of her to stop her escaping' the taller one replied. As the duo entered the clearing focused entirely on the prey, it was hard for them not to notice Timmy standing ahead of them… with a giant blue blackberry standing behind him like a guardian to some mystical realm. Everyone froze in place in this unfortunate stand-off, nobody dared say a word, everyone scared. Even the natural sounds of the Forest had taken a momentary hush. Bongo's instincts started to activate as she slowly backed up to the tree lines, but the novelty of an oversized rabbit had now fallen into insignificance of what stood ahead of the two children.

'Now stay calm… I can explain' Timmy said in his kindest, softest voice to the newcomers, mouths wide open, frozen solid. The smaller of the boys said, 'What is THAT?' his shaking hand slowly raising to point at Alan 'My dear boy, 'That' has a name, I am Alan, and I am a Quibbleberry. Now if you would be so kind as to stop pointing at me, it's incredibly rude… and do close your mouth young man, I can practically see what you had for breakfast' Alan stated in his poshest voice. The smaller boys quickly closed his mouth 'Ethan, don't move!' Kieran said. Alan's attention was now drawn to the taller boy 'That must make you… Kieran, was it? Its lovely to meet you, I am Alan, Alan the Quibbleberry… the 1381st' he said with a grin holding out his hand for a handshake. Timmy hadn't met Kieran and Ethan before. He had seen them playing football when he went to see Jackson, but based on their apparent ages, the older looked to be in the year above him, and the younger to be in the year below. Certainly not in his group of friends. Ethan was slowly backing up; Kieran was making the same movements. Timmy tried to defuse the situation 'We are not going to hurt you, I am Jackson's friend, I saw you earlier playing foot...' before Timmy could finish, he was interrupted with 'AAAAAAHHHHHHHHHHHH' in sync from the two boys, who then turned around to escape as quickly as their legs could carry them. Timmy then turned to look at Alan 'Well, that could have gone better' Alan, looking lightly rejected 'Well that's disappointing, I was on my best behaviour then. What rude young men'

'What do we do now?' said Bongo gently approaching the pair. Timmy stroked his chin and tried to think 'I don't know, they will probably run back to... JACKSON! I can call Jackson to try and intercept them!' He reached into his pocket to take out his phone. Pulling it out, as he raised his phone to a vertical position, the screen came into life. 'MUM MOBILE - 23 Missed Calls' How had he not noticed her trying to call him. The wind from the operation must have muffled the vibrations, this was bad 'Oh no, I'm in real trouble now' Alan looked at the screen over Timmy's shoulder, not being able to read 'What's happened dear boy, has Jackson tried to call you?' Timmy was unsure how to answer, he knew he would be in trouble with his parents now 'No it's my...' Timmy was interrupted by the sound of the phone coming into life. MUM MOBILE CALLING. He looked at the screen for a few seconds trying to figure out how to answer the call. He slid his finger across the screen to answer and held the phone to his ear. 'Hello, mum?' the panicked voice through the speaker responded 'Timmy! Where are you, what's happened? Are you ok?' Timmy tried to sound as calm as possible 'I'm fine mum, just got a little held up. I'll be home as soon as I can' The panicked voice on the other end replied 'Timmy, where are you? We need you home, it's your Gra…' then silence. 'Hello… Mum… Hello?' Timmy lowered the phone to look at the screen to see the phone shutting down. It then displayed a red battery symbol with a striking red line through it. 'That's not good' Timmy said deflated.

Timmy's thoughts were probably not where they should have been. They weren't concerned with Alan's safety, the fact that his parents were worried and looking for him. They weren't worried about his phone now being dead, and not being able to contact anyone. He wasn't even thinking about the implication of now being seen, and the mass panic that was about to ensue once news got out of them, and where they were. All he could thing about was the last word he heard his mum say, It's your Gra… 'Gra…?' What could that mean? It's your Gra…titude? It's your Gra…vy boat? It's you Gra…dually decreasing battery?' what could it have been? Alan then put his hand on Timmy's shoulder 'Everything alright young Timmy?' Timmy was still staring at the blank lifeless screen of the phone in his hand. I'm alright, I just wish I knew what my mum was going trying to say' Timmy didn't even realise what he had just said, his mind was too distracted. 'Hmmmph' Alan exclaimed like being punched in the side.

Timmy immediately turned round, suddenly realising what he had just said. 'Wow, that was a surprise, which didn't feel the way it usually does' Timmy was quick to reply 'Oh Alan, I'm so sorry, I didn't realise what I just said, it slipped out by accident. How do you feel, where does it hurt? Did you say it felt different?' Bongo was now at Alan's side to try and comfort him again. 'Yes, I'm fine now, it was just a surprise. Before it was like being punched when a wish was made... but this time... it feels like... like... it feels like part of me has been ripped off, and a lot more painfully. Timmy took two steps back to try and located where the wish has taken its toll. It was clear, Alan's side again. Only this time, the capsule hadn't deflated, it has disintegrated, like an over inflated balloon leaving unrepairable remains, barely recognisable as a capsule. These were having a more serious effect on Alan. 'I'm so sorry Alan, that looks so painful, and it was only a small wish. Perhaps mixing your juice with Hericum, has had a dangerous effect on you?' Alan nodded 'I don't know if I can be trusted with this power anymore, should I transfer it to someone else?' Alan shook his head 'One thing at a time young man, let's just focus on the problems at hand for the moment' Alan had regrouped himself, and stood up straight. The wish had been granted; Timmy was granted the memory of the whole conversation from the other end of the phone before it died. He heard it in his mum's voice 'Timmy, where are you? We need you home, it's your Grandparents, there's something you need to know about them, they've… Timmy? Timmy? Can you hear me? Timmy? He's gone'

Grandparents? Timmy had not thought about his grandparents since… Timmy had never thought about his grandparents, nor had he ever needed to. They were never present in his life, and aside from a token gesture birthday and Christmas gift once a year, never needed too. He knew that his dad's parents died before he was born before his dad even met his mum. They were spoken of occasionally, a picture of them sat on the rear quarter of a blue convertible car hung in the wall in the living room. From the stories he was told by his father, his grandad, a bricklayer by the name of Jack Tumblewhisk, worked all hour's god sent on building sites around the county, His dad would often point out buildings that his grandfather had laid some bricks on, and let him into secrets, like 'That building there your grandfather was one of the bricklayers on. He placed a silver penny between two of the bricks near the top for luck.' The story Timmy heard of him was that one day, whilst on a building site building the local courthouse and police station, he suffered a major heart attack.

The story he was told was that his grandmother, a beautiful woman with long hair called Margaret was heart-broken. She raised his dad until he left home, and although lived a few years beyond him leaving home, passed away peacefully in her sleep. This was all before Timmy's time and was a story he was told from a young age. But his mother's parents were never spoken of, never discussed. Timmy had asked about them a couple of times, usually when he received the regular financial present from them but never got a conclusive answer. He once overheard a conversation, a little fragmented, but learned their names, Michael & Christine Deebey. He had no other facts then that. His mother never answered any questions and very quickly changed the subject if it ever came up... She would certainly never try and contact Timmy to discuss it, that was the strangest part of it all.

Finding out what his mother had said just raised more questions, and why now? What could have possibly happened that they needed him? Timmy then felt a hand on his shoulder 'Young Timmy, we need to do something soon before those two rather rude lads, reach the beach and alert every one of our presence. Perhaps we should chase after them?' Timmy was brought back down to earth with what was happening 'You're right. Err, You and Bongo stay here, I'll go after them and try and explain' He started to run along the path, but Alan stopped him. 'Perhaps it would be safer if Mrs Bongo and I make our way back down to the lakeside the way we came, in case anyone come here looking for us now?' Timmy paused for a moment, and said, 'Good idea Alan, you go down to the lake that way...' pointing to the opening that Hericum had formed along a practically nonexistent path 'And I'll take the track down this way where the boys went' Bongo nodded 'But don't leave the lakeside, stay there, we can't risk anymore chance encounters just yet. I'll come find you!' Alan nodded and replied, 'Very good young man, we will wait for you there, be safe' and Timmy ran off down the path to try and catch up with Kieran & Ethan, knowing full well that they had quite a head start, as Bongo and Alan made their way down the flattened grass track formed a short time ago down to the lakeside.

Chapter 16:
We May Have a Problem, Mrs Bongo

There was a silence in the air as they walked. 'How are you feeling now Alan? Bongo said walking beside him through the undergrowth. 'It's a strange feeling my dear Mrs Bongo. It's like, it's good to be myself again, feeling the size I do, but it doesn't feel like me, hollow and full at the same time. It's like I can feel Hericum, not as me… I don't suppose that makes sense at all does it?' Bongo tried to be as sympathetic as possible. 'I can understand that Alan, it sounds like what has actually happened' Alan replied 'That's true. I'm sad I didn't get to say goodbye and thank Hericum for saving my life. I would very much like to find out where he has been buried when we next see Pob, so I can pay him a visit' Bongo nodded and agreed.

The ground was very uneven walking back down the hill and felt a lot steeper going down then coming up it. Bongo was conscious of Alan walking, especially in his weakened state 'Are you doing alright Alan, it's a bit steep here, do you need to rest?' Alan was touched by Bongo's concern 'Don't you worry your pretty little ears about me young lady, I'm a tough old berry!' The pair finally emerged from the woods to the grassed area at the foot of the woodland. An expanse of wildflowers, before the sand started near the water's edge. Alan made his way to a tree stump near where they had emerged from, and sat down, taking a moment to take in the view of the lake 'It really is lovely down here' Alan said taking in the feel of the evening sun on his face, cooled by the gentle breeze, he hadn't actually taken a moment for himself since Timmy relieved him from the bush, and it was very much needed. He slowly opened his eyes to adjust to the light, and looked at Bongo, she was doing the same, just taking a few seconds to… exist. Alan's attention was then drawn to the spot he washed up on the shore, the footprints around it, Hericum's trail, and the juice he had lost… the juice he had lost? There was a lot of juice, puddles everywhere when he left, but now, there was hardly anything. Sporadic patches, but it had all been removed. Alan's glance now turned to an inquisitive stare. There was more than this when they left. This could be a real problem, seeing what the juice had done to Vixen and Hericum… Alan now scanned the area for clues.

Bongo was enjoying the silence, the noise of the water in the lake. She slowly opened her eyes to expect to see Alan doing the same, but he was not. He was frantically looking round at the ground. This bought Bongo back to reality with a crash. 'Alan my dear, are you ok?' Alan ignored her entirely focusing on his surroundings 'Alan, what's wrong?' she said as she hopped over to where Alan was sat in a state of clear distress 'There was more here, lots more' Alan said starting to panic 'It was everywhere, and now there's none. We need to find out where it went.' Alan got to his feet. And started to move around the shoreline as if looking for clues. 'Tell me what's happened? What's gone?' Alan was clearly getting distressed. 'Vixen was a product of eating the Quibbleberry, Hericum was because I gave him a small amount of juice a few times. When Vixen attacked me, I lost a lot of juice, some in the water, but there was a lot on the shoreline here while I lay' as he pointed to the outline he created in the sandy bank 'But it's all gone, it's been taken, or worse yet, eaten by something. This could mean another creature is about to change?' The look of fear then spread to Bongo's face; Alan was right.

Bongo then scoured the bank to see if there were any signs of what had happened. 'ALAN... LOOK!' Bongo was standing over the area where he had laid, and where most of the juice should have been, pointing at something in the sand. 'Look at these, are they... footprints?' Alan turned to look closer, they were footprints. They weren't Timmy's or Pob's, they were from an animal. They certainly were not from Hericum, and they looked like Bongo's, but far, far too small. Big back legs, with two central front legs, which clearly hopped up to the juice, looks like into the juice, and hopped out the other side. 'Was that from you my dear? Alan said to Bongo. Flattered to have been considered small 'No Alan, these are tinny, and they move off in that direction, look' she said pointing at the ground. Bongo followed the footprints along the sand and stopped a few feet away, the prints were getting bigger. 'Alan, I think you should see this' Bongo said with a degree of concern. 'The footprints, they are getting bigger! Something has had all the juice that was spilt, and made its way down the shoreline, and…' She followed the tracks further; they had become bigger than hers, they were very big. They both followed them further to what looked like a crater where whatever the creature was, it had passed out. They both stood looking at the dip in the sand. 'What do you think, Alan?' Bongo said. 'I think, we may have a problem here, Mrs Bongo.'

They booth stood in silence for a few seconds in silence before continuing the trail beyond the crater. Their eyes scanned upwards to see where the creature had gone. The footprints had now evolved from a hop to a walk. Large hind feet, one foot in front of the other, a stride which took a sudden right turn into the water and disappeared. They turned to look at each other, each knowing what the other was thinking. 'Perhaps it will be alright. Vixen ate some older berries and became something vicious… Hericum had some of your juice and was wonderful and gave his life for you. If something has evolved here, it would be from your juice. Perhaps we are alright? But we need to find out.' Bongo said to Alan reassuringly. 'I think you're right my dear, we need to find out more, but there is definitely something out there' They both turned to walk back the way from which they had come.

Alan went and sat on the tree stump that he had been sat on earlier, and Bongo joined him and sat on the floor beside him. They both looked out onto the lake, both in complete silence trying to digest the news they had just discovered. 'I need to be more careful with anything I spill. That's now three creatures that have come into being because of me, and not all good' Bongo looked up at Alan 'Don't be so hard on yourself Alan, you had no way of knowing. And Vixen was not your fault at all, not even your berry juice to start with. You managed to make me what I am, and I've never been happier to have met you' Bongo always had a way of calming the situation, even her tone was exactly what it needed to be 'You're very kind Mrs Bongo' he said looking down at her 'We should tell Timmy when he gets back' Alan said, and Bongo nodded. 'I do hope the young man is doing ok and managed to catch up to those two young boys. He seemed quite disturbed by the call from his mother, do you know what happened?' Alan shook his head 'I'm afraid not Mrs Bongo. He accidently wished to find out the whole sentence, and there was something about his grandparents wanting to see him. I'm not sure how that would be disturbing.

I never had a grandparent, not really, just a mother bush and lots of siblings' Bongo smiled 'I didn't know mine either Alan, or how many brothers and sisters I had… but I know there was a lot. Even when I was in the pet shop Timmy got me from, the family was too big to take note of one another' she said thinking back to her younger days. They both sat in silence for a few more minutes. 'But we have each other now, and I hope we always will' Bongo said to Alan reaching up to hold his hand. The scene was almost romantic between them both, as they looked at each other, nothing around them mattered in that moment, framed by a sun setting over the lake behind them.

Bongo looked at Alan's side, where the last wish had taken its toll. The sorry looking capsule hung a deflated balloon, pitifully hanging with a scar across which had been repaired by Pob. 'What did it feel like Alan? When Pob was fixing you. Did it hurt?' Alan looked down at the floor, trying to recall what it was like. 'I remember sitting down, and I can remember when Pob was delicately fixing me. It's kind of a tickle, but I was so weak and in pain from my injuries, it didn't really register. I can then remember the silence before, like the calm before a storm, I knew it was going to hurt, but I had all but given up by that point. My life force was almost gone. The last wish that young Timmy made hit me hard, and everything was a blur after that. But I remember, whatever was going on, it hurt.' Bongo looked up at him intently listening to his words 'The thing I remember the most, that I will always remember, is how Hericum never made a sound. I felt like I was screaming in pain, but it must had been so much harder for him. He was so strong, and although our time together was brief, I will always be so grateful to him.'

'We were very fortunate to have met Pob, otherwise we may have lost you too Alan' Bongo replied putting the emphasis on all the things they should be grateful for. Alan smiled and agreed with a quite nod. Alan looked along the shore and noticed the boat that Timmy, Pob and Bongo had arrived on. 'Is that how you got here? In fact, how incredibly rude of me. How did you get here from the Forest? You managed to escape Vixen's hunt? Young Timmy and I tried to find you, but you were too fast!' Bongo then preceded to explain what happened, the chase, the collar, the river and floating out into the lake. 'I saw you from the water, I saw you fall when you were attacked by Vixen, there was nothing I could do to help, it was truly horrific to watch. And then to find you washed up on the shore, was such a relief' Bongo said. I wonder what happened to Vixen, do you think she is still out there?' Alan mused. 'We saw her too washed up on the shoreline. She stood up, but looked, smarter... more intelligent, more evolved. She must have gotten what she wanted from the berries and walked off' Alan then contemplated this for a second. 'I wish her well. She wasn't evil, she was just led by her primal instincts, and if I have now given her some enlightenment, I wish her well' Alan said proudly 'Although I do wonder where she went. Not too keen to find out if I'm right and she doesn't want more of me!' he said with a mischievous smile. 'Well,' Bongo said, 'You weren't the one she was trying to have for her tea, were you?' Bongo said with a sarcastic tone.

'Now now, she was only giving in to her hunting nature. To be honest I doubt we will hear from her again. With evolution and enlightenment, comes intelligence, and appreciation for all life. I suspect she is very sorry for what she has done, and perhaps too humble to come back and bother us again' Bongo looked back at Alan 'You're far too nice Alan, let's just hope our paths don't cross again' Alan looked her in the eyes and said 'I doubt we will see her again' Alan broke the gaze, and they both looked back at the lake, and sun setting over it, blissfully unaware that there was something looking back at them, two orbs sitting just above the water line out into the lake, watching them with sinister eyes.

Chapter 17:
C'mon You's Two!

Timmy ran down the path in the direction of the two boys he had met earlier. What could he possibly say to them? He had to think of something, but he had catch them first. If they get to Jackson first, Jackson knew I wanted him to meet him and had someone to show him… I need to just get down there first and see what's happening. He ran down the track to the main path and immediately turned left to run down the hill. There was a faded signpost at the end of the track pointing to the play area, but this was not only barely legible, but also buried with vegetation. Very few people were aware of the park's existence now, which is why it gave a good sanctuary for them for a bit.

Timmy gathered momentum that he hadn't banked on as he ran down the hill, barely able to keep vertical but managing to maintain his speed. He reached the bottom of the path and turned right sharply expecting to see the two boys running up to the rest of the football players, but he was too late for that. They were all standing in a crowd listening to

Ethan and Kieran explain what they had just seen, and very likely with additional dramatic effect. He slowed down and approached the crowd slowly. The two boys had their back to him, and the others were stood listening to *the amazing tale of the monstruous beasts of the forest*. He could start to hear the story the closer he got '…Massive blue monster, with oozing blue blood. Teeth that could tare your skin off with big red evil eyes…' Timmy rolled his eyes as he edged closer '…And an evil minion servant rabbit. With long fangs and brown fur. It tried to rip my head off…' Timmy was standing immediately behind them by this point. 'And I suppose they were controlled by a small boy too, were they? I read about this on the internet. It's an old wife's tale of the *Blue Beast of Quibbleton Forrest*. Supposed to be joined by his evil master, as small boy…' Timmy couldn't think of a name for the boy quick enough '…and his evil pet rabbit!' The two boys both turned around to see Timmy standing between them, their mouths dropped to the floor. 'I've heard the stories too, but I'm smart enough to know the difference between a fairy tale and reality' The two storytellers both raised their fingers to point at Timmy 'You!' Timmy faked surprise 'Me, what?' The crowed were losing interest by now.

'It was you with the beasts!' one of the boys mustered the courage to accuse. 'Me what?' Timmy had never had an interest in acting before, but he was impressing himself with this performance of nonchalance. 'You were the one with the monsters!' The other boy said with a shake in his voice. Timmy laughed out loud 'You think I'm the evil child beast master? Ha, I'm flattered. I'm scared of my own shadow, can't even get my pet... (He stopped not wanting to associate himself as having a pet rabbit) ...to eat' Some of the lads had returned to the makeshift football pitch to resume their game of football. 'Timmy!' Jackson exclaimed realising who it was. He circled round the boys to go and see his friend 'Can you believe these two? Full of tall tales... Back on the pitch you's two!' He turned back to Timmy 'Have you come to play some footie? Did you find your friend?' Timmy gestured Jackson to walk away with him, away from the two boys 'I did yes, and I'd like you to meet them' frustrated Jackson said 'Again? But I want to finish this game! I already missed a penalty when I went with you last time' Timmy had decided it was better not to force him again and take the luxury of getting away with being caught by the other two children as a win. 'Well if you're sure, maybe we could meet up another time and I can introduce you to my new friends' Both happy with the decision the other person had appeared to make, Timmy raised his hand to bump fists 'I'll see you at school next week, you done all your homework?' Jackson raised his fist to bump with Timmy's 'Nah, I'll leave it till Sunday night, that always works', they both turned around and walked in the opposite direction. Ethan and Kieran still standing in shock staring at Timmy as he walked back along the shoreline, Timmy turned round as we walked away and gave them wink. 'C'mon, you's two! Back in Goal Kieran!' Jackson shouted picking up the ball to carry back to the pitch.

Timmy didn't want to walk along the shoreline, knowing full well that at least two of the boys behind him were watching him, so he gracefully turned left to return back up the path the way he came. He walked round the corner until he knew he was completely out of sight before running up the hill. Running up was a lot harder than running down it, but he eventually reached the fork to leave the path and return to the play area down the track. He took a sharp right turn where the hidden incomprehensible sign was and ran into the clearing. Once there he didn't stop and ran straight for the opening formed by Hericum earlier and followed the beaten track back down the hill to the lakeside where he had instructed Alan and Bongo to wait for him. He was met with the uneven surface of the slope, harder to keep his balance once he gathered momentum going downhill again, but he managed it. As he started to approach the bottom of the track, where the surface started to level out, he saw the silhouette of Alan and Bongo sat side by side holding hands, watching the sunset over the lake.

'Alan! Bongo!' Timmy yelped with exhausted breath coming to a stop. They both turned round and welcomed Timmy back. 'My dear boy, welcome back. Did you sort the problem with those two frightfully rude boys?' Alan asked as Timmy came to a stop just behind them. Gasping for air Timmy said 'Yeah, I think so' Bongo breathes a sigh of relief 'Oh how wonderful, well-done Timmy, my hero!' she said reassuringly. 'Right, we need to get back to see my parents, I need to know what my mum wanted' Timmy said with trying to think of a plan that wouldn't get them into more trouble. 'Very good master Timmy, but I think there is something you should know first' Alan said with a hint of concern in his voice. Still gasping for air, Timmy replied, 'Really, what now?'

Timmy looked at the two who were clearly hiding something 'Well my dear, we think there is another creature out there who has been changed by Alan's juice' Timmy held his breathe for a moment to clarify what he was being told 'What? How?' he exclaimed. 'Well, when you found me on the beach, injured from Vixen's attack, and haemorrhaging berry juice, its highly likely I may have spilled some on the floor just over there where I laid' Alan said pointing to the spot on the shoreline where he was found. 'And you see, now it's gone' Alan said.

Bongo then clarified further 'We found some footprints leading up to it, and then walking away from the little that was left, and walking along the sand, getting bigger and bigger until it collapsed. Whatever it was, then stood up and walked into the lake' Timmy asked, 'What sort of footprints?' Bongo then explained 'They looked like rabbits, but much smaller at the start… Hopping along and then standing up and walking at the end. But whatever it is, it was big!' Timmy tried to work out exactly what it was he was being told 'So where is it now? In the lake?' He stood up straight for being bent over trying to catch his breath. He took a long look at the body of water ahead of him. 'That's where the tracks went!' Alan confirmed. Timmy walked up to the spot where Alan had laid. The odd spots of juice sprinkling the area, but nowhere near as much as had been there before. He saw the tracks leading up to where most of the juice had gathered. And then the tracks that left the scene along the sand. He would see a sizable crater just in the distance where something had fallen to rest.

Timmy turned back 'Any ideas of what it could be?' he asked. 'I'm afraid not young master Timmy, we were just trying to surmise that ourselves' Timmy looked back at the crater 'Another Rabbit?' Bongo replied, 'Too small my dear' Timmy thought a little more 'Something from the water?' Alan confirmed 'That would make sense, it came out of the water, and looked to return to it.' Timmy then turned back to the pair 'Something small that hops and lives in the water? A Frog?' Alan agreed 'Yes young master, that could be it' They all then got to their feet and stood gazing out into the water for some kind of clue where the amphibian could be' Timmy then approached the water's edge and said 'We need to find out their intentions, I don't want to be followed and ambushed like we were with Vixen' Bongo then replied 'We were discussing this earlier, the dried berries made Vixen evil, whereas juice from Alan made Hericum nice' Timmy thought about it, 'I don't think we can make any assumptions at this point. We need to be careful of what it could be' He approached the water more and yelled 'HELLO! We know you're out there. We want to talk with you' No response.

Timmy tired again 'HELLO! We saw your footprints in the sand, I know how confusing this must be for you, we just want to talk with you!' No response. 'We just want to be your friend; we just want to help you!' No response. Timmy turned round to talk to Alan and Bongo 'Maybe we should leave, they don't want…' Alan interrupted Timmy mid-sentence 'WHATS THAT?' Timmy turned round quickly and saw what the two were looking at. The water was rippling like something beneath its surface was making its way towards the shoreline, like a torpedo, swaying from side to side, up and down, just enough to raise the water's surface, and then drop down beneath it again. There was something there, and it was definitely making its way straight towards them.

Timmy started to back up, Alan and bongo started to edge backwards the closer and closer the surge in water seemed to get. As it approached, the shallower water, the surface broke revealing two eyes poking up, then a big head. It was still quite far out; it would be huge. As it got to the shallower water, the beast stood up, it was indeed a Frog. 'GRRRRRROOOOOG!' The beast bellowed. Teeth glistening in its open mouth. Timmy, Alan, and Bongo could only look up in amazement at the creature. 'GRRRRRROOOOOOOOOG!' the monster bellowed again. Alan was the first to reply, 'Hello Grog, pleasure to meet you, my name is Al…' 'GRRRRRROOOOOOOOOG!' Alan was interrupted and looked at Timmy 'How very rude!' Timmy raised his hand to calm Alan and carried on the introduction 'Please stay calm Grog, we want to be your friend' Grog's big yellow eyes gave nothing friendly away, Grog granting them an audience, was frustrating enough to him. He stepped forward closer to intimidate them. Instantly, the frog's eyes shot to the side of Alan where a young rabbit had hopped into view, completely oblivious of the collection of creatures sat on the lakeside less than a few meters away. Timmy, Alan, and Bongo all had their back to the small woodland creature, it was only Grog that noticed it.

No sooner had Timmy realized that he had lost the frog's attention, its mouth started to open slowly, and in the blink of an eye, his tongue shot out of his mouth like a bullet, targeted with militant precision directly at the innocent rabbit. The bulging red end of the elasticated tongue hit the rabbit unawares like a freight train, smashing it against a rock behind it. In shock, the rabbit had neither the time, strength of brainpower to realise what had happened, before tongue started to retract like a power cable to a vacuum cleaner once the button had been pushed. The poor creature was now airborne attached to the tongue hurtling like an arrow through the air, past Bongo who was still trying to understand what was happening, grazing the top of her ears, before its final decent into the waiting mouth. The whole ordeal barely lasted 5 seconds, and the frogs mouth closed with a chomp. A gasp, Timmy, Alan, and Bongo all shared a face which had jumped from a welcoming comfort, to fear. All three in unison started to take a couple of steps back, eyes fixed on the beast Infront of them as it started to enjoy its food.

The trio had reached the Forrest line by the time the frog had opened its eyes and realized that they were starting to retreat. 'Grog hungry… Grog want more!' he said eyes firmly fixed on Bongo. Timmy could see what he wanted and gestured to Bongo to get behind him. Alan being the larger of the three started to move in front of Timmy and Bongo to protect them 'No sudden movements, lets slowly make our way back to the Forrest. Grog had now lowered himself into an attack position, front legs now planted on the sand, eyes and face targeted with hungry intent. Grog's mouth started to slowly open revealing what was left of his earlier snack, Tongue moving into position like a surface to air missile adjusting its position to follow its target. Bongo was now out of view, behind Timmy and Alan, but none of them were safe, Grog wanted to feed.

Grog propelled himself forward a few meters closer, but to a position in clear view of Bongo to the side and armed his tongue to the target position. The leap forward was small, and clearly nowhere near his capabilities, but enough to get a better unobstructed view of Bongo closer to the tree line. Grog's mouth started to open again, and the tongue dripping with goo, and fir prepared to fire at her. Grog's eyes squinted as he made is final instinctive calculations on the time to fire. Both Timmy and Alan were too far forward to be able to move in between Grog and Bongo before it was too late. Grog's mouth was now full open, tongue ready to fire, the seconds turned to silence… interrupted by an unwelcome, but very familiar voice being screamed from the trees 'BONGO!!! RUUUUUUN!'

Chapter 18:
My Grog

Little Deedee was never allowed a pet, she was six, and didn't have the responsibility in her to care for another life. All her friends had older brothers and sisters and were lucky enough to have pets of all kinds, but Deedee had no siblings. Her parents had been allergic to most animals, so they constantly refused the request. Deedee was sat in her garden one evening looking at the pond of the house into which they had just moved. She had seen it from her bedroom window, but never had the opportunity to inspect it closer. Today was her first (Semi) solo visit to play in the garden under the watchful eye of her mum who was hanging out the washing. Deedee looked at the ponds surface, it was muddy, and slimy and very smelly. Any life that had been swimming around it had long since gone.

Deedee watched the bugs skimming the surface of the water, and wondered what it would be like to be that small. Could anything be lurking in the depths of the pond? She looked into the black cloudy water for any signs of life, but there was nothing. As she sighed and chalked the mission to find life up to a failure, she started to turn around, a splash came from the ponds surface. Deedee bolted and looked to see what had fallen into the water… a frog then rose to the surface and seemed to float, treading water, looking up at the human figure investigating. Deedee moved in for a closer look, but the frog retreated to the other side of the pond.

Deedee walked round the below average sized pond to see where the frog had headed. As she looked at the water closer, she realized that the water's edge was full of bubbles… moving bubbles. They were tadpoles… hundreds of them, thousands of them, in various stages of development. From frog spawn to embryos, to tadpoles… and a few in advanced stages of development. Deedee leaned in for a closer look, and reached down to touch them, they didn't retreat. Could these be the pets she desperately wanted?

The next day, Deedee went back to the pond, and the day after that, and the day after that. A week had passed when some of the tadpoles had sprouted legs and were evolving out of the pond. 'Look mummy, they're getting bigger!' She had told her mum about the little creatures a few days ago so she had joined her today to have a closer look. 'Wow, look at them Deedee, do you know what they are?' She looked at the water 'Fish?' she said with a childlike innocence. 'No sweetie, they are called tadpoles, and they will become Frogs…' Deedee looked at her. 'Can I have a Grog mummy?' She looked back at the house, and said, 'Wait here, let me see what I can find' Her mum got up and walked back to the house as

Deedee continued to stare at the hypnotically moving mass. The tall woman walked slowly up to the pond with a small Tupperware container, and a spoon. She knelt on the floor next to Deedee and lowered the container into the water, away from the frogspawn, to fill it with water, and then handed the spoon to Deedee to collect some of the tadpoles. She very unskilfully took a scoop of the small black creatures and lowered them into the box her mother was holding. Half a dozen of the small black tadpoles dispersed into the water. 'That will do Deedee, let's take these indoors to watch them grow' Deedee followed her mum into the house and into the kitchen, and watched as she placed the Tupperware tub on the windowsill, where Deedee could see the little animals evolve.

It had been a few weeks, and Deedee had watched the tadpoles evolve legs, arms, and increase in size to baby frogs. They had evolved to a size, clearly out growing the box they had lived in for their time indoors 'We need to set them free now Deedee, shall we return them to the pond' Deedee had watched and grown attached to her new pets over the weeks 'Aww but mum, can I keep one?' Her mum was aware of how fond she was of the little frogs, so reluctantly accepted. 'Ok sweetheart, we will free most of them, but you can keep one in the container until it's too big to stay' The pair went outside with the container and the same spoon they had used to capture the creatures. As Deedee tilted the container to delicately release all but one of the frogs back into the pond with all the others, she was very careful to make sure she kept one. The tadpoles disappeared into the swirling mass, indistinguishable from the rest, but Deedee was able to keep one back. She used the spoon to add some more water from the pond before she would top the rest up from the tap when she got back. She finally had a pet of her own 'There you go, what are you going to name your new frog?' Deedee looked back at her 'My Grog?' she said unable to properly pronounce the 'F'. 'Grog it is' her mum said with a smile, and they both walked back to the house where Deedee could keep her new pet on the windowsill of her room.

Deedee had been the proud owner of a baby frog for some weeks, and it was now the weekend. The sun was shining, and it had been discussed a few days earlier that they would take a picnic to the lake. A regular tradition the family undertook when their busy schedules allowed it. So, they packed their car, and made their way to the lake car park. Deedee was sat in the back of the car, with a small Tupperware container on her lap, with baby Grog inside. It wouldn't have been their preference to allow her to bring with her the creature, but in order to avoid a tantrum, her mum let her bring the frog with her. The car journey to the lake was uneventful, Deedee's dad didn't drive anything exciting, it was an average estate car, a beige one, and her mum was just happy to be out. She had packed a picnic to take with them, which included all the usual things you would expect to find at a mediocre picnic. Deedee sat in the back on her booster seat with nothing but a plastic tub with a lid partially attached on her lap. Inside swooshing from side to side in the water was her young frog, Grog. If the car went round a sharp enough corner, Deedee had to hold the tub up to avoid losing much of the water, but she would get some more when they got to the lake.

The car pulled into the car park and docked in its usual station when they visited. They all exited the vehicle, Deedee with the tub in her hand, and her mum removing the picnic supplies from the boot. Once they were all assembled, they began the walk down the path to the lake. It was a familiar route, and there was not a lot of talking that involved Deedee while they walked the path. A few minutes later, the lake came into view. Not wanting to break routine, they approached the lakeside, and turned to the left to the designated picnic area, hoping to reach the same bench they always had done. The whole area was clear, so they headed straight for the bench at the back, completely out of view of anyone.

It was quiet and tranquil, and they liked it that way. 'Mum, can I go play near the water with Grog, and top up his container?' Deedee asked, 'Okay honey, just stay where I can see you' Her parents then sat at the bench and from the picnic bag, her mum pulled out a book she was half way through reading, and with a mischievous look, also pulled out a Cribbage board, and a deck of cards 'Fancy a game?' she said to Deedee's dad, hoping for a response that would mean they wouldn't be sitting in silence on their phones or with her nose in a book. 'Sure, I've not played this in years'... But Deedee didn't care, she was already making her way to the water's edge with her box in hand, carrying it like it was the most valuable box in the world.

As Deedee got to the edge of the water, she sat down on the gravel, and placed the box beside her, before removing the lid. There was still plenty of water in Grog's box, and he just sat there, enjoying the still from the very bumpy ride it was for him to get to this point. Deedee reached into her pocket and pulled out a chocolate bar she had sneaked from the picnic bag whilst in the car. She tore it open and started to eat it. From where she was sitting, she could see along the beach to some children playing football in the distance. She was far too young to be able to join them but hoped one day she would be old enough to be interested in doing something like that, all she wanted was to do was play with Grog. Deedee turned round to see her parents' playing cards at the picnic bench behind her, mainly just to check they were still there... they were engrossed in a game of cards, laughing, and joking, clearly something they had not done in a while, and being rekindled. As she glanced down at her very unimpressed frog, not moving, looking miserable... was it even alive? She nudged the box, and the water rippled making Grog blink. Satisfied he was alive, she looked out at the lake, contemplating what she could do now.

After a few seconds, a rumbling noise came from the woodland behind her, breaking the tranquil silence. Deedee turned round to see leaves and sticks blowing in the wind above a certain section of the woodland. Her parents were already looking at the disturbance, muttering something to each other, and pointing inquisitively. It looked like a localised small-scale tornado, blowing bits of tree up into the air, from what she could remember, was the vicinity of the play park she had visited a few times. It had been a long time since she had been there, but it was definitely around that area. Her parents had now gotten to their feet as they helplessly looked on at the natural anomaly. 'Deedee, we better go!' shouted her mum, Deedee jumped to her feet hastily, not realising that she had knocked Grog's box on its side, ejecting Grog out of the box onto the gravel. Deedee looked down at what had happened. Grog, landed on his side, and flipped himself over to his feet. One large leap and he would be in the lake, they both knew this. Deedee started to reach down to pick up the slimy amphibian, but she wasn't quick enough, Grog was already in the air, making a bid for freedom. SPLASH! Grog had landed in the lake with ease and was already swimming away faster than Deedee could observe, a few seconds later, and he was gone, off into the water to hunt.

'Deedee come on!!' her mum yelled already packed and wanting to leave in case the storm got any worse. 'But mum, Grog has escaped!' Her mum was already stomping over to the disobedient child 'We have to go; it's getting dangerous here. We will get you another frog, but we need to go now!' Her mum grabbed her by the arm and pulled her back to where her dad was already striding to the path back to the car park. 'MUM! Grog has gone into the lake!' Deedee didn't even get time to pick up the box… they were now heading home.

Grog had already swum for freedom quite a distance, what he thought was out into the lake, but was actually along the coastline. His natural instinct was to swim, not how, not why, not where, just swim. But his defence mechanisms were now in full flow, he was very exposed to predators in the water like this, so when he felt a sandy ground beneath him, his swimming turned to hopping… out of the water to find cover and food. He was rapidly running out of energy; the swim had taken it all out of him. Each jump forward felt like he was running on fumes. He had at best five more jumps before he needs to rest. He leaped forward and landed in a puddle with a splash. But this wasn't a normal puddle, it was thicker, sweeter, and seemed to cling to him. His mouth was open, and he had already taken some of the fluid in. It was pleasant, and he wanted more. He took in some more, and more, and more, there was loads, and he just kept consuming it. It never seemed to be enough. Eventually, the point came that there was no physical way he could consume anymore… he tried to, but it just wasn't possible. Something was happening… he… he could hear his voice in his head. 'What's happening to me, I'm so angry' he hopped forward a few leaps, into another puddle 'I need more of this, but I can't drink it. I feel heavy…' he felt himself grow bigger and bigger… growing bigger meant he could drink more. He opened his mouth to guzzle faster as he felt himself swell. 'I am so

Angry! I've been a prisoner all my life! I am a Frog, 'Grog' is so insulting, others must suffer, I am so Angry!' He had drained the puddle he was sat in and was able to look at it from above. He could see the dark purple juice dripping off him. 'I'm hungry, need to eat something' He looked around him from this new vantage point, everything looked so insignificant. He mustered up all his energy to stand on his hind legs, standing tall, powerful, and poised to destroy anything in his way. As he stood there, he looked out at the lake that had saved him a few minutes earlier.

Grog managed to lift one foot and move it forward, then the other followed. As he propelled himself forward, he started to look for something he could destroy, or something he could devour. He needed to quench this rage that was now brewing inside him. He looked back out at the lake, flies were no longer going to cut his insatiable appetite… but fish, that could work. He stopped in his tracks and walked towards the water. This rage and anger were growing, he didn't know why he was so angry, but he wanted to eat first. He walked into the water, thinking of all the possibilities that lay ahead of him, the suffering he could cause, the torment he wanted to inflict, it all gave him… satisfaction. He slipped beneath the water's surface and propelled himself forward, mouth open, listening for movement. He knew he had to refine his hunting skills now because of his size, stealth was no longer an asset, he needed force, speed, and strength to capture his prey, something he could feel growing in him in abundance.

After a few minutes, Grog was in the middle of the lake treading water. He had not eaten much, aside from a few Carp he had managed to spear with his tongue. This was not enough, so he floats with his eyes just above the water line, looking for signs of life. A gull was flying overhead, circling obliviously looking for fish, Grog started to open his mouth, as his tongue assumed the attack position, following the flight path of the bird, anticipating its trajectory… and then… the tongue came out of his mouth with unqualified accuracy, knocking the bird out by the impact to its body. Once secured, the tongue shot back as quickly as it had left, bird stuck helplessly to the swollen end of the tongue. Straight into Grog's mouth. Easy prey, but not at all satisfying. He returned his head to just below the water line, floating motionless when… 'HELLO! We know you're out there. We want to talk with you' bellowed in the distance from the lakeside. 'Ahh, food' Grog thought… It was time to eat, as he started to propel himself back to the shoreline.

Chapter 19:
Oooomph

The feeling of remorse was overwhelming, it's never ok to take another life, hunt and mutilate it the way she had done. Her heart ached in sorrow for the animal she was, and the murderous deeds she had carried out because of her insatiable hunger. She walked through the trees, not knowing where to go, nor knowing what to do. He face, cheeks and paws were still stained with the Quibbleberry juice, she looked at her paws and just felt unclean, as it served as a reminder of her brutality. What had she done to poor Alan, He can't have survived the fall, let alone the attack, how could she have been so cruel to him. 'I am a monster!' she stopped and sat under a tree dropping to her knees with tears flowing down her face. The juice she had craved so badly must have given her a conscience and she didn't like feeling this way, she needed to repent for her actions, but needed to wallow first. She howled a sombre groan at the sky.

Starting to lick her fur to clean herself of the dried Quibbleberry juice she was smothered in. she could feel the effects of it as she swallowed it. Pulses of intelligence and enlightenment surged through her, each adding to her remorse from what had just happened. She paused and watched a frog hop passed her, no appetite, and even if she did, she had no intention of taking another life because of her hunger. She watched through the tears as it hopped off under a bush, and then continues to preen herself until she was clean. After a few minutes of reflection of what she had done, she again got to her feet and wondered off into the clearing ahead of her through the trees. She could feel the wind blowing through the trees like there was a storm nearby, but she couldn't think of anything else but the hate for her actions, and the humiliation for the way she had been, walking without direction or intent. As she reached the other side of the clearing, a surge of nausea cam over her 'I need to rest a while' she thought to herself, so she found a small patch of land out of sight and curled up into a ball to sleep as her eyes slowly closed.

She was awoken by a burst of wind that startled her, wide awake. She opened her eyes and raised her head, alert. The clearing ahead of her had a small sandstorm, a cloud which looked like it was lowering itself below ground. This cloud, with what looked like a blue tint, seemed to be digging down into the ground. Soil was flying everywhere as the cloud dug deeper and deeper into the ground. As the cloud disappeared below the ground level, although it looked like the trees, it was now clear that the green behind the cloud was in fact a large mass, a lump of motionless green. What was going on? Then the noise from the cloud... stopped, the cloud dissipated into the breeze, and a large hole in the floor came into view. Then, on the holes edge one hand came up, then a second, holding the side, before a flat cap rose out of the ground. Vixen instantly recognised Pob before his thick glasses came into view. Pob pulled himself out of the hole and got to his feet. 'Ahhh, that should do it' he said turning round looking back at the hole in the ground 'A heroes grave if ever I saw one! Now a quick brew, a few words and we'll lay you to rest soldier.'

Pob reached into his overalls pocket and pulled out a battered thermos, unscrewed the lid, and dutifully poured what was left of the contents into the cup, barely half full. 'Well would you look at this for a fine kettle of fish… Not ideal but it'll 'ave to do for now' he took one sip, downed the lot, and followed it with a very disappointing sigh. 'Nope, but that will have to do for now' he said as he returned the cap to the flask and put it back into his overalls front pocket. Pob then walked over to the green mass that lay the other side of the grave. He rested his hand on it, and muttered something sombre under his breath that Vixen couldn't quite hear. It sounded like a poem, or a prayer, but she couldn't make out the words. Then Pob stepped back and turned to walk around the other side of the green mound. Vixen could no longer see him… had he gone, she needed to know what was happening, so she stood to her feet when all of a sudden, the green mound started to lift off the ground, and then she noticed under it was Pob, holding the mound aloft, with no effort whatsoever. He was tiny by comparison, proportionally and scientifically unable to lift something of that size, but he was defying the laws of gravity somehow and carrying the mass forward to the open grave. Then in a single hop, jumped into the grave with the mass on top of him 'Oooomph' came out of the whole 'There you go chief, your time to rest now' and then he jumped back out of the hole, and turned to look back into it. Pob removed his hat, placed his right hand on his chest and lowered his head in silence.

Vixen just stared at Pob standing there in in respect for two or three minutes. Then the silence was broken by Pob returning the flat cap to his head and waving his hand to the head of the grave where a faint, floating yellow light ignited the air and a floating gravestone appeared. Vixen looked back at Pob, and the headstone disappeared. She looked back at where it was, and it reappeared. It was only in view when she is looking directly at it. Pob then started to utter some words aloud, and as he did, they became written on the stone. He spoke the works…

> **HERE LIES HERICUM, THE CATERPILLER BRAVE,**
>
> **IN HIS NOBLE SACRIFICE, FOUND HIS ETERNAL GRAVE,**
>
> **HIS TIME WAS SHORT, YET HE LIVED SO LARGE,**
>
> **YOU HEALED OUR FRIEND, YOUR DUTIES DISCHARGED**.

As the word left Pob's lips, they were inscribed on the illuminated headstone. Then he paused for a moment and turned to walk around the grave… which turned into a sprint, then a run and finally he was a blue ring which expanded creating a dust storm that seemed to return the soil that had been scattered over the ground from the excavating he had done earlier. This carried on until a small mound of earth was left where the grave once was. The cloud slowed down, and the blue ring slowly became a blue light running round, then Pob jogging, then walking before coming to a complete stop at the foot of the grave.

Pob took the pipe from his pocket and put it in his mouth 'Might nip for a quick Brew at TM-HQ before going back to see the Boy, the Big Fella and the princess, Rest in peace my friend' and with that he took two steps backward, clapped his hands, and disappeared in a flash of light. Vixen waited a moment to see if the coast was clear, before emerging from the scrub. Tentatively she approached the freshly filled grave site. Constantly looking around as she approached the foot of the grave where Pob had just disappeared from, she looked up at the head where the yellow gravestone appeared. Although she couldn't read what the words said, she could remember and recite Pobs words aloud from earlier. 'Hericum the Caterpillar? What could have made a caterpillar so large, they are small by… ooooh, Alan' she said as she looked at her paws. She continued 'Noble sacrifice… Healed our friend?' Did Hericum sacrifice himself for something, or someone? Could Alan be alright after my brutal attack, was it him Hericum saved? I need to know that he's ok and ask for his forgiveness. And poor Bongo, she must have been terrified when I chased her. They are the only ones who can forgive me' She looked back at the grave. She turned, and walked over to the corner of the clearing where some flowers were growing, she picked up a handful and returned to the foot of the grave 'We never met, Hericum, but my actions may have forced you to sacrifice yourself, so I ask your forgiveness' as she lay the freshly picked flowers on the soil. She stood for a moment, and slowly turned to walk back to the opening in the clearing she had entered through.

She walked along the path she had forged on her way to the clearing, contemplating the words on the headstone 'You healed our friend…' every time she recited this to herself, she felt a wave of happiness that there is a chance that was about Alan, perhaps he was, ok? 'But what am I going to say to them' she said aloud to herself 'How on earth am I going to ask them for forgiveness. I wouldn't forgive me for the way I acted, that's for sure!' She paused for a moment at the next clearing to sit and think about how she could approach them, softly and unthreatening. Perhaps it's something to think of more closely when she arrives, to assess the situation. So, she got to her feet and carried on walking towards the lake.

As she approached the lake, she could hear voices, familiar voices. Bongo's voice was very distinct and well spoken, she was pleased to hear her… and a male voice, it was Alan! He was ok! Vixen felt a wave of such relief that they were both ok. She creeped closer and found a position behind one of the trees out of sight, where she could observe and wait for the safest time to softly approach them and ask their forgiveness. There was no Timmy, and no Pob, and both Bongo and Alan looked distressed by something they had seen on the beach… It looked like they were following footprints along the water's edge, but she couldn't quite see. They then walked back along the edge of the lake to sit together for a moment. She had decided that now wouldn't be a good time to break cover, as Timmy and Pob were not there, it may have looked threatening, so she waited patiently. The image of Bongo and Alan sat watching the sun set was almost romantic, maybe in a different life there could have been something blossom between them, but where was Ti… oh, there's Timmy. She saw Timmy come running out of the trees, looking exhausted and eager to see them. She wasn't close enough to hear exactly what was being said, but it looked like some worrying news had just been delivered to Timmy. Timmy then walked up to the water's edge, flanked by the other two and started shouting at the water, this was very confusing to her, so she slowly made her way to hide behind another tree closer to them to hear them, and get a better idea of what was happening.

She approached a tree immediately behind them and could get a better view. Timmy shouted at the water 'HELLO! We saw your footprints in the sand, I know how confusing this must be for you, we just want to talk with you!' There was no response, who was he shouting to, but he shouted again 'We just want to be your friend; we just want to help you!' Again, there was no response from the water. Timmy turned round to talk to Alan and Bongo and said 'Maybe we should leave, they don't want…' By this point she could see something coming out of the water, Bongo had seen it too and had interrupted Timmy midsentence to alert him. The beast rose out of the water in front of the three. Vixens heckles immediately went up sensing the danger. She could tell a predator when she saw one. It looked like a giant frog, towering over them. They were clearly trying to communicate with it, having no idea of the danger she could sense they were in. She needed to help them, but as she was thinking how, a rabbit hopped out of the trees in front of her, she had completely missed being entirely focused on the meeting happening before her. She could see the beast had noticed it and was preparing to attack… and she was right. The Frog struck the helpless rabbit with its tongue and sucked it back into its mouth, before devouring it. This clearly shook-up Timmy, Bongo, and Alan, as they were starting to retreat backwards towards her, while the beast was eating.

They would never outrun it, they were in danger, and she had to help. As the frog finished its snack, it was obvious it now had a hunger for something else, most likely Bongo with it now having a taste for rabbit, and she could see in its eyes what it was after, it was clear to all as Timmy and Alan also tried to use themselves as shields for Bongo, but the creature was positioning itself to strike. It pounced forward to a position at the side of them giving it a clear line of attack on the rabbit. It was now sat closer to Vixen, so close that she could smell it. Her trained nose could also smell the Quibbleberry juice on him, so she surmised that this could have been another creature brought into existence from consuming the juice. She didn't have time to think about that now, she had to strike, and strike now while it was distracted and before it attacked Bongo. The monster started to open its mouth to strike, the slime dripping tongue ready, still littered with fur and blood from its previous attack, lined into position like a laser guided gun. She squats down ready to pounce, it was now or never so she yelled 'BONGO!!! RUUUUUUN!' and leaped forward allowing her predatory instinct to kick in, completely ignoring her new enlightened peaceful nature. She flew through the air, over Bongo, teeth on full display, and aiming for beast, catching it unaware. The frog had closed its mouth by the time it realised what was happening, and by then it was too late. Vixen had sunk her fangs deep into Grog's neck and was attached like a leach. Grog was knocked onto his back by the impact. Arms up trying to grasp Vixen with its hands, but her bite was too tight, and now her claws had taken grasp on Grogs side. The pair wrestled on the floor, predator, and predator in brutal attack. Grog tried to roll around on the floor to loosen Vixen's grip on him, but it was no use, she was now feeding on him. She managed to interrupt her bite long enough to shout again 'BONGO!!! RUUUUUUN!' at the three bystanders taking in the battle before them.

Grog was flailing around on the ground losing the battle, one of his hands landed on a large rock on the sand, and he instinctively clasped it and swung it onto Vixen's head. This disorientated her, but she took the blow. Grog swung again at her with the rock, this disorientated her more, easing the attack on Grog enough for him to get to his feet. Grog kept smacking Vixen with the rock, which took its tool enough for her to loosen her bite on him. He dropped the rock and grabbed her with both hands and threw her to the ground.

Covered in his own blood and chunks bitten out of him, he turned to go and pick her up, but she was already on her feet and pounced at Grog again, taking out his hip and dropping him to the floor again. The pair rolled around on the ground, itching closer and closer to the water's edge. Vixen managed to run around Grog, like a plane circling a ship, attacking, and retreating, attacking, and retreating, until Grog was able to catch her and pin her to the ground. Vixen was still able to take chunk's out of Grog, each of them deteriorating at the same pace. Strength versus stealth and agility. Timmy knew they needed to run.

Chapter 20:
Shut Her Eyes with A Smile

Timmy had had enough time to be able to see what was happening, enough to realize the danger they were all in, he grabbed Alan's hand and turned to Bongo and said, 'We need to get out of here!' Bongo was already turned to start running, Alan was still watching in amazement at the battle unfolding before them. 'Alan, we need to go, NOW!' he pulled at Alan's hand and they both turned round and joined Bongo, running as fast as they could in the opposite direction. By the time they had entered the trees, they had lost sight of the spectacle happening on the lakeside and were out of sight of the danger. Bongo was already leaps and bounds ahead of

Timmy and Alan forging a path for them but increasing the risk of losing the pair. 'Bongo, slow down, we can't keep up' Timmy yelled at her. She wanted to slow down but her primal instinct to run was difficult to overcome. Bongo reached the play area clearing they had just come from, and stopped for a moment to make sure it was safe. Timmy and Alan burst through the trees behind her, grateful to see that she had stopped, so they could catch their breath and regroup for a second.

'She saved me!' Bongo said in shock. 'Vixen saved me, I hope she's ok, should we go back and help?' She asked Timmy and Alan gasping for air. 'I don't think that would a good idea my dear. Grog is dangerous, so we need to get as far away from him as possible' Although Timmy agreed with Alan's logic, he wanted to see if Vixen was able to defend herself after having saved them. He looked at Alan 'I could sneak back and see if they are finished?' Alan looked disapprovingly at him 'We really should keep running young sir, but if you feel you must know, perhaps you could use a wish, you could wish to know if she's, ok?' Timmy looked at Alan in shock 'Absolutely not! You're only just back to being healthy. I think that if we just go and see if she's ok, it would be much better than if I wish to know if she's ok!' Alan agreed, but was then brought to his knees by a shooting pain in his side as he granted Timmy's wish 'Alan, what's wrong, I didn't make a wish… as he recounted exactly what he had just said… he had 'Oh Timmy, no!' Bongo said realising what had just happened. 'Oh, Alan I'm so sorry!' Alan was bent over in pain as the wish was granted. A memory had appeared in Timmy's head, it was of Vixen and Grog on the lakeside, Grog was in a pool of blood laying semi submerged in the water, lifeless. Vixen was laying a few paces away beside him, covered in blood, barely breathing. 'I think Grog is dead, and Vixen doesn't have long left to live. It looks like she has killed him' Timmy said sorrowfully. Bongo immediately ran back along the path she had forged, back down to the lakeside. 'Bongo, WAIT!' Timmy yelled, as both him and Alan started to chase after her.

Bongo was back at the waterside in a matter of seconds, running straight up to the brown fur pile that lay on the sand. Briefly checking that there were no signs of life from Grog before approaching Vixen. Her eyes were closed, and she wasn't breathing. 'Vixen, Vixen! You saved me!' There was no response from Vixen. Bongo placed her paw on Vixen's side to feel for her breathing, there was nothing. 'Vixen, please speak to me' Alan and Timmy had finally caught up with her by this point, Timmy made his way over to Grog to make sure he was gone. Grog was floating by this point and starting to float out into the lake. The further out he got, the further beneath the water's surface he started to descend, he was dead, Vixen had taken so many bits out of him, blood was everywhere, he was gone. The seagulls had already been taking dives at him for food. He stood and watched with relief as his body slowly slipped beneath the water's surface, there was no way he could have survived. Timmy turned around to go see Vixen. 'Timmy, she not moving I think she's gone too!' Bongo said with a tear welling up in her eye. Hers and Vixen's relationship had been troubled at best, but

Bongo was so grateful for her sacrifice to save them. 'Vixen, please speak to me' She said. Vixen's eyes started to open as she exhaled the last of the air in her lungs, and she rolled her head to look at Bongo who hadn't noticed she had come round. 'Please forgive me' she whispered in a strained voice to Bongo 'I am sorry for what I was' she finished. Bongo looked at her and knew she didn't have long left. Alan then answered for them all 'We forgive you Vixen, and thank you for saving us' Vixen rolled her head and shut her eyes with a smile, she knew she could rest now… and she was gone.

Timmy, Alan, and Bongo all took a moment of silence, standing over Vixen. 'What do we do now?' Timmy asked, 'We should give her a burial, it's the right thing to do' Bongo nodded in agreement. Alan said 'Do you know where Hericum was buried? We could bury them together' Timmy looked at Alan 'I don't know, Pob took him off to be buried and he never told us where.' Timmy looked at Bongo 'Well I should say we find out. We need Pob back, and he can help us lay her to rest' Timmy looked perplexed at Alan 'I agree, but he's gone now, and I gave him my TM-DL box back' Alan looked deflated, still tender from the earlier wish. 'Well then we will have to do it the old-fashioned way then' Alan turned around and walked back up to the wood line and started to dig a whole with his bare hands in the sand. Bongo started to make her way over to Alan and stater to dig with her paws next to him. Timmy sat and watched, admiring their efforts, then got to his feet and wondered over to help them dig. They were two feet deep when their silence was interrupted by a very welcome voice from the tree branch above them. 'Diggin' fer buried treasure are ya? Strange 'ol place to dig fer treasure… Usually found on a beach by the sea not a lake, thas where the pirates buried it. Supposin' you 'ave a map though, then you'd know where to go!'

All three of them looked up at the branch and with a Joyous cheer, they all chanted in Unison 'POB!' He dropped from the branch to the floor 'That'll be me! Ere' on my customer care return visit to check ya all doin right, was gonna wait till the morning, but 'ad a strange urge to pop and see ya tonight. So, let's get started then…' Pob reached into his overall front pocket and pulled out a wooden clipboard, twice the size of the pocket, and detached a ball point pen from it, and clicked it. 'Right then, 'ere we go. Question one, on a scale of one to ten, how likely are you to recommend your Task Miner to a Friend? Cuh, what a stupid question, I mean, who wouldn't want a Task Miner, I ask ya!' Timmy interrupted him 'Pob, we need your help, can you stay?' Pob looked at Timmy a little confused 'Would that be a 10 then boy, that's grand' as he circled the ten on the clipboard 'Right Question two, did your Task Miner give a full explanation for the services they provided? Knew a guy once, right moody he was, never got more than a five fer this one. So, what do ya think of ya 'ol mate Pob?' Bongo Glanced at Timmy and back at Pob 'My dear Mr Pob, we need to know where you buried Hericum, and can you help us bury Vixen there?' Pob looked at Bongo 'Oh dear, that sounds like an eight to me. Ne'er you mind, there are no wrong answers, your feedback is important to us' Pob begrudgingly circled the eight on the clipboard.

Pob then broke his concentration from the clipboard, partly driven by the fact he was trying to be more helpful, and looked down at the hole they were digging 'Reckon you'll need to go deeper then that if you be lookin' to find you some treasure! Let me finish this an I'll gi'yer a hand… Right Question 3, how did you hear about the Task Mi….' At this point Alan put his hand over Pob's shoulder and interrupted his flow 'Mr Pob, we are so pleased to have you back with us, and we need your assistance with something. Would you be able to help?'

Pob looked up at Alan. 'You wanting another free service? I gi' you a free one already! Not running a charity 'ere you know. You're 'ol mate Pob is savin' up fer a house, and still got a long way to go! Needs to get me all tens on this 'ere survey to 'elp with that!' Alan replied, 'If young Timmy here wished for the house you wanted, would you stay and help us for a little while?' Timmy looked at Alan 'No Alan, you can't!' Alan held his hand up and said 'We could have used Mr Pob's assistance on several occasions, I think he should stay with us' Pob lowered his clipboard and looked at Alan 'So let me get this straight… If 'un I go an stay with you lovely folk, you'll wish fer a house for me? How long was you thinking of keepin' me in yer service?' Alan looked at Timmy, and back at Pob 'Well, how long do you think it would be before you can save enough for that house you want?' Pob stroked his moustache with his thumb and forefinger 'Well, thinking on how much I've already saved, and the rate of cash I'm getting… oooh, I would guess only about…' he whispered some numbers under his voice 'Maybe another 754 earth years, or there abouts… thas takin' into account sick days, holidays, scores of less than 10, maybe add the odd pandemic's in there to lower demand… Yeah, I reckon thas about accurate' Alan looked at Timmy and whispered 'I can take the hit'.

Timmy looked at Pob 'So if I…' He paused a second to review he's terminology 'So if I get you the house you want, will you stay with us and help for as long as I need, let's say 10 years at most?' Pob looked at Timmy surprised 'You what? You're telling me that if I hang around with you lovely folk fer only 10 YEARS! Then you'll get me my little cottage by a lake… 10 Years? 3,652 Days including leap years? 87,648 Hours? Gordon Bennet, I've had holidays longer than that, I 'ave!' Timmy looked at Alan 'With Alan's permission I'll get you the little house, and you can stay and help us' Flustered, Pob couldn't think how to answer calmly… almost speechless he mustered the words… 'Ummm…. Will there be tea?' Timmy smiled 'Will give you as much tea as you can cope with' Pob stood in shock completely silent, dropping his clipboard and pen to the floor 'Well then, I reckon you've gone and got yerself a Task Miner! 'Appy to be of service to ya's' Timmy said, and first to business, can you help us bury Vixen over there, where you buried Hericum?' as he gestured to Vixen laying behind him. Pob turned around and saw her. 'Isn't that the young fox that caused all that ruckas today?' Bongo looked up at him 'It was Mr Pob, but she saved us from a monstrous beast that was trying to kill me' Pob looked back at Bongo 'In that case, it would be me honour to help ya' Pob looked down at the pit they were digging 'Is that what you was trying to do here?' Timmy looked at him and nodded 'Well that won't do will it now, let's do this right!'

Pob walked over to Vixens lifeless body and looked at her. 'Well little miss let's get you to rest' he reached down and picked up the fox's paw, removed his flat cap, placed it in his front pocket and rested the paw it on top of his head. He glanced at Timmy and yelled 'Back in a jiffy!', stepped back and clapped his hands and both him and Vixen disappeared in a flash. Timmy looked at Alan 'Are you sure you can take a wish like that? You're already starting to show signs of damage' he looked down at Alan's sides, each equally deflated. 'My young Timmy, I won't have long for this earth anyway. Having Pob around you will be a good thing when I am gone. And by the sound of it, I would say we are saving him a good few hundred years!' Timmy smiled. A flash and Pob was standing in the centre of the three dusting his hands off. 'Right then, can't carry you all I'm afraid, not the young fella I used to be, need to walk it. Not far, just up this 'ere hill' Pob started to walk, and Timmy, Alan and Bongo started to follow him. 'Not walked in a while, little legs ya see, should be good, get to blow away the cobwebs' Pob said strutting ahead of the trio.

As they walked up the hill at a slow pace because of Pob's speed, Timmy's mind was taken back to the phone call from his mum. Why were his grandparents back, what could they possibly want with him? He's completely forgotten about their existence, and now they were here, and his mum sounded distressed by it. Something was going on and he needed to find out what. 'Are you alright young sir?' Alan asked Timmy 'Me? What, oh yes, I'm fine. Just thinking about that call from mum' Alan looked at him 'I see, well let's lay poor vixen to rest and we will go home to find out what's going on.'

They arrived at the clearing where Hericum was buried a few hours earlier. The sun was very low in the sky, and they could barely make out the disturbed earth of Hericum's grave 'Is that where he is buried?' Timmy said to Pob 'Yep, thas his grave there. There's a summoning headstone, but you need to look directly at it' They all looked directly at the head of the grave and the illuminated yellow headstone came to light, with writing on, the epitaph Pob had recited earlier. The three looked, Timmy was the only one capable of reading, so he read it aloud to the others. 'That's lovely Pob, thank you. Pob tipped his cap 'Lets lay Vixen to rest' as he started the process of excavating the grave next to Hericum's.

Chapter 21:
Her Villainy Undone

Timmy, Alan, Bongo and Pob all stood beside the freshly filled grave waiting for Pob to inscribe the illuminated headstone. Pob was muttering something under his moustache, and he waved his hand towards the headstone and the inscription appeared on a glowing yellow headstone.

> **BENEATH THIS STONE, VIXEN LIES IN REST,**
>
> **ONCE DEEMED EVIL, NOW HER HEART CONFESSED,**
>
> **IN ONE SELFLESS ACT, HER VILLAINY UNDONE.**
>
> **SHE GAVE HER LIFE TO SAVE HER FORGIVING ONES.**

The words wrote on gravestone as if being written by a skilful calligrapher. The three watched them being inscribed as Timmy read them aloud. Alan and Bongo smiled in agreement. 'That was beautiful Pob' Timmy said. They all stood watching for a moment or two before Pob broke the silence 'There she goes, now what's next young Timmy? You Wanting to get home?' Timmy and Alan all took a step back and started to walk round to Pob. Bongo stayed where she was, head bowed in silence. 'Mrs Bongo, come on now, it's time to go home' Alan said gently to her. She looked at Alan and turned to hop over to him. Pob joined them all as they made their way to the opening in the clearing to get back to the track.

Timmy and bongo were walking side by side up the track to the car park, with Alan and Pob were walking behind them, engaged in their own conversation about TM-HQ, and what some of the busy body bureaucrats were like. Timmy realised they were now walking past the spot where they first encountered Vixen, and had the standoff before Bongo made a run for her life. 'Bongo, how did you escape Vixen, must have chased you for a long time?' Bongo, unphased, responded 'She did, and she was a very good hunter. I would not have escaped if it weren't for my increased size, I was able to leap further and run faster. It was only when I had to stop, and caught my collar on a branch, she was able to catch up to me' Timmy watched her as she recounted the chase 'She was distracted, and I was able to run away again. It was then when I fell into the river and carried downstream to the lake' she said 'I saw Alan get attacked and wished I could help but couldn't swim fast enough… then you came and rescued me from the water' she said looking up at Timmy. 'I remember' Timmy said as they continued to walk along the path. Bongo looked back at Alan 'He's been through quite a lot today… well we all have. These wishes are killing him, and I don't want to lose him' Timmy looked at her suspecting she was growing sweet on Alan 'He will be fine, we have Pob with us now so I'm sure he will be with us for quite a while yet' Even though Timmy knew this wasn't true, he managed to reassure himself by saying it out loud.

Timmy hadn't given any thought to what they were going to do when they reached the car, and how they were going to get home. The sun had almost set, and the individual trees were indistinguishable from each other. The sky was a dull blue with silhouettes of tree branches swaying in the wind. As they approached the car park, it was easy to see that there were a set of car headlights on, illuminating the car park and the entrance to the path they were descending on. Timmy and Bongo slowed down to stop. '…And you see chief, that each task miner has a TM-DIL which means that they could summon you anytime! You could be sat on the toi…' Pob was interrupted mid-sentence by almost bumping into Bongo 'Oh, I'm sorry princess, everything good?' Pob said. Timmy pointed to the car park ahead of them 'Looks like we will need to wait before we can leave, we don't want to be seen again' The four of them stood looking at the headlights just ahead of them. 'I can nip ahead and see what the crack is chief? I'm now at yer service' Pob said already taking two paces back ready to clap his hands. 'Hold on Pob, at ease soldier' Timmy said to Pob 'I'll go, it may be my parents waiting for me' Timmy started to walk along the path 'You sir, are you sure this is a good idea? I think we should all stick together' Alan said. Timmy stopped and looked around

'There! You three wait behind that bench for me, it's dark and you won't be seen by anyone, I will come back to get you' Timmy said pointing at a bench to the side of the path. Timmy started to walk away from the trio who were still looking at the bench 'I won't be long' Timmy said as he walked towards the car park. 'Be careful Timmy' Bongo shouted as he left. Alan was the first to make his way over to the bench, followed by Pob. Bongo followed shortly after.

Timmy was at the edge of the car park before he glanced back to ensure they were all out of sight. There was indeed a car sat in the corner of the carpark with its lights on, and two figures standing beside it, he instantly recognised the car, and the figures. His dad was standing to the side looking at his phone as if texting someone, whilst his mum was pacing back and forth with the phone to her ear. It was too dark for them to notice he was standing there, so he took the moment to quickly assess what they were doing. It looked like his mum was trying to ring someone, and was unable to get through, and his dad was now answering his phone, looking uneasy. His mum was still pacing back and forth trying to get through to someone. Timmy took a quick look back along the path and scanned the rest of the car park before making his move toward the car, where he would no doubt be seen any second now. 'OH MY GOD, TIMMY!' his mum yelled as she ran over to him. She swooped him up and carried him off the floor 'I was so worried about you, WHERE HAVE YOU BEEN?' she said as she carried him back to the car and his waiting father 'My phone battery died, I was fine' his dad hadn't broken his concentration on his phone call, like he was trying to negotiate a hostage situation to the recipient on the other end. His dad glanced up at Timmy, and smiled giving him a wink, and carried on with his conversation. Timmy's mum was now carrying him to the car door, where she opened it and placed Timmy in the waiting car seat 'Mum, we can't leave yet, I have something to tell you…' His mum wasn't listening, entirely focused on the mission to get Timmy home 'We need to go home, I'll get you some tea, and we have some people we would like you to me' his mum said buckling his belt. 'But mum, wait. My friends are waiting for me up the p…' SLAM! Timmy's mum shut the car door. Timmy tried to open it, but the child locks were doing exactly what they were supposed to do.

Timmy's mum had now walked round to the other side of the car to where his dad was standing on the phone. He couldn't make out what she was trying to say to him mid phone call, but it wasn't working, she wasn't getting through to him. As he was watching his parents try and engage in conversation, which his dad wasn't entertaining, he noticed a shadow coming from the back of the car as the boot lid opened slowly. 'Didn't think you was gonna leave without us did ya?' Pob said as he appeared in the boot behind Timmy's seat. Timmy smiled with relief as he felt the suspension take the strain of Alan slowly getting in the car boot followed closely by Bongo. Pob then grabbed the boot lid, and stealthily closed it. Pob reached for a blanket in the boot and placed it over Alan who was trying to keep as low as possible so as not to be seen. Bongo had already found a small alcove of the boot to hide in. 'Hope you don't mind us joining you master Timmy, was getting a bit cold up there in the woods. Knew a guy, left outside all night, had icicles on his nose by the morning, don't fancy that much myself' Timmy looked back at him 'Not at all Pob... I'll get you a cup of tea when we get back!' Pobs face lit up like a child in a sweetshop 'Gawd bless ya young man. You know how to keep a Task Miner happy!'

Pob noticed Timmy's parents move towards the car doors, and dutifully ducked down behind the seat out of sight, and Timmy faced front as the front car doors opened. 'Timmy, have you had a good day?' Timmy's dad asked as he closed the door behind him 'Yes dad, it's been... good' Timmy replied as his mum closed her door and started to fasten her seatbelt. Timmy's dad put the key in the ignition and started the car 'Good man' he said as he pulled his seatbelt round him to fasten it 'Has your mum told you the news yet?' he said. His mum turned to look at him, knowing the answer. 'I haven't yet love. Timmy, it's about your grandparents, Nanny Christine, and Grandad Michael. We know you have never met them, and we haven't really talked about them much before but... well, they are coming to see us' Timmy's dad leant over as the car started to pull away and interjected 'They are here' Timmy's mum's face dropped with the realization of something unwanted scheduled to happen, actually happening. 'Really? They are early!' she replied to him. Timmy's dad nodded in agreement. The car rolled to the exit of the car park before stopping at the road. 'We are going to meet them at The Stoat' Timmy's dad said, 'THE PUB?' she replied trying to digest this new information. Timmy's dad nodded in silence as he looked both ways before driving the car out of the car park. Timmy had no tangible input into the conversation and could only look left to right at them as their conversation evolved. They both sat in silence, looking forward as the car drove the short distance down the road to the pub car park. Timmy's mind took him back to earlier that day running past the pub car park on the back of Alan, with Bongo giving chase, hoping the man who had seen them run passed, had either left or forgotten the incident. Timmy could hear some faint whispering coming from behind him, barely audible 'Psst… What's a Pub? Don't reckon I've seen one of those' Pob said in whisper 'I'm not sure Pob, must be some kind of fantastic meeting ground?' Alan's hushed voice replied.

The car slowed as it approached the pub, and slowly turned into the car park to look for a space. There were plenty to choose from, as the car park was rarely at capacity. Timmy's dad selected a space close to the building, parking next to the only other car in the car park… a big black, very expensive looking saloon shaped car. It wouldn't have looked out of place with some diplomatic flags on the front, and a police escort. Timmy noticed the prominent registration plate 'DB 1' proudly displayed on the front of the car. 'Looks like they are here' Timmy's dad muttered 'I think you're right' his mum said nervously. The car came to a stop next to the limousine, and his dad turned the key to turn it off. He looked at his mum concerned 'Are you sure you want to do this? We can do it another time when you're ready, it's been a long time' he said reaching out to put his hand on hers to comfort her. She sat looking at the car, 'No, we need to do this, we can't delay it anymore' she replied with a sigh. Timmy just looked on, wondering what could be happening. They all sat in silence for a moment, preparing for something, nobody wanting to move first. Timmy's mum was the first to break the scene, she unclipped her seatbelt and reached to open the door. His dad looked at Timmy, before doing the same thing, as they both exited the car. Timmy's car door was opened, and his mum reached in to unclip him from his seat, without breaking her gaze on the building, which was lucky as she didn't see six pairs of eyes looking back at her from inside the car boot.

His dad came round to hold her hand, 'Out you get Timmy' which he dutifully did. Timmy glanced back into the car and whispered 'Wait here' to the trio in the back, before closing the door behind him. Pob and Alan's eyes peered through the rear window watching as Timmy and his parents slowly walked towards the entrance to the building. 'Well, what do you think is going on here?' Alan whispered 'Can't say I have the slightest, big fella. It's all a bit strange' They both glanced at each other. 'Well, they could have left the radio on, or cracked a window open for us' Bongo chirped in. They both looked at Bongo who was sat in the corner, wrapped in a blanket. Alan looked back out the window as they all walked into the building, his dad holding the door open, and his mum and Timmy walking in before being followed by his dad. The door closed behind him, and they were gone.

Chapter 22:
The M.O.U.

Timmy followed his mum into the building. The smell of stale alcohol was the first thing he noticed. It was dark and gloomy, the wooden floors creaked underfoot as they all walked towards the bar. An old portly man noticed them walk in and make his way along the empty bar to greet them. Timmy knew him as Mr Shuttleworse, the land lord. Never having spoken to him before but had seen him around town. 'Evening Mrs Tumblewhisk, this is a nice surprise. What can I get you?' Timmy's mum was too busy looking round the pub for someone, to notice the offer. Timmy's dad approached the bar. 'Billy, nice to see you again. What can I getcha?' the bartender asked him. 'We'll have a drink in a second, has there been anyone else in here tonight?' Billy asked the bartender, who looked over Billy's shoulder at the table behind the door. Before Billy could turn round, '…Suzanne?' a well-spoken lady's voice came from the back of the pub. Timmy's mum slowly turned round to look over Timmy, to see a well dress couple sitting at the table looking at them in surprise. 'Mum?' Timmy's mum uttered with a whimper in her voice. The woman sitting down in a long black dress, perfectly preened and styled hair, red lipstick, and high heels, slowly stood up, and the pair just stared at each other, each too speechless to speak. Next to the well-dressed woman, sat a man in a very expensive suit, a white shirt, and a grey tie, looking at the pair, then focusing on Timmy's dad 'William' he uttered in acknowledgement of the man standing at the bar, who responded humbly 'Good to see you again Michael' who nodded accepting the compliment.

The two ladies were still frozen solid facing one another, until eventually they both, in sync, started to walk towards each other. Billy followed Suzanne to approach the table, Timmy just stood to the side, purely an observer to this overdue meeting. Suzanne and her mum were now embracing after overcoming an awkward do-we-shake-do-we-hug moment when they first reached each other. The man in the suit was resolved to stay seated, to get up and be excited by this would be too vulgar. Billy went over to shake his hand during the lady's embrace, which he was happy to accommodate. They each had a glass of white wine on the table in front of them, untouched and chilled, which Mr Deebey followed the handshake by taking a sip out of the glass, completely unphased. His attention was then drawn to the young boy standing to the side, unintroduced and looking a little awkward. Suddenly his stern unimpressed demeaner shattered, and an approachable smile shot across his face 'And who is this handsome young man?' he said looking at Timmy. Christine was mid-embrace with her head on Timmy's mums' shoulder when she opened her eyes to look directly at Timmy. 'And this must be Timothy?' she said with an excitement in her tone 'I prefer Timmy' he managed to utter in response. Christine turned and approached him, kneeling down to his level. 'Well now, I apologise, Timmy. It's wonderful to finally meet you. My name is…' she said hesitant not knowing what to say, having never met a grandchild before 'My name is… Nanny Christine, I'm so pleased to meet you' By now Michael had risen to his feet and was standing over his wife. He then lowered himself to the same level, his well pressed suit clearly uncomfortable at having to perform a manoeuvre like this 'And you can call me Grandad Michael' he said in a friendly and approachable manner whilst holding out his hand for a handshake. Timmy took the hand and offered it a little shake. Timmy's dad asked, 'Can I get you both a drink?' before noticing the glasses on the table 'We're fine thanks' replied Michael without looking.

Timmy's dad then asked the same question to Timmy's mum who replied with a short 'Just a coke' He then approached the bar to place the order. Timmy's mum had made her way to Timmy to place her hand on his shoulder 'Timmy has been so excited to meet you' which Timmy knew was a lie but didn't want to break her stride. Michael offered 'Well come and join us young man, we have lots to discuss.' Both Christine and Michael rose to their feet and walked back to their table followed by Timmy and his mum. 'Come and sit next to me Timmy, I want to hear everything about you' Christine said to Timmy who patted the bench seat between her and Michael. Timmy's mum had sat down on the chair opposite and was quickly joined by his dad carrying two cokes and an orange juice, placing them on the table and sitting down on the other chair. Timmy sat flanked by the two well-dressed adults not knowing where to look 'It's wonderful to finally meet you Timmy, your grandad and I have been looking forward to meeting you for so long. It's just unfortunately, we work very hard and have to travel all over the world, so it's been very difficult to find time to come and see you' Timmy's mum and dad glanced at each other, reluctant to take this as an excuse, but each agreeing with a glance that they wouldn't interrupt, for Timmy's sake. Michael then turned Timmy's face to him 'For you see Timmy, we work for the government, a department called the Ministry of Unnatural, looking for strange things, magical beings, creatures… well… not from this realm. It's our job to look for signs of strange and other worldly things, and we received several alerts from this area' Timmy's dad didn't like the pace this was going at 'Perhaps we should save this until we get home?' he said to be met with Michael raising his palm to him, closing his request.

Christine then turned Timmy's face to her 'You wouldn't happen to know of anything happening round here that's been a little… strange, would you?' Timmy's mum then interjected 'Mum, we should really talk about this at home' Michael then raised his hand again to her. He then turned Timmy's face to him again 'For you see Timmy, we try to ensure the protection of the planet from these magical beings to ensure we all have a happy, unaffected life. The M.O.U. has been in place for hundreds of years, hunting down wizards and witches, and countering their spells. We would hunt them down and… well… make things better' Christine then turned Timmy's head again 'So if you know of anything that's been happening in this area, it's so incredibly important to tell us' Timmy then raised his hand to remove hers from his chin. 'I've not seen anything I'm afraid' he replied. Michael looked unimpressed with the response 'Quite' he muttered. Timmy then reached for the orange juice on the table in front of him to take a sip. All five of them then, in perfect sync, took a sip of their drinks, and returned them to the table. 'Would you like to come see our house?' Timmy's mum asked, 'Its only round the corner' Christine broke her stern demeaner and replied, 'Yes dear, that would be lovely' Michael exhaled, as if he had just been presented with a mundane chore to be completed, 'Yes, perhaps we should' He reached into his jacket pocket and pulled out what looked like a black tile and held it before him as you would a smart phone. Timmy watched in amazement as green hieroglyphs appeared writing across the tile 'Nothing new has happened, but we must stay vigilant my dear' he instructed Christine who dutifully nodded in response.

Michael retuned the tile to his pocket and rose to his feet followed closely by Christine. Timmy and his parents remained seated, still finishing their drink. Billy finished his drink first and said 'Come on Suzy, lets show your parents our home' with a hint of sarcasm that they had never visited before. Her and Billy then rose to their feet looking at Timmy waiting for him to finish. Christine and Michael had already made their way to the front door to leave and had stopped waiting for their guides to arrive. Timmy placed the glass on the table and stood up to follow them to the door. 'Cheers guys, good to see you!' The bar man said as they all walked out the front door. 'See you later' Billy said as he closed the door behind them. All stood outside, they started walking to their cars. 'You're both looking well' Christine said as they walked. 'Thank you, Christine' Billy said in response, not noticing that being called by her first name had aggravated Christine slightly. As they approached the cars, a bleep and the drivers and passengers side doors of the car opened gracefully to receive the with welcoming lights inside. 'Perhaps little Timmy would care to ride with us?' Michael asked with a hint of command 'Well that's up to Timmy, what do you say chief?' Billy asked. Timmy didn't know how to answer, knowing what was in the back of his parents' car, undoubtedly looking back at them right now 'I'm not sure…' Not being given the opportunity to answer anything further then that 'Nonsense, in you get' another beep and one of the rear doors graciously opened welcoming him in.

Timmy reluctantly approached the open door, being ushered in by his grandparents. He took a seat on the enormous leather bench chair, velvet lined doors, and twinkly lights in the roof lining offered a magical glow 'Don't forget to fasten your belt Timmy' Michael advised as he pushed a button on the door and it slowly and carefully closed shut.

Timmy looked out of the tinted rear windows and was completely unable to hear what his parents and grandparents were saying. The silence from the triple glazed windows offered absolute quiet from the outside world. Timmy's parents and grandparents were just outside the car exchanging a strained conversation, Timmy had no idea what they were talking about, but could only watch their expressions. His attention was then drawn to the rear of his parents' car, he could only see the top of the blanket that covered Alan, barely moving. He was able to take this moment to think about what his grandad Michael had said… '…*we received several alerts from this area…*' surely that couldn't be related to the wishes, could it? What alerts? What could the err… Ministry of Unnatural was it? What could they have that could detect these things? Nanny Chris, and Grandad Michael were now getting into the car with him, and his parents were then getting into theirs.

Timmy stayed focused on his parents' car in case they noticed anything in the boot. 'Right young sir, shall we go?' Michael said in his posh voice. He reached down to push a button in the centre console… nothing happened. He then slid a lever down just behind the steering wheel, and the car slowly started to roll forward in complete silence, he wasn't even sure the car was moving, it was so smooth and quiet, more of a polite gesture. Michael effortlessly encouraged the steering wheel to rotate, which it did with ease. There was nothing offensive about driving this vehicle it would seem. Timmy peered out the window to see his parents' car in front of theirs, bellowing smoke out if the exhaust, clunking along, which now looked extremely outdated by comparison.

'So, Timmy. Tell me about your day. What have you been doing? I understand from your mum and dad that you've been down to the lake. Did you get up to much?' Christine asked inquisitively. 'Not much. I was at home completing my chores, and my friend Jackson called me up, and invited me down to the lake to play football' Michael asked 'Football? Are you a big Football fan?' Timmy turned to look at the two, and noticed Christine was writing something down in a notebook while he was talking. 'Errr, no not really. There were a load of boys from school there, and I wanted to get out of the house. Jackson is my only real friend' Timmy could just about make out what Nanny Chris was writing, it looked like.

1. *Jackson (Friend) mobile phone…*

2. *Football at the lake…*

3. *Chores list from Suzanne, Home (Morning)…*

4. *Lake, friends, Quibbleton forest (Afternoon)…*

He has to be careful what he said. 'Did you play football, who won?' she asked. 'No, I just watched. Not much of a football fan you see' Christine seemed happy with that response. 'What sort of phone do you have Timmy, we were thinking of getting you a new one… can we see yours?' Michael asked. Timmy reached into his pocket and pulled out his phone 'It's not the latest one, but the battery is dead now, so I can't use it till I get home' Christine turned round to face him holding out her hand 'Oh no, do you mind if I have a look?' Timmy paused but couldn't see any harm in it as it had no charge 'Sure if you like' he said handing her the phone. Grandad Mike then pushed a button on the dashboard and a leather lined shelf ejected from the centre console, split into two revealing a screen above it, with a little black button on the base. Nanny Chris then lay the phone on the platform and pushed the button. The platform glowed and electric bright blue, and the screen above it burst into life displaying and flashing the word 'Scanning…' in blue letters.

After a few seconds the screen displayed 'Complete' Nanny Chris picked up the phone and handed it back to him 'Here you go Timmy, it looks fine' Grandad Mike then pushed the same button again and the platform returned to the dashboard. Timmy looked at his phone, which proudly displayed in the top corner '100%' next to the battery icon. Before Timmy could look up, he realized that they were then rolling onto his drive behind his parents' car. Grandad Michael brought the car to a stop, pushed the same button in the centre console he had pressed to start the car, lowered the leaver behind the steering wheel and pushed another button on the dashboard with a strange door shaped logo on it. All three doors opened allowing them to gracefully disembark the vehicle, shining a light onto the floor beneath each of the doors he had previously not noticed. It was a logo for M.O.U. with a target in the centre underlined with the writing MINISTRY OF UNNATURAL. He could see that the door in front of him has the same projection. Timmy jumped out of the car, giving a simple gesture to the door to close, which it dutifully obliged and closed behind him.

Chapter 23:
More Dangerous Alarm

Timmy got out and ran up to his parents' car, as they were both getting out, he could see that neither of his grandparents had left their car but were both looking at something displayed on the dashboard. His dad was now walking up to the front door to unlock it, and his mum was slowly walking up to the black limousine at the bottom of the drive, she paused not wanting to disturb them in what they were clearly engaged. Timmy opened the back door of the car, and whispered 'Are you guys ok back there?' The first response he received was 'Young Timmy, I cannot over emphasize how much I would like a brew right now! Do ya know I've not gone this long without a cuppa for a lot of years, it's not good for a Task Miner to be without one. Knew a chap a few years back, tried to come off Tea, cold turkey as it were, he slept for weeks, never was the same after that' Pob said exasperated. Timmy looked around and saw that his dad had unlocked the door but was now walking back up the path to see his mum. 'Ok' he said, 'If you can quietly jump to the kitchen, I'll keep an eye out, but BE QUIET!' Pob got to his feet 'You don't have to tell me twice!' He took two steps back, with the limited space provided, clapped his hands, and disappeared. 'Timmy looked at Alan and Bongo 'Are you guys, ok?' Bongo replied, 'I'm a little car sick my dear, but I'll be alright' Before Timmy could ask Alan, he was interrupted by a siren sound coming from his grandparent's car. He looked up and could see something flashing reflecting on their faces. His parents were now walking up to the car concerned by the alert. Nanny Chris and Grandad Mike had noticed that they were walking towards their car, and in a panic, grandad Mike pushed some buttons to power down whatever was flashing, whilst they both quickly exited the vehicle.

They both shut the doors and intercepted his parents before they could reach the car. Timmy noticed his parents' car shake a little as Alan tried to move, he had to get Alan and Bongo out of the car before they were noticed. He walked back to the car, where he had left the back door open, and peered his head in. 'You need to keep still until they are all out of sight' he said to Alan. 'I'm sorry young man, it's not particularly comfortable back here you know, but I will try and keep still' Timmy looked to the side 'Are you ok Bongo?' She nodded, clearly eager to get out of the confined space. Timmy turned to look up at his parents when there was a flash, and Pob reappeared 'Cooooor blast, that was a cracking cup of tea dat! Ya know them brew's that are absolutely spot on. Well, that was one of 'em. So! How are we all doing?' he said, clearly refreshed. Before Timmy could respond with a request to be quiet, he was distracted by the noise of another alarm going off in his grandparent's car. Grandad Mike and Nanny Chris also noticed the alert and broke away from their conversation with his parents to rush back to the car to see what the alert was. Timmy looked back at Pob, was he the one causing the alarms by jumping? Timmy looked up at the limousine, where his grandparents were engrossed in a screen on the car dashboard, discussing and analysing whatever it was they were looking at. 'My dear Timmy, would you mind if we get out of here soon, I'm becoming a little claustrophobic in the back here?' Bongo asked politely. 'Yes Bongo, just a moment, I want to test a theory.'

He turned to Pob 'Mr Pob, would you mind going to the kitchen to get me a glass of water?' Pob looked back at him a little confused 'Water? You want me to go get you a glass of… Water?' Timmy nodded 'Yes please Pob, I'm really thirsty' Pob looked at Alan and Bongo 'You want a water? No teabag, no milk… in a glass, not a mug?' Timmy nodded again 'Well thas a rumen, you sure?' Timmy nodded again a little exasperated this time. 'Very well Master Timmy, I shall go get you a glass of… Water' Pob rose to his feet and started to walk out of the car and passed Timmy 'Wait, could you jump, you know, so you're not seen' Pob looked deflated 'Well, a jump seems a little bit of a waste of my energy, but as you wish' He took two paces back and clapped his hands… flash and he was gone. Timmy looked up at the limousine, and heard an alarm go off again, exciting his grandparents further. His parents were just standing watching, waiting for them to leave their car. After a few seconds, flash and Pob had returned with a half full glass of water. 'Here you go

Timmy, one glass of plain, flavourless, cold and unsweetened… water!' Timmy took the glass as he heard another alarm come from the limousine. Nanny Chris and Grandad Mike were clearly getting very excited, pointing at the dashboard, and writing notes.

There was no way he could get them out of the car without being seen right now, he had to think of something. 'Please Timmy, I need to get out of here, I need to get out now' Bongo was panicking and squirming, clearly in distress. 'It's ok princess' Pob said stroking her back 'There there, it's alright, nothing to worry about. I knew a Floodle once, she was claustrophobic, ran around in a panic, fell off a cliff, poor little mite' This was doing nothing to calm her. Timmy looked back at his grandparents, they were staring back at him, not saying a word, but watching him intently. Timmy had to do something now.

He looked at Alan with a look of apology, Alan knew what he was about to do. 'I'm sorry Alan, but I wish you three were out of danger' Bongo looked at him in despair 'Timmy, NO!' Alan squinted his eyes in pain, and the three of them faded away until they had all disappeared. The sudden relief of weight on the car's suspension raised the car off the ground a few inches. They were gone. The silence was then filled with a louder, different, more dangerous alarm coming from the limousine, accompanied by a red flashing light. Timmy looked up and his grandparents were striding over to him, like a freight train, completely ignoring the alarm and the siren, straight passed, and ignoring his parents, walking directly towards him. He felt like he was in real trouble, but his friends were safe… wherever they were.

Nanny Chris came straight up to Timmy with a forced calming smile, which was definitely not calming. Grandad Mike went to investigate what was going on in the back of the car. He reached into his suit pocket and pulled out a device resembling a milk bottle attached to a games console controller. He pointed the top of the bottle at the boot of the car, like a makeshift gun clumsily put together. A beam of light projected out from the top of the bottle creating a screen floating in the air above it… making various beeping tones. He digested the results, looked at Nanny Chris and gave the tinniest nod. She, understanding the gesture then turned to Timmy 'How would you like to come and see where we live? We have lots of toys and games you could play with, and a big bed. Perhaps you would like your friend Jackson, or any other friends you have to come along too?' Grandad Mike had now approached them 'Your father tells me you have a pet, Rabbit; can I see him? You could even bring him along if you would like?' he said looking round for some signs of the pet. Suzy then offered assistance, and to distract from the request to take him away 'Timmy, go and get Bongo to show your grandparents' she looked at her parents 'He really is a very good and well-behaved rabbit' Timmy wasn't sure what to do next 'Err, ok I'll go get her' as he ran off through the gate to the back garden. 'Her?' Suzy muttered.

Timmy was finally out of sight. He ran to the rabbit hutch knowing full well that there would be nothing inside.

Unhooked the hatch to the door and opened it. He looked around to make sure there was no evidence from the chore list escapades earlier, everything looked fine. Then ran to the fence at the bottom of the garden to peer over and see if there were any signs of life there, perhaps that's where they had reappeared? Nothing. Just some flattened grass where Timmy sat and was forced to do his homework. Where had they gone? This was yet another situation that he should have chosen his words more wisely. He looked back up the garden to the gate he had just entered via. Grandad Michael was standing there watching him. He could see Nanny Chris was talking to his mum and dad, but she was holding something in front of her mum, as if hypnotizing them but shining a light into their eyes, and his grandad had been able to break away from the conversation and was now walking down the garden to him.

He was looking around as he walked 'So where is this Bongo, I'm looking forward to meeting him… or is it her?' As he backed Timmy into the corner, he got down on his knee, a gesture that his well pressed suit struggled with again. 'Listen my boy' he said in an authoritative and menacing tone 'I am well aware of what's been going on here. We've detected a few level three transit jumps on this property in the past few minutes, and a category seven level production, or 'wish' (he said in inverted comma's) event a few moments ago. I also have reason to believe that a Leporidae category species has been brought into being by one of these events, and they need containment before an infestation breaks out.'

He moved his face closer to Timmy's 'So where is your rabbit, Timmy?'

Timmy looked over his shoulder at the hutch with the open door. 'She's gone. She must have escaped when I was at the lake. I was then looking for her. She usually finds her way out of the garden under this fence, perhaps you could help me look?' Michael looked at him disbelievingly and said 'Hmmm. Quite' as he got back up to his feet, Christine and his parents walked into the garden behind him. His dad looked at his vegetable patch 'Huh… I'm sure I had more in there than that. Timmy, you haven't been touching them, have you?' he said curiously, but nobody was listening. Nanny Chris came up to Timmy and said 'Its ok Timmy, I've asked your mother, and she has said you can come stay with us for a few days. Timmy looked at his parents who seemed to ignore the statement, like they had been told this fact and could do nothing about it. 'No need to gather your stuff Timmy, we have everything you need, come get in the car with us' Timmy couldn't do anything as his nanny had already grabbed his arm and was starting to pull him along the garden path. 'But mum, I don't want to go' his mum in a semi trance replied 'Its fine Timmy, go with your nanny, she will look after you' she said with no emotion in her voice. His grandad followed shortly behind them back up the garden. His mum and dad didn't move and stayed in place, waving at them as they left the garden.

It was pitch black by now and as they approached the limousine, the headlights illuminated the area, and the doors opened welcoming them inside. Nanny Chris gestured Timmy into the back seat, and closed the door behind him, locking him inside. His grandparents then entered the car from either side to the front seats, and closed the doors behind them, shutting out the outside world. Timmy could still see through the tinted glass, his parents standing at the bottom of the garden, faintly illuminated, still waving at him. 'Right Timmy, come with us' Grandad Mike said as he pushed the button in the centre console, which seemed to do nothing, and turned the wheel as the car rolled cautiously backwards down the drive. Timmy felt helpless sat in the back of the luxurious car, nobody saying a word.

He couldn't see where they were heading when they left Winkleford, as it was pitch black, he had lost his barings a few miles back, and could be anywhere. Why had his parents been so ok with them taking him? Where were they going? But most importantly, where were Alan, Bongo and Pob? He looked out the window into the black, looking for some signs of where he was. He looked at the front of the car, his Nanny was reading some notes, and his grandad was entirely focused on the road, not a word was uttered between them. 'I'm thirsty, can we stop for a drink?' he mustered up the courage to ask. His nan reached forward and flipped a switch on the dashboard, which opened a compartment in the back of her seat. Inside there were three bottles of drink, one water, one orange squash and one cola, as if by magic. He reached forward and released the bottle of chilled orange squash. Nanny Chris never uttered a word; she then flipped the same switch and the hatch door abruptly shut. Timmy just held the bottle and looked out the window. Then a familiar voice came from behind him 'Well my days, what a fancy carriage this is. Feel like the king sat in 'ere, will 'ave to get me one of these! What do you reckon they retail at? Maybe Pob should use his savings for a house and splurge on one of these beasts if you're wishing me a house instead?' Timmy turned round in a panic, Pob was sat beside him 'Pob!' he yelped. His Nanny Chris turned round and said, 'Did you say something sweetheart?' looking at Timmy, and not noticing the Task Miner sat beside him. 'No, nothing, I just burped' His Nanny didn't look impressed at all and turned round to carrying on reading her notes.

Timmy looked at Pob and said 'What are you doing here? Can they see you?' he whispered as quietly as he could to not be heard. Pob was looking round in wonder at the car's interior 'Hold on chief, this doesn't feel right' Pob clapped his hands again and disappeared in a flash. Timmy checked that his grandparents hadn't noticed anything, then another flash and Pob was sat on the bench seat next to him in a tuxedo and bow tie 'That's better, much classier' he said. Timmy smiled at the effort he had put in 'Can they see you?' he whispered. 'Pob looked at him through his new monocle. 'Of course, not boy, I'm your Task Miner, I'm only visible to people you subconsciously want to see me. I've also taken the liberty of disengaging those fancy sensors and contraptions in the front of this car, so they don't know I've arrived, I hope that's ok?' Timmy looked at the front of the car 'Very clever' he whispered. 'So, what's the crack 'ere, what have I missed?' Pob replied.

Timmy was so pleased to see Pob, but his concern was quickly drawn to the others. 'Where did you go? Where are Alan and Bongo?' he said as quietly as he could not to disturb his grandparents. 'Well, you see, you wished us to be somewhere safe, and I was sent back to TM-HQ. That was an awkward chat, as I don't work there anymore. Not best pleased to see me either, not so much as a leaving card, quite put out if I'm honest. Knew a guy once…' Timmy interrupted 'Yes, but where are the others?' Pob was never a fan of being interrupted, but continued 'Well, ya see, that was my first thought too. So, I jumped to where the big fella had gone, and he was in a clearing in the forest. Not one I'd seen before, I'm afraid to say, he's not in a good way. He was laying on the floor, not moving very much, that last wish has really done a number in 'I'm. So, I left him to sleep for a bit to get some rest' Timmy's heart sank at hearing this. 'What about Bongo?' he said quietly continually checking the front of the car so that they hadn't heard him. 'Not good news there either I'm afraid, couldn't find her. Did me normal thing of requesting a jump to them, and it always works, but wouldn't with her. Strangest thing, never happened before, so came to you. Hope the princess is ok. And it's not the start of a failure for Pob. Knew a fella once, lost his direction like that, ended up living in a washing machine, never got over it, never knew where he was' Timmy started to panic, 'Can you take me to Alan?' he asked Pob, 'Sure thing my 'ol fruit. Put your mit on me 'ead' He removed his cap, and Timmy put his hand on top of his head. 'Let's get outta here!' He clapped his hands together and… Pob disappeared, but Timmy was still there.

He had disappeared, and an alarm had now been activated on the dashboard. Shutters shot up between the rear and the front of the car, and the windows turned to sheet metal. A screen appeared on the shutters in front of him with his grandad Michael's face on it.

'Ahh, Timmy my dear grandson. It appears you have activated the ORPS, or 'Occupant Removal Prevention System' for the uninitiated, which is fitted to this car, were you trying to escape? Quite impossible now, nothing can get in, or out.' The screen then changed to Nanny Chris 'I think there is something you're not telling us Timmy; this will all go a lot easier if you tell us the truth and let us do our job.' Timmy started to weigh up his options, and they didn't look promising. He would have to do what his grandparents have asked.

Chapter 24:
Descendants of A Wizard

Bongo slowly opened her eyes, stayed frozen in place. Her mind was taking a few seconds to assess her senses. Could she breathe? Yes. What was her temperature? A little chilly but ok. Could she hear any danger? No, it was silent. What was her position? She was laying down. Could she feel anything around her? Her face was laying on carpet, or something similar. It was dark wherever she was. As her senses slowly started to return to her, she remembered the panic of the claustrophobia from earlier. She'd never experienced a feeling like that before and never wanted to feel it again. Her eyes started to adjust to the darkness, she was laying on the floor in a cupboard or storage room. The carpet was soft, and very high quality. She slowly lifted her head up to get her bearings, she was definitely in a cupboard, a slither of light from the cupboard door gave her a better indication of where she was. She was able to get to her feet, and gently put her paw up against the cupboard door to apply some pressure and open it. It unclipped, and slowly swung open. As her eyes adjusted to the light, she was able to see what was beyond the cupboard. 'What a strange room' she said aloud, in a hushed voice. She peered her head outside, none of the walls were straight, they were curved upwards, like the room was a long, thin cylinder. The walls were brown, and there were seating areas to the front, and a wall at each end with a door in. The walls also had little round windows lined along them, this was a very strange room.

She poked her head out a little more, until she was fully out of the cupboard. The carpet under paw was very think and very soft. She hopped towards one of the seating areas, and hoped up onto one of the leather lined seats to see if she could look out of one of the windows. The room she was in was in a large grey, concrete, and steel room, she couldn't see much more than that. Silence. She looked around the room and made her way to one end to try and open the door, but it was locked. She turned around and started to head to the other end, but there was a noise coming from outside, footsteps on concrete, slowly getting louder and louder. She hopped back onto the seat to have a look. Two men in strange suits were walking towards her. She dropped to the floor and returned to her cupboard, closing the door behind her. There was a clink, clank, sliding noise, clink, and the floor started to wobble ever so slightly. She peered through the crack in the door, she couldn't see them, but she could hear them talking as they got closer. '…and I said to the chap, I will only have it in red, if it's the convertible. The guy said it would only come in black for the Spyder version, so I said *Then get it resprayed.* Trust me Stephen, I won't be going back there…' Bongo thought about how well spoken they were. '…Alright Gareth, you may need to lower your standards a little…' and they both laughed. '…So, what's this evening's flight plan captain?' 'I don't know, let me check, wherever they want to go I suppose. Most likely home. I don't think they wanted to come here in the first place' Bongo heard the sound of a door closing and the voices became muffled.

There was a loud noise of something dragging along the floor outside, like some big, heavy doors opening, as she could start to hear the wind rustling through the trees. This noise was then overpowered by the sound of an engine. Like the one in Timmy's dad's car, but these were A LOT louder, and a lot more powerful. They just got louder and louder. What was happening? She could see lights moving across the wall, like something outside was moving and projecting a light through the windows, she had to investigate. She emerged from the cupboard again, hopped onto the seat and peered out of the window, where she could see a car approaching. It looked familiar, and she recognized the symbols on the plate on the front, DB 1 looked like the ones on the big black car, Timmy's grandparents had. As the car approached her, she was sure it was the same car. The car came to a stop beside her room, and she could see the figures in the front were very recognisable. Michael and Christine opened the doors and got out of the car. There was a clunking sound as a door opened to one end of the room '…I will go and meet them Gareth…' and the sound of the door closed. She looked back out of the window and saw one of the well dress men approach Timmy's grandad and shake his hand.

Timmy's Nanny then opened the rear door of the car, and Timmy jumped out, looking very scared. She was holding his arm and not letting go. The suited man then escorted them all to just out of sight from where Bongo was sitting. She jumped down to the floor and returned to the security of her cupboard and closed the door.

She peered through the gap to see the door at one end open up and in walked Timmy's grandad, followed by his nanny with Timmy in tow. She sat him down on one of the seats and sat opposite him. The well-dressed man then followed 'Mr Deebey, we are just carrying out our pre-flight checks and we expect to be able to depart in a few minutes. Flight plan has now been logged and we hope you will have a pleasant return flight home with us this evening' Timmy's grandad didn't look impressed and sat down 'Thank you captain' he said to swiftly end the conversation. 'Now then Timmy. Is there anything you want to tell us?' his Nanny said to him. 'We will find out eventually. The ministry has investments in many different people. We have a track record of absolute success, and these unnatural events need to be eliminated' she said a lot less calmly to Timmy. 'You see my boy' Timmy grandad said from the other end of the room 'These events have been going on for hundreds and hundreds of years. We are the first and last line of defence to keep normality constant. To maintain your way of life. There are some malicious creatures out there, which we have contained. Why, only a few years ago, there was the *Beast of Quibbleton Forrest*, from your neck of the wood, as it were. We were able to step in and contain him, with nobody being any the wiser' He explained. His Nanny then continued 'And that wasn't even the worst from your town, one of our first assignments was the *Witches of Winkleford*, descendants of a wizard that lived locally, that was driven out of town many years ago for murder, but his children lived on in the area, in the shadows, waiting to rise again. They were successfully contained and now reside in our high security unit offshore. A very dangerous duo indeed' Timmy's grandad then got up from his seat, and walked over to Timmy, sat down next to him, leaned in, and said, 'So my boy, shall we begin?'

The intercom erupted into life '…Errr…. This is your captain speaking, we are potentially looking at some delays before we can taxi. We have received some reports of a storm on our flightpath…' Timmy's grandad then rose to his feet 'Oh for goodness' sake' he exclaimed, and walked to the front of the plane and flung the door open. Timmy's Nanny then got to her feet and walked to the other end of the plane. 'We'll continue this in a minute, your nanny has to go powder her nose' and she opened the door to the rear compartment, entered and closed it. Timmy was alone. Bongo then emerged her head out 'Psst, Timmy my boy. Are you ok dear?' Timmy looked down at her, and the biggest grin came across his face

'Bongo!! You're ok! What are you doing here?' Bongo whispered back 'I don't know, I was in the car when you made your wish, and then I woke up here' she said looking around to make sure the coast was still clear. 'What of Alan and Pob, have you heard anything?' Timmy whispered back 'I saw Pob, but he has gone and can't get back now. But I think Alan is in a bad way, he is in the forest' Bongo then had a look of worry 'Oh poor Alan. So, what do we do now?' Timmy looked at the door to one end 'I don't know but keep yourself hidden until I can think of something.'

The door to the end of the room then flung open and Nanny Chris burst out drying her hands. 'Good boy, stay calm' as she walked towards him to sit down. 'Fasten your seatbelt' she said, trying to assist him. Bongo sat in the cupboard peering through the gap at Timmy and his Nan, when his grandad came through the door at the end of the room looking at his phone. 'It looks like there is a problem at containment centre 8-12. Security have issued a breach of containment alert to… hang on the emails are still loading… breach in containment of section… 12… Unit… come on come on…' Timmy's Nan looked at Michael with a look of panic 'Please don't say nine dear' Michael looked at his loading screen 'Chris, it's nine' they looked at each other in fear 'we need to get there and help, the security won't stand a chance against them' Christine pleaded to Michael. 'Not until we are summoned to sweetheart, you know the procedure. In the meantime, we have this young man to deal with, so let's take you to our home' as he finished his sentence, the engines roared into life and the plane started to move. Michael sat down in his seat and fastened his seatbelt. 'Mr & Mrs Deebey, we are now making our way to the runway to commence taxiing. I have turned on the fasten seatbelts sign and kindly ask you to prepare for take-off' a voice over the intercom uttered. Timmy was trying to see if he could see Bongo, but there was no line of sight.

Christine looked at Michael 'they've broken out of containment, they will come for us Michael, like they vowed they would. We won't be as lucky to capture them next time!' She said clearly concerned. Michael looked back at her 'I'm sure it's a false alarm. And even if it's true, the witches have a lot of power, but they can always be caught' the plane had now reached the end of the runway and the engines started to whirl into life. Timmy could feel the plane start to move and the feeling of a rocket pulling everyone back into their seats like a punch to the chest was felt by everyone, except bongo who was unrestrained, and thrown to the rear wall of the storage cupboard. Faster and faster, then the plane started to tilt, and lift off the ground. They were now airborne. An experience Bongo and Timmy had never experienced before. Their ears went muffled as they started to pop under the change in pressure, as the plane rose to the heavens like a homesick angel. In any other situation, Timmy would be enjoying the experience, but he wasn't enjoying anything about this.

The plane levelled out, and a voice over the intercom announced 'Good evening, Mr & Mrs Deebey. We've now reached our cruising altitude of 14,000 feet. I'm going to go ahead and turn off the fasten seatbelt sign. We will be arriving at our destination in approximately 45 minutes. We wish you a pleasant flight with us today, and I will let you know when we approach our destination' this was followed by a 'bing' noise and the fasten safety belt sign turned off. Bongo had been able to get to her feet again and managed to get another look through the gap in the door. Michael and Christine had now moved to the back of the plane and were muttering something to each other. Timmy had moved seats and was trying to see Bongo; she pushed the door open slightly to show Timmy she was ok. Timmy held a thumbs up gesture to Bongo to visually confirm she was ok, and she nodded back at him. She was about to exit the cupboard, and see if she could get closer to Timmy, when there was a very small, but familiar flash of light come from behind her. She turned round to see, and there was nothing. Just an envelope and a small parcel, wrapped in paper, held together by string that wasn't there before. Perplexed by this; she pulled the cupboard door closed and picked up the envelope to see who it was addressed to.

In scrawling handwriting on the front, it read 'F.A.O. The Princess, Bongo' she clawed open the envelope and pulled out the contents. It was a folded piece of paper, the same colour brown as the envelope, and in italic handwriting it read, Dear princess. I hope you are well and safe. I can only apologise for not being able to reach you as normal, something's stopping me finding you to come get you. I was only able to send a very small transmission you see. So, I've been clever ya see, and sent my TM-DL through to you. It will be more of a *come find me*, then a *where is she* type deal. So, if you push that there button. I will be able to get to you. Ya see, Pob has been smart about this. Knew a task miner once, did the same thing. Got sent to Neptune, came back very strange. Odd creatures on Neptune ya see, he could never pronounce his 'S's after that, not good for a task Miner. So anyway, you push the button, and I'll come fetch ya. Yours, your ol' mate Pob (Dictated not read)'

Bongo folded up the letter and returned it to its envelope, then changed her attention to the little parcel. It was very well presented. She pulled the string, holding the other end in her mouth, undoing, and releasing the brown paper that unfolded in front of her, there was a small plain white box with no markings on it. She slid the lid off the top, and inside, wrapped in paper, was the black box she had seen Timmy use before. She lifted the red button protector and hovered her paw above the button. Was now the right time to summon him? Perhaps it would be better to do so when Timmy's captors were out of sight. She peered through the gap and could see Timmy's Nanny sat down on her phone at the other end of the room, and his grandpa had obviously gone through the only door his nanny had used earlier to powder his nose. Now would be as good a time as any to push the button. She pulled the door closed again and pushed the button firmly on the TM-DL... a flash from beside her and Pob appeared, mid-sentence '...Alan, not long now till you'll be at rest. Hang on a tick, hello Princess! Are you a sight for sore eyes. How are you doing beautiful?'

Bongos first thought was for Alan 'What's wrong with Alan? Is he ok?' Pob look at where he was 'Is this a cupboard? And… err… are we airborne? Not been in a flying cupboard before…' Bongo interrupted again 'Pob, tell be about Alan!' Pob drew his attention back to Bongo. 'Oh yes, the big fella. I'm afraid not, he doesn't have long left, the last wish really took it out of him, and I don't think even your 'ol mate Pob will be able to save him this time' Pob went to inspect the gap in the cupboard door. 'Ahh Timmy my boy…' Pob went to push the door open when Bongo stopped him. 'Timmy's grandparents are at the other end of the room' Pob looked at Bongo 'Well that's a pickle and no mistake. It's only Timmy that can see me, I'm his Task Miner. Let your old mate Pob go and assess the situation' he pushed the door ajar slightly and squeezed through the gap. Timmy's face lit up when he saw the familiar blue overalls walking towards him. Cautious of what his Nanny Chris was doing, he made no incriminating movements. 'Timmy my boy! Flying in luxury I see, only the best for you. Have you tried the caviar on these flights, not as nice if ya ask me. Knew a fella once, tried to…' he was interrupted by Timmy 'Pob, can you get us out of here?' Pob looked at him a little put out to be interrupted but looked around at the room. 'Let's 'ave a look shall we' he put his pipe in his mouth. 'Hmmmmm. I should think this is a C650… quite a plane. Broken quite a few speed records too for its size, I believe it can reach Mach 0.95, outstanding for its class' Timmy didn't want to interrupt him again, but had too 'Pob, can you get us out of here?' Pob looked around room and walked to the front of the plane 'hang on a tick, let me check out the cockpit' he took a couple of steps back and clapped his hands. Flash and he had disappeared.

Timmy then looked Bongo, who was sat in the cupboard in full view with tears flowing down her cheeks. He mouthed 'Are you ok?' To her, but she didn't reply. Michael then emerged from the door at the end of the room drying his hands. 'I've just received word' he said to Nanny Chris 'Edna and Evie have escaped' Nanny Chris then fell back into her seat with a look of sheer terror on her face. Pob then flashed into existence next to Timmy. He took the pipe from his mouth and said 'Yep, all seems simple enough. Nice plane truth be told. There are some additional countermeasures on board, but I think I've disabled them all now, so I can jump you both out of here, but only one at a time. I think you need to go see Alan now my friend' Timmy looked at his grandparents who were clearly distracted by the news they had just received. 'Get Bongo home first' he whispered. 'Very good young sir. I will be back for you shortly' Pob walked over to the cupboard and picked up the TM-DL and threw it to Timmy. 'Keep this just in case I can't get back' Timmy caught it and hid it in his jacket pocket. Pob walked over to Bongo, removed his hat, and placed her paw on his head 'Ready princess?' Pob took a little step back and clapped his hands, flash and they were gone.

Tommy's attention was then drawn to his grandparents again, relieved that Bongo was now safe, he kept one hand in his pocket with his thumb on the button of the TM-DL he had just been handed. Grandad Mike and Nanny Chris were sat opposite each other in silence, contemplating the news they had just received. 'You know they will come for us, hunt us down and…' Grandad Mike interrupted 'I know, but it will be ok, we are safe on board, The MOU has kitted these planes out with all the countermeasures we need' At that moment, a green storm cloud, looking like a micro-Tornado appeared in the air between them, circling, little lightning strikes, and forming a small vortex. From the centre of the vortex, which looked to have created a small porthole, a small ball dropped through, green and looked like it was made of glass. It suspended itself in mid-air a few inches below the vortex and emitted two directional beams of light, one at Michael and one at Christine. They looked at each other paralyzed in fear, Christine uttered the words 'They found us' as they both, along with the orb, and the green vortex all vanished. Was this the work of the two escapees they had been talking about? Edna and… Evie was it. Were they the Winkleford Witches they were so scared of? This was very low down the list of priorities for Timmy right now.

The fact was he was now alone on a private jet flying, who knows where, and he needed to get to Alan. He pressed the button in his pocket to summon Pob. The intercom sparked into life 'Mr & Mrs Deebey, this is your captain speaking. We are now about to commence final our decent, I am going to go ahead and turn on the fasten seatbelts sign, and thank you for flying with us this evening, we wish you a safe onward journey' a voice came from the chair in front of him. 'Well, he sounds like a nice chap. What's the plan then young sir do we…. Hang on a tick' he said looking round

'Weren't there more people on board a little while ago? Captain's just put the seat belt light on, best they return to their seats' Timmy looked at Pob, not interested in explaining 'Can we leave now please?' Pob hopped up on the table in front of him. 'As you wish young sir' he removed the flat cap and lowered his head 'If you wouldn't mind' Timmy put his hand on-top of his head 'Right then, make sure your trays are locked in the upright position, keep your hands and arms inside the cart… off we go!' Pob took a couple of small steps and clapped his hands… Flash, and they were both sat on the ground in a clearing in the Forrest. Bongo was sat next to a lifeless Alan in the middle of the clearing. 'There you are sir… right, where can a get a brew, I'm quite parched now.'

Chapter 25:
Pob's Rest

Timmy instantly recognised where he was standing, and his eyes were drawn to a patch of soil, made up of a browny green mulch with hints of blue. The morning sun had started to shine through preparing to project a beam of sunlight onto the patch which now stood a lifeless stick. This was where it all began, this was where he first met Alan. His attention was then taken back to Alan laying lifeless on the floor just beyond the former bush. He ran over to see him, and placed his hand on Alan's side to see if he was still breathing. He was, faintly. 'Alan, speak to me. Alan, how do you feel?' Alan rolled over and looked at Timmy 'I'm fine young man, but I need you to do something for me. You're not going to like it I'm afraid, but I need you to fulfil a promise' Timmy was confused by this request, until Alan looked at Pob. 'My boy, you made a promise to that man over there, which you need to fulfil while I still have some juice left. He has already helped us immeasurably, and we need to keep our promise' Timmy looked at Pob, who was pacing back and forth thinking about where his next brew would come from. Timmy looked back at Alan 'There must be another way to do this, we could build one ourselves, or wait until we find a way to heal you, we have ten years to deliver on my promise to him' Alan looked sterner at Timmy 'We keep our promises, and I am ready to deliver it for you, I have a few wishes left in me. I won't have long left for this world, so it's now or never' Timmy called Pob over to them.

'Pob, I think we are ready to deliver on my promise to you for your little cottage by the lake. Alan is ready to grant my wish, and I want to confirm what it is exactly you want?' Pob opened his mouth wide, so wide that the pipe fell out of his mouth and hit the floor 'YOU MUST BE HAVING A GIRAFFE! Alan can't possibly muster a wish like that. Now you listen here the pair of you. My commitment to you lovely folk is for ten years, as agreed. I'm sure we will find another way for you to fulfil your payment in that time, and in the meantime, I am happy to work with you until we find another way' Alan chirped in 'Pob, this is my choice, I will be granting a wish soon, and I would like it to be our obligation to you' Bongo interjected 'My dearest Pob, is there anything that you can do to save Alan again? There must be something that can be done for him?' Pob bent down to pick up his pipe, and put it back in his mouth, with a sharp intake of breath he said, 'Sorry princess, no can do, the last one was a miracle, and it worked, there is no way I can fix him again I'm afraid' She placed her paw on Alan's forehead and closed her eyes.

'Timmy, make the wish, while you can. I'm ready' Alan demanded. 'Don't be so foolish ya numpty! I reckon we will find another way to make payment. I can always go back to TM-HQ and carry on as I was. I will not let…' Alan interrupted Pob 'Make the wish Timmy, please, for me! You know of my wishes when my time is up, that's all I ask, now please, make the wish, please make it before it's too late!' Timmy could do nothing more than stare at Alan. Pob and Bongo both looked at Timmy to see what he would do. Timmy closed his eyes and faced the floor. 'Alan, I wish… for Pob to get the house he wants, built specifically as he wants, beside the lake exactly how he wants it, with as much tea in it as he can drink' Bongo said, 'Oh Timmy, no!' Pob exclaimed 'Gordon Bennet Timmy, there was no need for that!' But Alan looked at him and smiled in acceptance of the request. Alan lay back and closed his eyes, preparing for the pain that would now inevitably come. And so it began, Alan's eyes scrunched up in pain as a large portion of his remaining juice visibly drained from the last few capsules on his side. Alan muffled a scream by holding his breath. Timmy, Bongo and Pob looked at each other and back to Alan in sympathy for what had just happened. The pain was unbearable for Alan, but worth it to deliver on their promise.

Finally, the pain subsided, and Alan laid back with his eyes closed, a satisfied smile frozen on his face. Bongo looked up at Timmy 'Was that it? Was the wish granted?' Timmy and Bongo both looked at Pob 'Well, what happens now? Did you get what you wanted?' Timmy asked Pob 'Cor' blimey lad, I know just as much as you! Hold on a tick, let me have a look… I'm really gonna need a brew after all this!' Pob took two steps back, clapped his hands and disappeared in a flash. Timmy and Bongo then turned their attention to Alan. 'Alan, Alan, are you still with us?' Timmy asked. He wasn't breathing. 'Alan, come back to us' Bongo whimpered with tears flowing down her cheek. 'I… I… I think he's gone' Timmy said holing back his emotions. Bongo removed her paw from Alan's face and took a step back. Flash, Pob appeared next to them. 'He's only gone and done it! He's only gone and built Pob a beautiful little cottage by the lake! It's a proper nice at that! Had a little kitchen stocked full to the brim with tea bags from all over the world… Even had to have a quick brew. It's furnished in all the furniture I could ever want, even got a little name plaque on the wall 'Pob's Rest' Proper clever that! It's even got…' Timmy stopped his excitement by pointing to Alan. 'Alans gone' Pob stopped dead in his tracks and looked at him. 'You sure boy? He has a little colour left in them juice capsules' as Pob pointed to his side. 'Big fella, wake up and stop all this foolishness' But Alan didn't move. Pob stepped forward and tried to wake him 'Wake up big fella, I want to thank you for me cottage!' Alan lay lifeless. 'Big fella…' Pob said realising what was happening.

Pob stood up, removed his flat cap, and stood in silence beside Alan. Pob said in a whispered tone 'Thank you Alan' as he bowed his head in respect. Timmy, Bongo and Pob stood in silence beside the lifeless berry for what felt like an eternity, and for all they knew, it was an eternity. Timmy was the first to speak 'His wishes were to be buried and hopefully spawn into a new Quibbleberry bush for future generations of Quibbleberry's. Pob looked at Timmy 'I should think that's the least we can do for him. Can I suggest something too, there looks like a little juice left in there, I should think not enough to save poor Alan's life, but might just be enough for you to wish his request to come true?' Just a thought little man!' Timmy looked at the side of Alan. 'Then that is what we will do' Timmy said. 'Pob, would you do me the honour of digging a little hole to plant Alan in?' Pob replied with pride 'It would be my privilege young Timmy' as he replaced his hat and walked over to the spot next to the former Quibbleberry bush.

'I should think this spot will be good for him' He started to walk around in a little circle. The walk turned to a sprint, and then a run and then it was a full-blown blue ring as before. The ring then raised off the ground slightly, and then started to dig a hole just big enough for Alan. Mud and dirt were flung out from the ring as a small excavation was formed. The ring then returned to the surface and slowed down from a blur. To a run, to a sprint, then a walk, until Pob was walking round the newly formed pit, and then he stopped. 'There you go young sir' Pob said walking back to the group. Would you like me to do the honours?' Pob said, standing beside Alan.

'Just a moment' Timmy said. Timmy knelt down beside Alan and placed his hand on Alan's Hand 'Thank you for everything' He whispered. Bongo then hoped over to his other side and gave Alan a kiss on the cheek. 'Rest in peace my dearest' She whimpered through the tears. Timmy and Bongo then took a step back, as Timmy nodded to Pob to proceed.

Pob Approached Alan and picked him up with ease. He walked over to the open grave. He lowered him softly, laying him at the bottom. Pob removed his hat again and started to sing a song reminiscent of Amazing Grace but was clearly a task miner hymn in honour of Alan. Silence followed this, and the three stood in respect not saying a word. Timmy was the first to speak again. 'Alan, I thank you from the bottom of my heart for what you have done for us… And I wish for your wish to become a strong and thriving Quibbleberry bush to be fulfilled' The three all watched as the last drops of juice drained from Alan's capsules on his side. Alan's expression did not change. The ground started to rumble and the dirt that was flung out by Pob moments earlier, lifted off the ground and returned to where it originated from, slowly burying Alan in his shallow grave. The beam of sunlight redirected itself to the mound of fresh dirt and water began to drip from the sky, only above Alans final resting place, like an extremely localised storm.

This went on for a few moments, then, a seedling burst through the soil, a couple of inches tall, but the start of a new bush. The seedling grew, and grew and grew, until it was a few feet tall. Leaves began to sprout from the branches, and then it all stopped. Small buds had started to form, but nothing of a berry like size. Alan's wish had been granted. Bongo reached her paw up to grab Timmy's hand and the three stood in awe of the new plant. 'A fine fair-thy-well, to a very fine berry' Pob said proudly. Timmy, Bongo, and Alan all stood in reverential silence around the bush. Bongo looked up at Timmy and said, 'Come on Timmy, let's get you home. It's been a long night for us all' But Timmy didn't want to move. Pob walked over to Timmy's other side 'The Princess is right my boy, time to go home' Pob said reaching for his other hand. Timmy lowered his head and nodded, and they all slowly turned round and headed for the gap in the woodland they had used yesterday to meet Alan. The walk was long and quite back to the garden fence. 'It's a wonderful thing that has happened here today dear boy, a wonderful thing indeed. Alan has secured is species of plant life for another generation, perhaps even generations to come. His legacy now remains' Timmy nodded in silence to agree. As he wiped away the tears from his eyes, he looked at the two either side of him. 'So, what about you two? What will you do now? I don't know if Bongo can now live in her hutch anymore with the size she is?' Pob looked at her and smiled 'Bit rude ain't it princess? Why don't you come and live with me in Pob's Rest? Plenty of room for ya down there with me!' Bongo looked at Pob 'Oh Pob I wouldn't want to impose on you?' Pob laughed 'Don't be so daft princess!' You are more than welcome, there's plenty of room. What's your tea making like?' Bongo smiled 'Nothing I can't learn my dear.' They reached the fence and stopped. 'Timmy looked over at the house where he could see his mum washing up. There would no doubt be an inquisition when he walked in the door, but nothing he couldn't fabricate a simple story to get out of. 'I guess this will be where we part ways for not then' Timmy said to the pair. 'We are only down the road dear boy; I expect to see you soon!' Pob replied. Bongo looked at Timmy 'We are always nearby sweetheart. Don't be a stranger!' Timmy gave Bongo a long, tight squeeze of a hug, both reassuring each other that everything would be alright. He then turned to Pob and shook his hand. 'Not like the American way of fist bumping' Timmy said with a smile. Pob smiled back at him. Timmy then climbed over the fence and landed on the flower bed the other side. He turned round to look at them both. 'Shall we princess?' Pob said removing his flat cap. 'Very gentlemanly of you sir' Bongo said as she placed her paw on Pob's head. Pob then took two steps back and clapped his hands. 'See you soon' Timmy uttered under his voice as the pair disappeared in a flash.

Timmy then enjoyed the silence after a very long day, thinking of Alan and all they did together. A smile shot across his face as he remembered how he got his name from his English teacher Alan Kibble, and wondered if he would be able to look at his teacher the same way again. Timmy turned round to start the walk back to the house. He wondered to himself about Grog, and why he was so angry at them, then recalled the heroic actions of Vixen to save them. Then his mind was drawn to Hericum, and their brief encounter. No doubt he would chat to Jackson when he gets back to school about the events. Timmy's walk to the house was slow as he recounted the events of the day, and wondered if he would revisit Alan's bush to see if any more Quibbleberries would spawn? It was nice he was able to able to carry on Alan's legacy in a new bush.

Timmy looked up at his mum who was washing up. She saw him through the window and smiled 'Timmy! You're home' she shouted through the window 'How was Nanny and Grandad's?' Timmy would think up some kind of story to appease her and shield her from the truth. 'Billy, Timmy is home!' she shouted upstairs to Timmy's dad. As Timmy looked at the house thinking about what story he could tell his mum, but as he did, he noticed a green glow coming from behind the house. The clear blue morning sky has an eerie green glow to it. Timmy stopped in his tracks looking at the phenomena. The green glow was coming from a growing storm cloud. Vivid green and enveloping the area. It was the same colour green from the little cloud that captured his grandparents. The storm cloud grew and grew. Lightning bolts of vivid green burst out of the cloud, accompanied by the sound of two women laughing. An evil cackle that filled the air with dread.

A flash of light from behind Timmy, and a familiar voice shouted, 'What in heavens name is this supposed to be then chief, I'd only just put the kettle on?' Timmy glanced round to see Bongo and Pob standing looking in amazement at the cloud. Timmy knew exactly what it was as he turned to look back at the looming storm cloud 'I think it's the Winkleford Witches, they're back!'

Epilogue

The green glow subsided to complete black. Christine could vaguely make out a figure just ahead of her. It was where Michael had been sat, and the outline resembled him. 'Michael, is that you? What just happened?' Michael leaned a little closer to her 'There were supposed to be protection measures on the jet that should have prevented anything like this happening. Someone must have disabled them somehow' Michael reached into his pocket at pulled an old zippo lighter. It was a shimmering multicolored metal box, covered in scratches and scuffs, and looked like it had a lot of sentimental value. He flipped the lid, and after a few attempts at turning the wheel to spark it into life, it finally ignited.

He held the light up high to try and get his baring's, or to find something the light would reflect off... but everything was black. They both looked around frantically for some sort of sign or item that would give them a clue as to where they were. On the floor between them was what was left of the orb that had captured them moments earlier, it had fallen to the floor and smashed into hundreds of pieces. Christine bent down to pick a piece up. 'Don't touch it!' Michael exclaimed 'We need to be careful, these two are very dangerous and very powerful.'

'But poor Timmy, he will be left alone on the jet' Michael looked at her 'There's nothing we can do for him yet, we need to find a way out of here' Michael got to his feet, not realising what they had been sat on, there were two tree stumps which provided a support for them having arrived from the plane in a seated position. Christine reached into her handbag and pulled out a handheld black tablet which she held it up for inspection. As she did, a green cloud enveloped the item, and it disappeared out of her hand. 'Michael! It has gone... they have taken my portal!' and with that, a green cloud appeared and enveloped her handbag, and once dispersed revealed that the handbag had also vanished. 'Michael... My bag!' Michael reached into his pocket and pulled out a similar handheld device that then fell victim to the same instantly appearing green cloud, and vanished, followed by the lighter in his hand, and everything became dark again.

After a few seconds of silence, their faces were illuminated by a green cloud forming around each of their wrists and ankles, pulling them closer together and binding them like handcuffs. The green glow was enough to illuminate their faces, both struck with fear at what was happening. Michael was able to sit back down opposite Christine, and all they could do was look at each other trying to determine what they could do next. A young girls voice of about 30 years old erupted from behind Michael. 'We told you we would find you!' Michael turned round but could not see where the voice was coming from but recognized it instantly.

Then a second voice of early thirty's distracted them both from behind Christine 'We did Evie, and we said we would get our revenge' They both turned round to look over Christine's shoulder. The voice behind Michael replied 'We did Edna. And we are witches of our word, aren't we?' Michael tried to defuse the situation 'Ladies, it is good to see you both after so many years. How did you manage to escape?' Both the voices laughed. 'We are the Witches of Winkleford, and we are not destined to be bound by the confines of your prison, we did warn you' the first voice bellowed.

Christine begged 'Then why did you take us? Why didn't you just finish the job? I know you are more than capable' The second voice responded 'Oh, we are more than capable. And we discussed this at length, perhaps some kind of torture, or eternal confinement as you were happy to bestow upon my sister and me, but where is the fun in that?' The first voice then interrupted 'Well let's not rule anything out, Edna' They both laughed a playful laugh. Michael asked, 'Then what do you want with us?' two beautiful faces of young girls illuminated by the green glow of the shackles, came into view either side of them. One of them responded 'We want to know about your grandson's Quibbleberry!' then the second voice questioned 'We know about his wishes, and you're going to tell us how we can find them both!' Michael and Christine looked at each other in sheer confusion, as everything went dark.

> Timmy will return in book 2…
>
> ## *Timmy & The Winkleford Witches*
>
> Coming Soon

Support the author!

PLEASE REVIEW THE BOOK ON AMAZON!

Timmy and the Quibbleberry

About the Author

Justin B. Black is an architectural technician, and a qualified civil engineer from the east of England. An ambitious man and the father of two, who has never… ever attempted to write anything before. The idea for this story came completely out of the blue whilst he was sat in the pub having a quick 'Friday-Night-pint' and he believed the story had potential to develop. Always eager to try new things, sat down one Monday night with a pot of tea, to attempt to write it, and write it, and write it.

A man of many hobbies ranging from Boxing and charity fund raising activities, to cars, and being a massive self-confessed science fiction fan. From Star Trek, Red Dwarf, and (The Greatest Films of all time) The Back to the Future Trilogy. Found refuge in the writing process, as a retreat from all of life's problems.

Fun fact: During the covid lockdown, the author built a pub in his rear garden, and based on the BBC comedy series Bottom, named it 'The Foxy Stoat' which is the inspiration of the pub in this Story… The Stoat.

Printed in Great Britain
by Amazon